Mobius: Out of Time

by

Richard Thieme

Exurban Press

Minneapolis MN

2023

Cover Photo-illustration by Harvey Tillis. ©2023 Harvey Tillis Photography

Author photograph by Eli Omen. Copyright Eli Omen 2020, Creative Commons BY-NC-ND

Published by Exurban Press

Printed by The Workshop, Arcadia CA. Jeff Smith, Proprietor. Noel Smith, Layout/Production

ISBN 978-1-7362663-5-9

Also by Richard Thieme:

Mobius: A Memoir (Book One of the Mobius Trilogy) – Exurban Press. Minneapolis MN. 2020

The Mobius Vector: The Long Road Home (Book Two of the Mobius Trilogy) – Exurban Press. Minneapolis MN. 2022

"The Road to Resilience: Strategies for Playing Through the Pain" – *ICS2.* Nov-Dec 2018

A review of "UFOs: Reframing the Debate" - *Journal of Scientific Exploration.* Fall 2018

A Richard Thieme Reader - a 5-volume e-book anthology of fiction and non-fiction on Kindle. Spring 2016

FOAM (a novel) - Exurban Press. September 2015

Mind Games*, A Collection of Nineteen Stories of Brave New Worlds and Alternate Realities* - Duncan Long Publications. April 2010

Richard Thieme's Islands in the Clickstream - Syngress Publishing (a division of Elsevier). July 2004

UFOs and Government: A Historical Inquiry - Michael Swords and Robert Powell, with Richard Thieme, Clas Svahn, Vicente-Juan Ballester Olmos, Bill Chalker, Barry Greenwood, Jan Aldrich, and Steve Purcell – a work of historical scholarship on government responses to the UFO phenomenon from WWII to the present. *Anomalist Books:* San Antonio, TX: 2012

"Silent Emergent, Doubly Dark" in *Subtle Edens,* editor Allen Ashley, Elastic Press: Norwich UK: 2008

"I Remember Mama" in *New Writing, Volume One: An Anthology of Poetry, Fiction, Nonfiction, and Drama.* Press Americana. 2013

"Entering Sacred Digital Space" published in *New Paradigms for Bible Study: The Bible in the Third Millennium* from T. & T. Clark, Ltd. June 2004

"The Changing Context of Intelligence and Ethics: Enabling Technologies as Transformational Engines" in *Defense Intelligence Journal.* Published in an adapted version in the proceedings of the *New Paradigms for Security Workshop (NPSW 2008)* and as "Changing Contexts of Security and Ethics: You Can't Have One Without the Other" in *Ethical Spectacle.* January 2009

Speeches available at **www.thiemeworks.com**, You Tube, and via Google

A Selection from Reviews of *The Mobius Trilogy*

Pick this book up and you won't put it down.

An incredible story, pick it up and you won't put it down. Richard Thieme's level of consciousness and storytelling is spellbinding. A hall of mirrors, instead of hiding what's true, the mirrored kaleidoscope becomes the truth. An old Jewish proverb has it that 'story is truer than truth', here the turning and twisting story becomes the truth. Here lies our unseen contemporary history, told from the inside about the people who make history

Thieme writes Mobius with all the tragic beauty of a fallen Angel.

Richard Thieme, a legendary guru of young hackers everywhere and a guy excruciatingly well-versed in life in the bowels of governmental secrecy, manages a raw and at times even tender, deep dive into a world of secrecy and nigh capricious bureaucracy that extracts a great human price. Read it at your peril, but in doing so emerge ready to better treasure your simple and honest pleasures. Thieme writes Mobius with all the tragic beauty of a fallen Angel

An absolute must read

Richard Thieme's latest book 'Mobius' truly is a beautiful compilation of all the occupational mental warps one develops by spending a professional career inside that house of mirrors commonly referred to as the 'intelligence community'. He brilliantly captures what it does to a person when you spend your entire life compartmentalizing both the information in your head, as well as the people in your professional and social life. It's full of these odd little quirks and mental pathways you'll recognize all too well, and you can't help but wonder how he got into your head like that. In fact, he captures all of this so well, that I spent the entire last quarter of the book wondering.... "Who is Richard Thieme really?". At the same time, it's a strong and damning social critique of the ever-present surveillance society we live in, and the tragic plight of the modern whistleblower. An absolute must-read!

At an arms reach, I know this person.

Really great. It seemed so parallel to my experience. I lived on Fort Mead for 4 years and know my way around FANX, and the main building at Fort Meade, though I was over in the S building. I also had visited Langley, Navy Offices at the Pentagon, and at the Security Group Headquarters, so as the various descriptions came by I could imagine the actual places Thieme was describing. This all made the book so very real for me, as if it were all true and part of my life. I cannot recommend it highly enough.

The best example I know of what their careers do to spies

It is ironic. Spycraft fascinates us even as it leaves the inner lives of spies invisible. Put aside all the tricks of cameras and recording and all the drama of saving or accidentally wrecking the world.

There are few accounts of what these careers do to spies. Mobius is the best example I know of.

Imagine living a life so secret that your most closest intimate cannot learn the truth of what you do or what it is doing to you. Imagine changing identities like people change shirts. Imagine a world where those who you are spying on begin to spy on you with the most horrible and unappealable consequences. Imagine a world where even your own boss might betray you as Vice President Cheney did to Valerie Pflame. She survived; the fate of her overseas contacts will never be told. Imagine a career where you will never learn the real agenda behind your work assignments.

What does it feel like to live a lie as a career? What is the price that is exacted? It is more than alcoholism (though there is much of that.) The isolation takes some to suicide. More profoundly, these careers unground the people who live them. Some can pretend that the moral consequences of their work will not come to rest on their own souls. Others sink into crushing cynicism. This book is about what we ask of and do to people who are working for us.

Table of Contents

A True Story

An analyst at the National Security Agency read my short story "Zero Day: Roswell." "It reminds me of *Three Days of the Condor*," he said with a laugh, "the Robert Redford movie about the CIA analyst who read fiction to find out what was going on. Ninety-five per cent of your story isn't fiction, but you have to know which 95% to have the key."

Prelude

The Conclusion of The *Mobius Vector*. An establishing shot.

You should read *Mobius: A Memoir* and *The Mobius Vector* which flow into *Mobius: Out of Time* but if you skipped them, here is an edited version of the last chapter of *The Mobius Vector*.

<snip>

"Joe! I haven't seen you here before. God, how long has it been?"

Joe Pantaglia was sitting at the bar. I had been heading home but something made me turn back to the Barbican where Joe was waiting. Some would call it fate. I called it being thirsty.

Joe had worked in the visible light for a think tank and in the dark for an agency. He was a good guy, and as far as I knew, he wasn't a hostile. I didn't think he would be pissed off by what I had done. I'd find out by saying hello. So I said hello.

"Hello, Nick," he said with a smile that looked genuine. "I had a meeting down the street and I wanted a quiet drink. I don't think I've been here before." He looked around. "I like the vibe."

"It sounds like you need what my lady friend calls me-time."

"I didn't mean it that way. Sit down. What've you been up to? How long has it been? A year or two? More?"

"About a year and a half," I said. I slid up onto the stool beside. "Are you still connecting the dots?"

"On occasion, but in a new way. I shifted my focus." He looked around by habit, seeing Jake twenty feet away, no one else in earshot. He lowered his voice anyway.

"You know about remote viewing, I imagine?"

"I've heard stories," I said. "I was told about some hits that sounded stunning."

"They were, they are," he said. "You didn't know that I was involved with that, did you?"

"No. I thought the agencies phased it out when results were ambiguous. That's what Kit said."

"That's a cover story, Nick. It just went deeper underground. We wanted the Other Guys to think it was a bust. But it wasn't. But at the same time, it isn't simple. Learning the protocols takes time. Not everyone can do it. If you have a gift, thanks to genetics, then the training works. You learn by practicing and get better. Every time it works, your ability to do it ramps up. If you don't have the genes, no amount of training can get you where you need to be. You can do it some but not in a useful way."

"And you, I imagine, got results? Is that what you're saying?"

"Yes," he said. "Not every time, but enough." He looked around again and leaned in closer. It felt like the old days, when we made a decision to cross the line and talk out of school. "I am trying to grasp what happens when I do it, Nick–not so much the content, but the context in which it occurs. The data shows us the deeper structure of ... consciousness, I guess. Does that make sense? We saw a Russian boomer about to be launched from an inland facility which didn't make sense until they dug a canal to the sea–you likely heard about that one–but that isn't what grabbed me. What did it mean that we can do that? My field of perception changed. Spacetime on a new loom. Things were detected, yes, but the most important thing was that they *could* be detected. It called into question—I know this sounds woo-woo—everything I thought about the universe itself, the entire cosmos, everything."

"That's all?" I smiled. "I'm waiting for *Twilight Zone* music. What are we talking about, Joe?"

"You think I'm making it up. But I'm not."

I waited.

"For one thing, we detected an alien presence, Nick. Not just once. We confirmed the viewings with sensors, satellites, pilots in the air. They come and go. Nobody knows from where."

We had all heard rumors that "the visitors," as a friend at NORAD called them, were real, had been coming for decades, and had technology and power beyond our understanding. I told Joe that's all I knew. Nothing first hand. Which had what to do with remote viewing?

"Quite a bit, it turned out." He turned back to his drink. "That's all I can say. Remote viewing gets results, and the universe is a goddamn stranger place than I thought."

"OK," I said. He sipped his drink. Jake was wiping down the bar but was still far away. "So you were meeting with someone. About this?"

He paused, then turned and said, "A few of us are partners in a new venture. You remember Sylvia Warner?"

"Sure."

"And Hal McCutcheon?"

"Sure, of course."

"They're involved. We decided to create a remote viewing

business doing competitive intelligence."

"That's fascinating, Joe."

He seemed to be looking at my shirt. His gaze was lower, at any rate. He wasn't looking into my eyes. "You don't have a steady job?"

"No," I said. "I'm looking."

"OK, so listen, Nick, I know why you did what you did. I'm not a blindly loyal guy, I have my commitments like everyone else but I'm not a slave of the agency. I think you were right to do it. Somebody had to do it. We went way over the line. OK?"

"Sure," I said. "OK."

"OK. So you're a pretty intuitive guy. You might be useful. I'm just thinking aloud. Are you interested in learning more? We'd have to figure out how you fit, if you do—let's not get ahead of ourselves— but why not take a look?"

"You're serious?"

"I'm serious," he said. "If you sign an NDA, we can discuss it. Make up your own mind."

"Where do I sign?"

He finished his drink and slid off the stool. "Come with me over to the office. It's right down the street. We can talk more easily there."

You're a meaning-seeking freak, addicted to adrenalin, you don't do trivial, you don't do shallow. You want to live on the edges all the time.

"Let's go," I said.

And down the rainy street we walked, watching out for puddles, not discussing anything yet, looking like two old friends getting wetter and wetter.

"Say what?" Val said. "A mind reader? A fortune teller? What?"

"No," I said. "Forget the crazy stuff. They developed protocols for using clairvoyance. Maybe nothing will come of it, but maybe something will. If it works, it works. If not, what have I lost?"

"How well do you know him?"

"As well as you know anyone that you don't know, doing the work. He was a good analyst. I remember one time he connected a phone conversation with a guy going to some unusual place, a place he should not be going. That was all Joe needed to know what was happening. Once he helped a guy escape and nearly got killed. We worked together in Amsterdam. That's where we really connected."

"But your point is, this guy is smart and you trust him?"

"Yes. He did some amazing shit. I joked at the time that he must be psychic. I never thought that maybe he was."

Val slid the flap of the book jacket into her stopping place and closed the book and put it on the table. "Why am I not surprised that this is the kind of thing that shows up in your life? Nothing normal or ordinary, ever. I will say this, Nick Cerk, or whoever you are" (we laughed because she knew my real name), "living with you is an adventure."

I just shrugged. "It sounds really interesting. It's worth exploring, don't you think?"

"Sure. See what it is."

I met with Joe at the nondescript office—not a posh suite in one of the high rise towers but a second floor set of ordinary rooms in an older brick building a few blocks west of State. There were three floors of offices, a chiropractor, an acupuncturist, insurance agents, an association headquarters, people like that. A directory in the vestibule with letters that pushed into the black backing was missing a letter "n." The bathroom in the hall needed help. I took it easy on the stairs, holding the railing, practicing my new habit of self-care.

"When you describe what happened to you, Nick, at the agency," Joe said, "it sounds like you turned sort of inside out. That's what you'll have to do to learn the protocols, in a way, but more slowly and with discipline. You'll need to stay steady when the currents bounce you around. There's a lot of turbulence out there. Let's start with an NDA and then we can get to the real meat."

I signed the NDA and I listened to Joe, but I had to tell him to say things twice, because I couldn't grasp what I was hearing. My brain was trying to learn a different way of imagining the universe. I retained maybe twenty per cent of that first lesson. I felt like I was back in school and way behind.

\<snip\>

Mobius Out of Time: The End of the Journey will reveal how successful the agencies are at compartmenting knowledge, how totally out of the know we can be kept, even when we're working on a project, not just muggles but people with clearances like myself. What we knew fit into tiny compartments and we never knew what lay behind a thousand other doors. I had thought I knew not only a lot about the world but how the world itself was built. How the epistemological or ontological space was constructed. I did not. The world around me was not what I thought.

\<snip\>

Learning to do remote viewing meant allowing subtle barely perceived traces of data or information to tease my brain so I could draw a target almost without thinking, my hand moving a pencil on a blank piece of paper on my lap. I had to learn to not think. I felt suspended like a diver at the right buoyancy in the ocean. There was neither up nor down, just hanging in suspension in the void.

Joe taught me how to build a little big bigger box than the one I had lived in all my life. A little bit bigger box is challenge enough.

Spacetime doubles back on itself, effects precede causes, causality a casualty. It takes time to learn a new language. It takes time to grasp that precognition happens, that the past is present, that we live at the still point of the turning world.

I will try to say what I saw. You try to see what I mean.

I met the members of the team. I knew them before, but they were different than I recalled. In the context of our work, I changed as well, and Valerie noticed subtle shifts in my attitudes and actions. I introduced her to the team and she liked the team and the team liked her. One thing led to another, and when she found she had the right stuff, she joined the game as a player, not just watching. Our relationship shifted into a higher gear. We were willing to risk the leap from the cliff hand in hand.

I'll tell you about all that, and about Joe and Sylvia and Hal and the team, and Brian, and Jelli and Brad, in *Mobius Out of Time*. Valerie will tell her own stories. So will Brian and Joe and a little guy named Hugo Blau. Jelli too. I'll be an editor. So will Val.

You are my teachers, my colleagues and co-conspirators. We are all jesters wearing conical hats with puff balls on top, dancing in harlequin garb. We are all the living creatures that exist, blazing with light for a moment before we disappear beyond the far horizon, beyond the reach of the speed of light. But before we fall, we burn so very brightly. Before we lose the eyes with which we see.

Out of sight out of mind. Beyond the telling of the story. Beyond the momentary thought. Beyond the barely uttered words which wither with the ticking of the clock.

tick tick tick

tick tick tick

Interlude

A gift from the Algonyi tribes of central Africa: "Big dreams revolve around powerful archetypal images from the collective unconscious. ... Big dreams–significant dreams–are often remembered for a lifetime, and not infrequently prove to be the richest jewel in the treasure-house of psychic experience."

- Carl Jung, The Collected Works of Carl Jung (1948b, 76)

Chapter 1
Two Big Dreams

"Valerie!"

I shook her shoulder. Valerie barely stirred and I shook it again, less gently. She moved and turned away.

"Mn," she said.

Her eyes didn't open. I shook her shoulder a third time and said, "Valerie."

She turned toward my voice and her eyes blinked, then fluttered. She gazed dully at something I couldn't see and said, "Why are you waking me?"

"Valerie, I have to tell you the dream I had. What Jung called a big dream. I have to tell you before I forget."

Her eyes were open, looking at nothing. She lay on her side, her head on the pillow.

"You woke me up to tell me you had a dream?"

"Not just any dream, a big dream. Seriously. It's time to wake up anyway. It's after eight. Were you up late?"

She had been having trouble sleeping and sometimes went to the living room to read or watch a video until she could fall asleep again. Sometimes she ate a banana or a piece of toast with marmalade. Sometimes she stood at the window looking at the bare branches in the streetlight and the quiet street. The first snow had more or less thawed, leaving patches here and there, and the wind was calm. It looked like nothing was happening, but that was deceptive. Nature has lots of arrows in her quiver, some too small for us to see.

"No. I slept through the night. I would still be sleeping if you hadn't gotten me up."

"Sorry, I'm sorry, but listen–" I looked at her closing eyes. "Can you listen? Are you awake enough? Dreams like these don't happen very often. They're really significant when they do. The psyche has something important to say."

"You can't just write it down? You keep paper beside the bed, I thought for that purpose."

"It's too slow. I could look for the phone and dictate but you're a better recorder. The phone sometimes misses words."

"So do I," she said, "especially when I just woke up."

She rested her head in her hand, elevated just above the pillow. She had taken to sleeping with two pillows but one had slipped off the bed in the night. Realizing that, she turned in the sheets and leaned over the edge of the bed to retrieve it, then stacked the pillows and rested on the higher elevation. That made her neck hurt a little and she adjusted the pillows, her head, everything, including her morning mood. She looked at me with open eyes, trying to be kind.

"Go ahead. I'm awake."

"OK, listen ... the level of detail was amazing! It was a *long* dream. I haven't had a dream like this for years. The last time I did I was walking through a large beautiful house and there were a lot more rooms than I expected. The house was my psyche, obviously. I came into a study where a beautiful woman sat at a desk—my anima, right?—and I said, "I had no idea you were so wealthy," and she smiled. Her wealth was a symbol of my latent abilities, things I didn't know I could do. They emerged when I was ready, making midlife a very productive time.

"My psyche was telling me there was more to me than I had thought. I had a profound sense of possibilities.

"That was years ago. Last night I was in a house again, but it was so much bigger than the one in the earlier dream. It was a huge mansion, absolutely immense. It was my house. But really it was me—my self, my psyche, my soul.

"My hand held ten keys, seven for outside locks and three for inside locks. I unlocked door after door with the right keys. I had complete access to my interior.

"The rooms were spacious and beautifully furnished. They made Miriam's place look like a shack. There were two living rooms, both the size of banquet halls. There were tables of food like a medieval feast and servants serving food and drinks to friends and colleagues who appeared out of thin air. Someone gave me a piece of chocolate that was the best I ever had. I think the delicious food was a symbol of abundant life.

"The mansion was on the North Shore, maybe Lake Forest. The house was surrounded by beautiful grounds. Through an immense window I saw the lake, glittering in the bright sun. Then I climbed a spiraling staircase—spirals mean transformation when I dream them, and creativity, and change. I took the stairs to the second floor and explored a whole bunch of beautiful bedrooms. The master bedroom was huge with an immense bed, bigger than kingsize. There was rich dark furniture throughout and exquisite art and an antique desk. It was one of the old-fashioned kind with a rolling shutter that opened as it rose. There were cubbyholes with tiny books in every slot. As I sifted through them, they multiplied and the more I looked, the more there were. There were books I read and books I wrote and books waiting to be written. I sensed I would write a book about my life after I left the agency, a sequel to my memoir. I felt words flowing, waiting for me to write them. The river of words widened, flowing into the sea.

"Then the scene shifted, the way they do in dreams, and next thing I knew, I was up in a big attic, filled with furniture draped with sheets, and then—shift again!—I was going down to the basement. It was cavernous and dark, and there was a large sarcophagus where an Anglican archbishop was buried and a chapel with an altar. The darkness was dank and humid with glimmerings of death, but welcoming, not daunting. A tomb or a womb, pick one. I turned and climbed back to the banquet above, to light and warmth and laughter and conversation. Val, I can't tell you the joy I felt. I don't know what it means, only that something is coming, something is opening up, something is ready to be born. There is more to me, to everything, to the universe, Val, than I ever dreamed. It's about the work Joe wants me to do, and about us, about our next step. I had to tell you right away."

"Uh-huh," said Val sleepily, her eyes closing again and her head sinking into the pillow. "Keep talking. I'm listening." Then she was snoring softly and I was outside her awareness, the world of the dream fading in the morning light.

"I had to tell you," I said aloud to no-one there, "before I forgot. I thought I was hitting a dead end but suddenly there were paths. Which should we take? A customary one or the road less travelled? That's what you were talking about the other day, wasn't it?"

Valerie, of course, said nothing. She snored adorably, nostrils flaring slightly, a flameless dragon waiting to be roused.

I said more loudly, "It helps to know there are paths, even if I don't know where they're going."

Valerie stirred, deciding, I think, whether to stay asleep or not, half and half, but she couldn't help responding to my intensity and energy. She opened her eyes and rolled over to look at me. She must have been listening in her sleep.

"Your stories about being a whistle blower and Syntactic and Nat Herman and Miriam and everything, you want to put that in a second book?"

"Sure. Why not? It's all true."

"You did leave out a lot in the memoir."

"I did. I said the least untruthful things I could, but I didn't realize how much I didn't say. I want to tell more of the story. The real one, unabridged. People have emailed asking if I'm really Mobius. I want to get beyond the fun and games. I want them to know who I am. I don't want to be misunderstood."

"Sung by Nina Simone. It could be your anthem."

When I didn't respond, Valerie sat up and folded her arms around her upbent knees. "Good luck writing another book. You know what happens to so many writers. After the first book, they can't get it up again. I knew some at the Barbican and they all said the world of publishing had crashed. A publisher won't talk to a writer, they said. Publishers talk to agents but only the ones they know who bring easily sold stories. It's the way your friend Bill Webb described church. People don't want to be challenged, they want stories that put them to sleep. Even small publishers, they said, can't afford staff to reject the flood of manuscripts they'd get if they open submissions."

"Would you call the sequel fiction too?"

"Sure. If I told the truth outright, you know what they would do. You'd have to visit me in a supermax."

"I know," she sighed. "But writers I talked to said fiction is hard to sell unless you're a brand name, and you need an advance of at least a hundred thousand bucks. There's no—what did they call it?—blacklist? Books that stay in print?"

"Backlist."

"Right. They have to be blockbusters, like movies. Then they do a million sequels and the sheep bleat. Those writers sounded bitter to me."

"For good reason," I said.

"So that's the reality. Do it if you want to or if you have to, but don't expect miracles."

"When did I let 'reality' stop me before, Val? I've never looked outside myself for direction. I trust my inner compass. Things have turned out, pretty much.

"Val, my dream says I have a future. There were so many beautiful rooms and I have to explore them."

I paused to take a breath.

"OK then," I smiled. "Go back to sleep."

"Yeah, right."

She leaned back against the headboard. The headboard banged on the wall as it always did when she pushed it back. "You know, I had a dream too," she said. She looked thoughtful, looking past me, remembering her own. "I guess it was a big dream, the way you define it. It wasn't a house, it was galaxies and stars and it made my heart beat real fast. It sure made an impression. I'll tell you about it at breakfast."

"You'll remember it?"

"Yes. I think I will."

She did remember, as much as she could, not knowing what she might have forgotten. She described the world of her dream simply and with feeling. It was a vision of the cosmos, an expanding endless space. Stars igniting in clouds of dust, birthing life. Nebulae glowing with inner light. Novas exploding. Elements created through generations of stars. She described a universe throbbing with life. I could feel its pulse the way I feel mine, before I even touch my wrist, like a tympani in the distance. I became quiet as I listened, and when she was done, I sat there, taking it in.

She tilted her head quizzically.

"What?" she said.

I didn't know what to say. Her dream was a view of trillions of galaxies turning like pinwheels, making her dizzy. This was a Valerie I hadn't yet experienced, a woman with profound gifts. She didn't know, yet, herself, how magnificent she was, she was so self-effacing, nor did I have all the pieces then, but after we learned what she could do, her dream was clearly a vision of how she would break through her limits and as a remote viewer extend herself toward targets she would see, and touch, and feel. She would leave the comfortable rooms in which she had lived and venture forth into eternity. The future was a locked room, but she had the key, and the questions she didn't know how to ask would be answered over time. The future would reach back and prod her along the path that would transmogrify her past.

And I would come along for the ride.

Interlude

"The truth is, life on the face of it is a chaos in which one finds oneself lost. The individual suspects as much, but is terrified to encounter this frightening reality face to face, and so attempts to conceal it by drawing a curtain of fantasy over it, behind which he can make believe that everything is clear."

- Jose Ortega y Gasset, *The Revolt of the Masses*

Chapter 2
Jelli On a Roll

Jelli and Brad Mastipilo looked like an ordinary couple.

We met at coffee after the morning service. We all needed pastry to perk ourselves up–the portly prelate had preached that day and we were still numb from his loud shouting–and the bulletin said that Betsy Marshall had the job of providing munchies after the service. Her home-made donuts went fast and then you were stuck with scones from a Starbucks down the street. Blueberry scones were all they had unless you went early, and they were OK, but nothing to write home about. Betsy didn't drive so she never went to Panera, maybe a mile away, for maple scones thick with frosting. She hadn't learned to use her phone for deliveries so we were stuck with ingredients she could get at the store a block away and carry home. Her shortbread was good but the donuts were the best.

So Val and I hurried toward the spread in the basement and so did Brad and Jelli. We jostled together down the stairs. Had there been four donuts, it wouldn't have mattered, but there was only one. The pigs who sat near the stairway beat us to the trough. The four of us arrived at the table at the same time and looked at the donut, a singlet on a paper plate, then at one another. We all laughed, mostly to hide our disappointment. Brad fetched a plastic knife and cut the donut into quarters and gave one to each of us. The minuscule treat on a large white napkin looked like an island in the ocean.

We went to the coffee urn next and drew off coffee into styrofoam cups. We used wooden sticks to stir in a powder called a creamer and chemicals to sweeten the brew, then headed toward a table as if we were friends instead of an accidental happening. We introduced ourselves—I'm Nick, hi, I'm Jelli, hi, Brad Mastipilo, hi hello, I'm Val, hi Val—and ate our mini-rewards for sitting through a sermon worse than a Vogon poetry reading. We sipped coffee, smiled at one another, and waited for someone to speak.

"That was funny," Jelli said, not because it was but to get something going."The way we came downstairs, you'd think we hadn't eaten in days."

"It's because the donuts are free," Valerie said. "You come into a church, you regress, you're kids again, don't you think? At the Barbican, where I used to work, it didn't matter what it was, pickles, nuts, anything. If it had salt and made them want a drink, it did the job. People would never order a pickle but when it was on the bar, they gobbled them up."

"The Barbican?" Brad said. "Is that the bar on Milwaukee?"

"It was. Now it's called the Wild Rose. They call it a tapas bar. I liked it better the old way. I don't like having to translate food to know what it is."

Everyone nodded, everyone agreed. The way things were was always best, whatever they were.

We sat a moment in silence again, not uncomfortable exactly, but close. Not thoughtfully chewing, not attending to texture and flavor like a Zen monk focused on every bite, just sort of mindlessly eating our bites.

Silence like that never lasts long. Someone gets anxious and says whatever pops into their mind.

"So how long have you been coming here?" Jelli asked.

"A few weeks," I said, "we're trying it out. We like Bill Webb. We're looking for a place to hang out. Valerie and I," I nodded to my smiling mate, "haven't been together very long. We're exploring things that might work for us as a couple. It's funny, it's like a couple is a third person. I never knew that before."

"That's a good way to put it," Jelli said. "That's us too, there's me, and Brad, and us." She looked at Brad. "There *is* an us, isn't there?"

"Of course," he said.

"How long have you been together?"

"One year. More or less."

Brad said. "Yes. About a year. Officially."

"Are you from here?" Valerie asked.

"I am," Jelli said. "I grew up on the north side. On Barry? Near the park? Brad's–"

"From Edina," he said. "Edina Minnesota. Jelli has to be here for her job so we moved from the Twin Cities to see how it works."

"How long did you live up north?"

"We weren't up north," Brad said. "We were in Edina."

Jelli sort of laughed, sort of shook her head. "The north, for Minnesotans, means really up north. Up near the boundary waters. North of Brainerd, Bemidji, Hibbing. The Iron Range. I tried out Edina for six months, but luckily my job came through."

"I would have preferred to stay," Brad said. "I didn't have a choice."

Then it was quiet again. The donuts were gone and Val shook her napkin to get the crumbs in the center, then squeezed it shut around them. It opened a little like a reticent flower but kept its shape in the main, keeping the crumbs inside. She wasn't a neat freak as a rule, so she must have been killing time. Trying to think of what to say.

Trying to kill time is like stepping on a balloon that squeaks and bulges but doesn't pop and becomes all kinds of shapes. We can't kill time. Time doesn't die.

"Is your name really Jelli?" Val said.

"Jill, Jilli when I was a kid. I couldn't say it right and it sounded like Jelli, so it stuck." She sort of laughed. "Is your name really Valerie?"

"Valerie's my middle name. I like it better than the one I was given."

Jelli looked at me. "Is Nick Cerk your real name?"

I laughed. "More or less."

"It sounds like a private eye," Jelli said. "Someone in one of those books. Is it Czech?"

"Kind of," I said, "everything's a hodgepodge in that area. I'm a mongrel, I'm sure. I should do a genetic test and find out."

"I did one," Jelli said. "I'm a bunch of different things. My ancestry looks like a pie chart."

"Mine did too," Val said. "They said I don't like cilantro. I didn't need to be told that. I already knew it."

"It did say you lacked the brca gene," I said.

"Yes, that's true. I was glad to learn that."

"Do you think it was worth it?" I asked Jelli. "Did you learn anything interesting?"

She was about to answer when something unusual happened. Jelli had been friendly, loose, maybe a little nervous, trying to include herself, unlike Brad who was mostly silent, and it was like a screw tightened and her face tensed. She looked at her hands, worrying the napkin as she tore it into shreds. She put the pieces into a tiny pile but her fingers kept moving as if she was tearing more.

Brad looked alarmed. "Are you all right?" She didn't reply. "We should go." He was rising from his seat when she said, "No." She shook her head. "No."

"Come on outside, Jell, get some air." He was standing and leaning, his hand on her arm.

"No," she said. "It'll pass. Brad, sit down."

Her voice was tense and a little different. I don't know what to call it. She had been casual, as the occasion invited, but stiffened as if she was fighting some invisible force.

Val and I looked on, enjoying the normalcy-disruption. That's nothing to be proud of, but we were as intrigued as if a strange bacteria showed up in our petri dish. Sunday morning is pretty boring: get dressed, eat in a rush, hurry to the church to be annoyed by the preacher. Jelli's behavior was a welcome "look at that!" sort of thing.

She breathed deeply, making us wait, staring at her hands. Brad remained standing. Jelli ignored him.

After another deep breath, she smiled again and said, "OK." She was back from wherever she had gone. "I'm good."

Brad was still in motion like Duchamp's nude descending a staircase. He obviously wanted to leave. It was like he was fluttering all over the place.

"You're OK?"

"Yes," she nodded. "Brad, I'm fine." She looked around the table. "I could use some water. Would you please get some from the fountain?"

He took her empty cup, seeming relieved to have a task. He crossed the basement toward a water fountain near the stairs.

"OK," I said. "So ... wow. What just happened? Were you that upset by the sermon?"

"Right, that's what it was, the sermon," Jelli said. "Ha ha."

"Nick." Valerie said in a voice I was getting to know. She had been trying to add "not my business" to my filter. Once I cast off the shackles of agency life which made every word a work of art, the truth was exploding out of me. It was a brand new experience to be honest and straightforward. I had to learn how to modulate my output.

Jelli turned to Val. "Is he always so direct?"

"Often enough to make life interesting," Val smiled. "He's learning to be truthful. There's a story that goes with that, but it'll keep."

"I see," Jelli said. She didn't, of course. She sounded more like her old self, a friendly donut-loving church-going person.

"Something happened," she said, "about a month ago. My memory of it is not exactly blurred, but–well, maybe blurred is the right word. You know how when you remember things, you know what happened first, then what happened next? This is different. It's ... unusual. Sometimes it feels like it's not a memory at all but still happening. It's like I'm pulled like a drawstring shutting a bag. It jerks me back into the event itself. It's strange. I'm here and I'm there, too, watching myself talking to you. Am I making sense? It never lasts long and ..." she twiddled her thumbs on her folded hands. "Here I am. Maybe I should see a therapist."

Brad was back with her water. "Thanks," she said, and gulped down the entire cup, then wiped her mouth with the back of her hand. "I was telling them how I go into like a freeze-frame, like when the picture freezes on the TV."

He looked around to see if someone else was listening. "Do you think we should talk about that here?"

"Why not? I'm not *ashamed* of it, Brad," she said in a *Glenn Close Fatal Attraction won't-be-ignored* sort of voice. "They asked me what happened. It's not like I committed a crime."

Brad nodded, more to not contend than agree with what she said. "I didn't say you had." He looked at Val and me. "Not what you expected, right?" He forced a laugh. But it wasn't a light moment, it wasn't the nothing-to-see-here moment he wished it were. He put his hand on her hand and stroked it for a moment, and when she didn't respond he half-rose again. "We should be getting home," he said. "I have a bunch of things to do. It was nice to meet you both. You'll have to come visit."

Jelli laughed. "That's Minnesotan. It means you'll never see our place or look in our drawers."

Val did her best to keep them from leaving.

"What do you do?" Val asked. "Your work, I mean."

He half-sat back down, intending to give her a quick reply and get away.

"I sold a business based in the twin cities. I know the routine up there a lot better than down here. I don't have contacts here."

"They all grew up together," Jelli said, "in Edina. Kindergarten, high school, maybe away for college but then back, rinse and repeat."

"Not like Chicago," Val said.

"No," Jelli said. "Not like anywhere else in fact. Maybe Scandinavia."

"I'm looking too," I said. "My prior career is a done deal."

"What did you do?" Jelli asked.

"Me? I was a spy," I said.

Jelli laughed at my reply. "Of course you were. I was a ballerina"– funny because her body was anything but.

"I'm looking for work too," Val said.

That took our minds off Jelli's event. Until I brought it up again.

"I'm still curious–" I said.

"Time to get home," Brad said, rising all the way this time and waiting until Jelli slid her chair back and rose.

"Another time," Jelli said.

"Maybe we can do lunch?" Val said.

"I'd like that," Jelli said. They exchanged data, tapping their phones, and we said good-bye. A dozen others milled about the basement but we didn't know them and had no interest in barging into a conversation. So we left as well.

"That was actually the most interesting thing that happened this morning," Val said, once we were outside. "What was that was about?"

I had to shrug. "I don't know. Interesting, eh?"

"Like she was a marionette."

I was quiet for a moment as we walked toward our Prius, hoping no one had stolen the catalytic converter while we were at church. I squeezed her hand and said, "Honey, I'm learning more about Dasein and I'll share it if you want to hear. Joe has pretty much finished his informal orientation. I signed an NDA, of course, but what the hell. You want to know what he said?"

"Sure," she said."What did he say?"

Our strategy of holding-each-other-while-walking-to-stay-warm slowed us a bit but we made it to the Prius. The wind was like a hawk swooping down on exposed skin but the sunshine helped, although it was blinding. reflecting from cars, windows, mirrors. The Prius, thank God, heated up quickly. Sunday traffic was sparse, and I gave Val the story as we drove home.

Interlude
Questions Sylvia neglected to ask Nick

Tell me about yourself and describe your background in brief.

What type of work environment do you prefer?

How do you deal with pressure or stressful situations?

Do you prefer working independently or on a team?

When you're balancing multiple projects, how do you keep organized?

What did you do in the last year to improve your knowledge?

- "Common Job Interview Questions,"
Harvard Business Review, Nov. 11, 2021

Chapter 3
What Box?

The office we used, a suite (we liked to call it) in need of paint and better ventilation, was on the second floor of the Barclay Building, west of the main boulevard, a space that was way too bright with fluorescent light ("we have got to replace those lights" was the second thing I said). But when we turned them off, we were left with pale winter light through windows badly in need of washing. The low clouds stayed for weeks, it was either snowing or going to snow, and the corners of the main room were cobwebbed with shadows. A cool draft came under the door from the hallway and the wind whistled through the ill-fitting windows. ("The windows should be replaced," was my first comment, followed by looking up at the lights which sizzled and hissed and occasionally flickered. That's when I made the comment about the lights.) The place made a cubicle farm seem plush. On top of that, I could feel low pressure moving in from the northwest; my sinuses were never wrong and my face wore a pinched unhappy look.

I did not look like a happy camper coming to a formal orientation. It was not a great way to start my official meet-and-greet. When I went there with Joe, I hadn't focused on the ambience. I was locked into his narrative and could have cared less about the setting. The main room had a long table and metal chairs on all four sides; a hallway led to three smaller rooms, but I hadn't been down there yet. The walls were dingy, reminding me of the hallways at the agency, always in need of a fresh coat.

My anxiety about my suitability for the task and how much I wanted approval intensified my stress. I didn't know what the job entailed yet, but I wanted it, I wanted to be included, I wanted to be part of a team again. I wanted former colleagues to validate my skills–to validate, in fact, my insecure shaky self. Joe said the purpose of the meeting was to greet the team but I knew his invitation to join them could always be changed.

No one knew why it was called the Barclay Building. It had nothing to do with the condos on the South Side. We think it was a trader on the merc, a guy named George Barclay, who made a lot of money on inside tips, then practiced law on behalf of his former cronies, keeping their sentences light. According to stories in the Trib, he owned a number of buildings, likely as a tax dodge–he certainly didn't keep the building up–but the team didn't have a lot of funding, not at first. They were just getting under way, Joe said, apologizing for the look. It was more important that the place be mostly quiet. Once they signed a lease, they lined the walls of the viewing room with noise-absorbing material. We called the main viewing room The Bridge. Ideally viewers would hear nothing but the chattering of their own minds. The passing traffic on the street was far enough away to sound like the ocean in a conch shell. We soundproofed all the rooms as best we could, and while it wasn't as good as a real scif, it worked pretty well. We wanted to keep noise out and of course we wanted to be secure but we were a small tight group and counted on mutual trust, not technology, to keep our conversations close.

I learned too that once you had gone to the Bridge a few times, and knew you were there to view, your brain prepped you unconsciously as you walked down the hall. You shifted into the right frame and aligned with the task as you entered the room. The brain said, in effect, "I remember this; I know what we're doing here." If you didn't settle in, something was in the way and had to be identified. If you tried to push it aside, you wasted energy needed for the task. You needed to be free of distractions. The readiness was all.

Joe tried to arrange for facilities at Eglin but he didn't have the tickets and couldn't pull it off. He said their facilities were great–they had everything we would need down there–but he really wanted warm weather. Sylvia Warner however hated humidity, heat, mosquitoes and palmetto bugs, i.e. cockroaches renamed by a marketing team. "Besides," she said, "it'll all be under water soon. Here we're a mile from Lake Michigan. We'll escape the worst when the waters rise."

"The waters don't rise here," Joe said, "the lake freezes. Ice builds up on the shore. When the temperature is real low, the water mists like steam. If you pause to admire the beauty, your eyelids do ice over, but it's quite nice for a few minutes."

"Uh-huh," she said. "Thank you for sharing."

When I went for my first real sit-down with the big three, Sylvia was alone in the office, looking through a folder. Before I could say hello, she closed it and said, "Well. Good morning, Nick." She looked at her watch. "You're a bit early–anxious I imagine. You know the old adage: early is anxious, on time is compulsive, late is hostile."

"Yes," I smiled.

"Yes. Well. ... So. What did Joe tell you?"

"He outlined the game plan but not much detail. He told me some of the results in the semi-official program, the one they claim no longer exists. I think he wanted me to understand that the way I think needs an update. It reminded me of when someone gets clearances and learns that everything they thought was wrong, that everything they read in the Times was incorrect, that they had been working with people who knew more than they did and never clued them in. I got the feeling he was priming me for emptying my cup, as the Buddhists say, before refilling it.

"He said I might have a role here. We didn't discuss specifics. The main focus, of course, was remote viewing. We agreed to explore options. That was it."

"Nothing signed and sealed."

"No. I assumed you three would need to agree on anything important."

"We would. We all have to sign off on major decisions. Hal and Joe said yes. So ... let's get something straight right off the bat. All right?"

"All right all right all right," I drawled, to no effect, if I hoped to make her crack a smile.

"It's not a time for jokes, Nick. We stick to protocols; we do not color outside the lines. You have a reputation for doing that, you know."

"Improvisation, you mean. A practical necessity once you engage the enemy."

"Improvisation? No, rationalization. Listen, Nick: We have a business here. Our clients expect us to stick to our knitting. We keep relationships with clients close. Our reputation is everything. If methods are suspect, we'll be out of business overnight. Other intelligence veterans work for businesses or government clients and use what they learned inside and that's why they're hired. They use their connections. Our approach is not even borderline respectable. People will ridicule our work. It's hard enough to do remote viewing without dealing with that but that's how it is. So even though you're just exploring at this point and we're checking you out, you can't say one word to anyone. Understood?"

"Sure," I said.

"You can't have friends like Nat. You two talked about things you should not have discussed. You need to observe the rudiments of trade craft. We don't have the luxury of flexing. Our protocols are not elastic. If you need to talk about anything related to work, you talk to one of us."

"OK. I understand."

"That includes the woman you're currently living with, Valerie Patchett."

"You backgrounded Valerie?"

"Of course. She's a surprise—almost normal in most ways. The only red flags are the partners she picks. That guy named Pilgrim was a real case. Now you."

"Oh?" My eyebrows went up. "How is that, Sylvia?"

"The biggest issue is, she's content to be with you. That requires a particular temperament. It's like the Groucho joke, you should not be in relationship with someone who wants to be in relationship with you. The fact that she seems to love you, whatever that means, can affect your discipline or hers." She did finally smile. "The jigsaw puzzle pieces that make up your two psyches must have been cut with a bendy saw. It must feel like a fit. From out here, it looks rather neurotic. Glad you have her, Nick, but we have to be mindful of security concerns. She's susceptible to manipulation by certain kinds of people. I don't like the term but she's classically co-dependent. Which means she can't be trusted to keep her mouth shut. She goes all in at once when she picks up someone's distress."

"I think she can be appropriate. She knows what it means to be with me. She understands what made her pick someone like Pilgrim. She got plenty of counseling so she wouldn't do it again.

We talk about all that. Humans can grow, you know. She's sharp as hell, in her way, which is, yes, a little different, sure, but exactly what I need. She has a clue, Sylvia. Co-dependent? That means she intuitively gets things right away, she reads people well. I think she's honestly psychic, her intuitive leaps are so quick."

"I hope you're right. You'll be adjusting to our culture and she'll be adjusting to you as you do. People pass along adaptations like the flu. I don't want to get new-agey, Nick, but this work will transform how you think. Joe wasn't kidding. You'll go through what Hal calls a zone of annihilation that calls into question everything you think. Then you'll put it together again on the other side. We'll help you do that. We don't know how viewing works, just that it does. We have to explain to clients what we do, but all we have is metaphors. Hal quotes a poem about 'skipping the bounds of earth, climbing sunward, dancing the silver skies,' as if it describes our work—which it does in a right brain way. Once you have the experience, the metaphors make sense. But we have to tell clients a compelling story that sounds scientific. We do the best we can with that. We're also waiting on a decision by a guy who might help with funding. He speaks science, not science fiction.

"Nick, you'll try to figure out what's going on. You'll want to talk about it. We can help you connect the dots but the picture they'll reveal will not be what you expect. It wasn't for anyone at the agencies, once they got into it. Are you following me?"

"I am."

"If you have questions or concerns about anything, ask Joe, ask Hal, ask me. Capisce?"

"Sure. And by the way, it's nice to see you again, Sylvia."

"Don't be a wise-ass."

I tried again.

"Simon says smile."

Nope. Nothing.

"OK, Sylvia, we'll keep it all businesslike."

"I'm not dicking around, Nick. This is a serious business. We can't take a chance on you or anyone else fucking it up." She paused, deciding, I think, whether to pull out her next card. "Some stories follow you, Nick. The Brits, I understand, requested that you be transferred. The Director apparently complied."

"That's bullshit and you ought to know it. I was commended for what I did with the Brits and elsewhere too. Not in Poland, obviously. Those stories were invented after I blew the whistle on torture. You know they destroy you if they can, once you tell the truth. They attack your reputation, your character, everything, and invent things to support their assaults."

"And sometimes, where there's smoke—"

"There's someone with matches. They wanted to undermine my credibility. If I did half of what they said, I'd be in jail."

She had to know that was true. But I was still on probation. "If we weren't willing to give you the benefit of the doubt, we wouldn't be having this conversation. The three of us agreed, we'll take a chance, see how it plays out. If you don't fit, pick up your marbles and go home. Or we'll make the decision for you. That's the bottom line."

"I understand," I said. "Look, Sylvia, what Joe said really got me interested. I need a new direction and this might be it. We'll see. If I add value, we'll know it. But don't bring up the lies the agency spread. We all have histories. You had your own baggage, didn't you? Do you know what you were called at DOJ, after you left the agency?"

She reddened. "I heard a few names. I expected no less. I'm a woman. Do you know what it's like to work up through the ranks in a white male military culture?"

"I can't know first hand but I can imagine."

"There was no game plan for women. Christ, Nick, how many nights I nursed a drink through hours of drunken sexist small talk, trying to be 'one of the guys.'"

"You and I both built informal networks to do a task, didn't we, Syl? You, I understand, recruited whoever was valuable, academics, people from other agencies, whatever you needed to do the job. You might call that improvisation."

"There was no other way to do it. I suffer fools poorly, Nick, and I swam in a pool of fools. And I know what it does to anyone who has to work like that, including me. At Dasein, too, the results matter. People think remote viewing is balderdash. They think it's snake oil, Nick. And look at us: I'm a woman with as you say a 'history,' you're a whistleblower, and Hal ... how well do you know Hal? Did you know he talks to what he calls 'faerie?' He believes in fairies, Nick. He thinks they help him with his work. Ask him sometime for a taxonomy of the wee folk. Then hold on to your hat."

I had to smile. "I remember some of his stories."

"Well, that's how people think of remote viewing. Joe is the most normal of the bunch, and you know his story, too, don't you?"

I laughed. "Everybody does. But he was a good analyst."

"Which is why he had a career, despite everything."

"OK, so we're eccentric or high-on-the-spectrum. The agency is full of people like us. "

She finally really smiled. "Yes, but to normals, we look pretty odd. We have to remember that and protect the enterprise. Give them stories that make sense in their frames of reference. It's OK if they scratch their heads, so long as they hire us."

"So let's assume we all come to this with good will and know what's at stake. I know they tried to derail you. You outplayed, outwitted, and outlasted all of those bastards. So fuck 'em, Sylvia. Let those pricks walk all over one another to get to mahogany row. Fuck 'em all."

Her face had not exactly softened but it looked more neutral. I was willing to settle for that. Under all of her prickliness, she was damned good at what she did and earned our respect. Once you hear someone's life story, you stop judging them and have compassion. You get that had you been in their shoes, you would have done the same things. You say "I know" with a different tone of voice. They get it. They get that you know.

"OK," she said. "We understand each other, then." She extended her hand. We shook with mutual firmness. "Welcome to Dasein Inc. Now, until we're all here, why not get some coffee? We'll meet at ten."

"You brew it here? Or use pods? Or what?"

"Jordan's is right down the street. Turn left out of the door. They use a good strong roast. Try it. I'll get back to this work I have to finish before tonight."

With none of the other guys around, it seemed like a good idea.

Interlude

And all that has existed in the space of six thousand years:

Permanent, & not lost not lost nor vanishd, & every little act,

Word, work, & wish, that has existed, all remaining still In those

Churches ever consuming & ever building by the Spectres

Of all the inhabitants of Earth wailing to be Created:

Shadowy to those who dwell not in them, meer possibilities:

But to those who enter into them they seem the only substances

For every thing exists & not one sigh nor smile nor tear,

One hair nor particle of dust, not one can pass away.

- William Blake, *Jerusalem*

Chapter 4
The Perils of Caffeine

Jordan's was an independent coffee shop. The first impression was thrown-together, not too slick, a club house for the neighborhood. Inside the door were cork boards covered with flyers and business cards, stuck over one another with pushpins and thumb tacks (drawing pins, we called them in England, which took me a while to learn). Cards were covered by other cards but it didn't matter because no one read them anyway. Cell phone numbers on tags had been pulled off for cleaning walks, shoveling show, hiring a nanny, finding lost cats. The mess implied that we were a community, not just a coffee shop. Nothing looked new, everything looked comfortable. The easy chairs angled toward each other at a fire place was a nice touch, the flickering flames looking almost real from a distance.

I ordered a mocha latte and was surprised when instead of squirting in syrup the barista used fresh chocolate, ground with a pestle, and poured the espresso over it. It really was quite good. I sat alone at a table near the window and looked out at the streetscape I would come to know so well.

I was in an unusual mood and the street seemed like a dream. The city was transmuted by mist which made it seem otherworldly. The old brick of buildings across the street was weathered and the stuff of artistic photography. I thought of photos of red wooden doors with paint flaking off or lights at the ends of hallways. The street had its own personality, having absorbed the emotions and long-forgotten behaviors of thousands who had passed by. The coffee made my brain perk and I felt alert and aware as I watched people pass by the window, indifferent to the fate awaiting the planet when the sun would expand and become a red giant and swallow the earth.

tick tick tick

I knew nothing of psychometry, not back then. I still thought in terms of old-school physics. Feelings did not adhere to things, is what I thought. People passing on the walk did not sound like rain. They were silent, muted by the window and occasional traffic. Whatever they carried in their pockets told no stories, however long the objects had been there. No one could pick up feelings or scenes by holding someone's object. Those were things I knew for sure.

I picked up feelings easily, but never questioned how. In my agency work, I intuitively knew how people felt and used it to advantage. Empathy was just another tool, friendliness a lure like twigs and boughs I could lay across a pit and wait for the crash of branches when they fell.

One person stopped in front of the window and looked inside. Our eyes met for a moment, then he looked past me at the counter and the tables. I turned to look where he looked. A back door led to a patio of sorts but the door was closed because of the cold. A hallway led to a restroom, I guessed. Pastries were displayed behind glass at the counter, some plates left empty to show us what we missed. The barista was busy with an order. A young woman in a blue parka and blue and white woolen cap with a blue pompom on top was waiting for a flat white. The espresso machine steamed and hissed, and he worked the spout with a rag until it was clean, then layered milk onto the brew with care. She dropped a dollar into the jar and went with her coffee to sit and work.

I turned back around. The passerby was short and heavy and wore a threadbare winter coat. He wore no hat and his hair was mostly gone. His face was reddened by the cold or some disorder of the skin, rosacea maybe, I don't know. His hands were in his pockets so he may have been wearing gloves, maybe not. Whatever he hoped to find, it wasn't in the shop, and he turned away and walked on up the street.

I never learned his name nor what he had done with his life. He wasn't a person of interest. He was one of the millions we ignore every day who swarm around us like gnats. I left him on the edge of awareness where he would soon disappear from short term memory. Almost everyone I met except a few lived in that fog, slated for removal by an automated timer.

Memories are altered by the way our brains store lossy versions. We call them memories to stabilize, homogenize, and make less painful the past we want to think we lived. They are the training wheels that keep the bike of our lives on track. Negative impacts have a high priority. They remind us what to fear while positives pass through awareness like neutrinos. When we're stressed, we don't even form short-term memories, much less encode them for long term storage, and the few we do encode pop like bubbles in foam. If an event is not threatening, it's background noise. If we want to remember "good" things, we have to focus intensively. Meditation counters the negative energy of real threats and imaginary fears. It placates the demons that otherwise torment us. We try to counter entropy, doing our best in a battle that's already lost.

The present is as elusive as the past because there is no present, only the recent past which the brain reports to my conscious mind as quickly as it can but always with latency. Memories align with the world I build out of expectations, core beliefs, assumptions about reality so fundamental I don't know I have them. My worldview is consistently renewed and unless some trauma knocks me off my feed, it's one I prefer to believe.

Trauma did knock me off my feed. I took the advice of my betters like a doctor who had nightmares from Abu Gharib and a meltdown after truckloads of bodies passed him on the road after a tsunami. He gave me a short list of things to do and they do help, but they don't erase the images and sounds. I suddenly think of a guy on a leash who could barely crawl to a tiny box where we crammed him into confinement in the dark. If I knew of a drug that could erase those thoughts selectively, I'd take it in a minute. The only ones I know will carpet bomb my memory and I don't want that. I don't want to be a blank slate. I'm doing the best I can, and I hope remote viewing will not add to my burdens. I hope it will take me out of time, out of my troubled state of mind, to interesting places. I need a vacation from my brain.

I'm getting ahead of myself. Reflection on memory and time came later. That morning as I waited for the meeting I knew little about viewing. After Joe and I met at the Wild Rose we hurried through the rain to the office, and after I signed an NDA, he gave me a preliminary briefing. I felt like a ten-year-old who had walked into a calculus class.

Let me bring you up to speed. Here are my notes on what he said.

I want you to know what you're getting into. Remote Viewing 101. When you look at the possible sources of data that come directly to us, the categories blur. Clairvoyance might be clairvoyance or it might be psychometry. It might be ESP. It depends on how accessible, how available, the feelings or thoughts are, if not from someone thinking them, then imprinted on the environment. Feelings do adhere to things. That sounds crazy but they do. How else can we retrieve them when no one's at the site? I think of them as modules, looking like folded proteins, but that's for my convenience. I have no idea what they're like. But it gets worse. Precognition is real, which takes some getting used to. Most impressions come in "real time" but we receive them from the past or future too. Causes sometimes follow effects. Events occur at discrete points in spacetime, and each has unique coordinates. Each exists in its own frame of reference. Each is happening now, but its own now, not anyone else's. They are never simultaneous, as you might guess.

At that point I said, might guess? Joe, what the hell?

Just listen, Joe said. Get the basics first, OK? When we do remote viewing we apparently access a variety of sources but it's hard to distinguish one from another. We get thoughts from people's minds and feelings embedded in places and sometimes events that happened in the past, more rarely from the future. We've done it enough to know what's happening but not why or how. The logs inside the agencies are full of documented sessions but they don't explain how it works.

If we're picking up data from a person, is it someone there 'now,' or one who was there, or one who will be there later? How does transmission move from their now to mine? If we tell people this, they'll cart us off to a padded cell. We have to translate what we do into words they'll understand. We have to use Newtonian tropes. We have to pretend we have a clue.

As Joe spoke, waving his hands and expostulating rapidly, I jotted notes as quickly as I could, as if transcribing a foreign language to translate later, using a dictionary, google, or a chatbot. I couldn't think about what he was saying, only take it down and plan to go through it later.

We think consciousness is non-local, Joe said. The universe might in fact have thousands of non-local connections. They might be rapid-communication channels which would mean the universe is conscious. That's a big idea, right? Otherwise it's too big to think or become conscious, but if those channels move data faster than light, they shrink it down to size.

Let me say it another way. We're fetching impressions from somewhere. But the picture depicts a thing or event. It doesn't depict molecules or atoms. The lines or dots or arcs we draw turn into patterns that make sense in a macro way; we see images of silos or crashed planes, not particles. Somehow the impressions come to us at a level that relates to our structures of cognition and our interests or intentions. It's as if the universe is written in machine language that transforms itself into natural language so we can understand it. But who does the translation, Nick? The remote viewer? Or is it implicit in the process itself? Do aliens receive impressions tailored to their different brains? This is the "what the fuck is happening" part of remote viewing. How does information transform itself on the fly so human minds can apprehend it? Is the level of abstraction determined when the packet of data is opened by a mind, the way a particle or wave becomes one or the other when observed? Do all possible levels of abstraction travel together superposition-like and unpack when the receiver looks?

Here's an example, Nick: remember the Bill Higgins case? You heard about that, I imagine, the story went everywhere.

Is that where the viewer found the room in Lebanon where Higgins was held captive? He described how Higgins was tortured, didn't he?

Yes. The same guy described the Lockerbie flight and the explosion–before it happened. After the crash, we knew what he meant. Wow, right? So why did he see inside a building in Beirut where Higgins was held and not the bricks or the atoms themselves? We don't see atoms, we don't see quarks, we see something meaningful to us. Is there some self-organizing principle that makes that happen? When a viewer drew a new kind of boomer before we knew it existed, was he getting it from the site or from someone's mind? The more we learn, the stranger it gets. God does apparently play dice with the universe but the dice are loaded and sometimes hidden. Is calling entanglement "spooky action at a distance" the best we can do? Does entanglement as a term untangle what is happening? I think not, Nick. I think not. And by the way, Einstein was talking about quantum mechanics as a whole when he said that, not entanglement.

I nodded as if I understood. I said "I know" a number of times, a placeholder for "I don't have a clue."

Think about psychometry, Joe said. We define it as feelings or images adhering to physical objects. Good psychics pick up the feelings and relate them to scenarios. I talked to a neighbor who told me an odd story. She was on a tour in Spain and going through a courtyard in the bright summer sun. When she crossed to the shade near a wall, the temperature fell, she got really cold. She shivered and went back into the sunlight. She asked what was going on and the guide said that's where Franco's men shot prisoners. How does fear and terror stick in stucco? How are feelings embedded in a wall?

All we have are questions, Nick. We're not even close to answers, Data doesn't arrive in a package with a bar code. For all we know, feelings cling to dust mites.

I laughed at an image of feelings hanging by their fingernails to floating motes in a swirl of Brownian motion, their dangling legs flailing, but it wasn't funny. It wasn't the ideas that were hard to grasp–I read plenty of science fiction, which was how it sounded– it was Joe's contention that multiple dimensions interpenetrate the ones in which we live.

But it worked well enough to gather intelligence. No wonder research into remote viewing was hidden in black budgets with cover stories nested in plausible narratives. Remote viewing, like UFOs, was debunked to keep it secret, even though others, like the Russians, were doing it too, just as they knew about UFOs for as long as we did.

I told Joe I had a hard time trying to stay attentive. I was getting a headache.

Get used to it, he said. I want you to see why this is more than a job. It leads to a new way of seeing things. As intelligence pros, we learned to live outside the consensual realities of the herd. We knew how to move between worlds and manipulate beliefs to our advantage. At the agencies, our work was driven by self interest, political shenanigans, the need to control and dominate. This is an existential threat to what we think is real. People get scared when the underpinnings of their beliefs are pulled out and the whole thing comes tumbling down. But science does that, time after time. We have to follow the data. We have to follow science. We have to believe in reality.

OK, take a break, Nick. Our brains can't think impossible thoughts for long, can they? We can't handle too much reality. That's also why we need one another to reinforce that all this exists, so we won't regress into obsolete models. At the same time, we're struggling to invent a language to make sense of what we're finding, to clients, yes, but also to ourselves.

Joe and I were alone in one of the smaller rooms. The dirty windows were streaked with rain. The walls were a dingy color that lacked a name. The sheet vinyl flooring ought to have been replaced. I felt pressured by his intensity and the meaning of his words. Remote viewing as a practice was one thing; understanding what it meant was the crazy-making part.

Joe was stretching my thinking in ways that felt insane. Spacetime was pockmarked with feelings that we can retrieve. Events we intend to see come into view like the grin of the Cheshire cat. Our three dimensional world with Euclidean shapes is only one way to think; the universe has lots of possible shapes like balloons that can be twisted into ducks or dogs. During a viewing, locks morph to let keys fit while the keys are on their way to the door.

Help me understand, I said. How does it happen?

That's the the wrong question, Joe said. I'm trying to tell you, Nick, that we share a consensual hallucination like cyberspace a la William Gibson. But he might have said the same after speech or writing or print. We've always lived in a consensual hallucination. People who know it are called shamans. We thought of naming Dasein Shamans-R-Us but thought it was presumptuous, never mind meaningless. The key thing is, we can work with what we're finding and make it practical and useful.

What does that mean, work with it?

He tried to suppress his impatience. I was usually the one wanting others to get to the point. I was learning how it felt to be the dumbest guy in the room. Joe forgot what it took to learn a new language.

It doesn't matter *how* it happens, he said. The important thing is that it does. Focus on that. We can use what we learn to bootstrap ourselves to the next level of the game. I'm speaking from experience, Nick. I am not making this up. Talk to the guys at SRI. Talk to Swann, talk to Puthoff, talk to Kit, talk to McMoneagle, they'll tell you. "Work with it" means we apply what we learn in a practical way.

I could see the honey and smell the honey but I could not for the life of me reach the honey. I felt like a UFO researcher who had been at it for decades but still had trouble believing what he knew. Each event had a sheen of newness about it, as if it's unique instead of one more data point in a well-documented set. We reject evidence that threatens us. Denial cushions the shocks that would shatter our equanimity. Earthquakes like that can wreck a society. Scientists retreat to former models to keep themselves sane, too, they follow emotions as often as rational facts, just like the rest of us. They too are caged in group-think.

So the paranormal is normal? I said. We need to change how we think? Is that the bottom line?

That's right, he said. Good. You're getting there.

We also want you to read about time. The way we think of time changes when we do viewing. We don't know what time is, only how to define it for different ends. The frame of reference, Einstein said, determines how time passes for someone in that frame. We have trouble holding four or five dimensional models in our minds. We know better, but we retrofit the data for a non-relativistic universe.

All this verbiage is theoretical, Nick. We pretend we're philosophers or physicists but we don't have the training. So we focus on practice. In theory, theory and practice are the same, but in practice, they're different. Pixels will populate your mind during a viewing like a pointillist painting painting itself. You'll sketch an impression of what you see. You'll tease it from the context in which it was embedded. You'll connect the dots or the dots will connect themselves. Then we'll analyze it. It's really that simple.

I wondered if I could do it. I thought of my friend Edgar Mitchell. His sister-in-law told me the family thought he was crazy. He spent years trying to tell people what happened to him on the return trip from the moon. He fluctuated from one state of consciousness to another for three days. In one mode, everything was connected. In another, things were separate. That everything is connected is not a surprise, he said; the odd thing is that we think they're separate.

The hiss of the espresso machine jolted me back into the cafe. I left my meditative state and heard conversations, smelled coffee, felt the hard wood of the chair on my back. I was back in the world of sensations, the world of my now.

I turned my attention once more to the view through the window. I thought of the man who had looked in. He had hoped to find something in the coffee shop that might make his day a little better. He wore an aura of despondency: the plight of aging on display. Soon enough—a few months, a few years, what did it matter?—he would be gone and forgotten. He knew he was almost out of time—but how can we be out of something we don't have? Time is embedded in consciousness. Consciousness is embodied. We are time-bound body-bound travelers transiting a landscape that keeps changing.

I thought of the guy as lonely, patrolling the cold streets, eyes on the pavement, minding where he stepped. When he was gone, I felt an absence on the sidewalk where he had been walking, a residue of energy. I imagined his despair as he searched for a handhold on the wall of life he had to climb. The impression he left on the landscape was like a scrap of paper in the wind. Then the street waited once again for people or cars, some going to work, some going home, some going nowhere. Waiting without hope, because hope would be hope for the wrong thing. The city was an empty vessel, waiting for humans to fill it. Traffic flowed two ways. The arrow of time, too, flows both ways. Janus looks forward, Janus looks back, but there is no Janus here and now. There is only a convenient self that unfolds like origami. Our selves are built of modules like Indra's jewels, mirrors reflecting mirrors.

Cold terror froze me abruptly. I couldn't move, my breathing became shallow, and I was a prisoner of my memories, chained to the wall of time. I thought of Higgins in his chains, tortured to death for pleasure and a purpose. I thought of one of our captives who had died—an "oops death" we called it—when a three hundred pounder bounced on him too many times. I breathed deeply, in and out, in and out, until I returned to the ordinary. My fear eased in the consolation of the coffee shop, normal people around me, the pale light of the plain day.

I would ask for forgiveness if there was someone to ask.

There is no innocence to lose nor paradise to gain. There is only negotiation.

I am trying so hard to burn clean with a blue flame.

Work with new colleagues might help me escape the nightmares of my past. Dasein promised a life on the edge, which I needed, but on a sunnier side of the street. The numinous has always drawn the moth in me to the flame. I can do Icarus one better; I can fly close to the sun, even get singed, but live to flutter another day. I may be wounded, but I can still fly. I am willing to be burned in pursuit of Promethean fire. I am willing to be chained to the rock.

Based on Joe's lecture, a new cornerstone for the edifice of reality would come to me through remote viewing. But it would take time to become a touchstone to which everything else relates. It takes time for a new idea to squirm its way through denial.

Joe told me one basic fact with all his words: remote viewing was real.

And suddenly I wanted to try it. I wanted to see what I could do on my own.

In retrospect, that was idiotic. I should have read the fucking manual as Joe tried to tell me.

I closed my eyes. I gave myself time for the darkness to faintly glow. I tried to detect people passing on the walk. I thought someone was right in front of the cafe. I followed the image to the corner where they waited for the light. I thought it was a woman– middle-aged, hatless, hair streaked with gray, about five feet four. She was anxious to cross. She shifted from one foot to the other, shivering in the wind.

Then she disappeared.

I had no way to know if I was seeing someone or imagining that I was. I tried to remember the storefronts, doorways, empty walks that I passed on my way from the office. If someone else was walking toward the cafe, maybe I could feel their presence, the way we know when someone is looking at us. I pushed my awareness out into the street, seeking the sense of a person. I was of course doing everything wrong. If I thought I would learn viewing by doing, it wouldn't be by doing *that*.

Then I heard again the sounds of a normal morning in a coffeeshop. I heard a chair scraping on the floor, the espresso machine at full roar, the clanking of plates. I felt a chill on my face as the door opened and closed slowly.

I wondered if someone really had been on the corner, waiting for the light to change. I wanted to go see if they were walking down the block. I started to get up but a voice interrupted me.

"Is one enough?"

I opened my eyes and turned toward the barista. Although there were others at random tables, I knew he was talking to me. I sat back down. The windowlight obscured the interior of the shop, with patches of brightness and shadow. I saw him looking in my direction.

"One is enough for now," I said, "and thanks for the good chocolate."

"It makes a difference, doesn't it?"

"It does. It's really good."

"You know what's in that syrup?"

"No I don't. Do I want to?"

"Probably not," he laughed.

Our talking heads were like two paper cups with a string between them, the kind of walkie-talkie we made when we were kids. Our connection was minimal, the string tending toward slack. You had to pull it tight to make a connection and I didn't want to do that. Then the espresso machine roared into action, smothering conversation.

The barista was young and thin, a runner I imagined or a cyclist, working out for distance, not for bulk. He wore a plaid woolen shirt with the sleeves folded on his arms. He didn't have the muscle of a lifter or a gym rat. He had a full head of dark hair and didn't wear glasses unless he wore contacts. When the coffee-roar was done, I asked, "What's your name?"

"Kyle," he said, his voice too loud because he spoke by habit over the din of the coffee machine. Valerie and I did that when one of us muted the TV and the other was already talking over a loud announcer. "What's yours?"

"Nick," I said. "Nick Cerk."

The exchange placed me securely inside the small world of the coffee shop. I was embedded in the life they all led without giving it a thought. I looked around. Pictures by local artists were on the walls, water colors, nothing very special. A couple were portraits. There were photographs too, the artsy kind that everybody took—street lamps in the park, faces reflected in the Bean.

The woman in the blue parka was working on a laptop. The espresso machine had stopped making noise and I heard her tapping, typing away. From the street I heard the steady traffic sounding like a rushing stream. I suddenly felt comfortable in the coffee shop, calmer, less anxious about the coming meeting, less anxious about everything. I felt at home for the moment in a world that felt benevolent.

Good moments are as good as bad ones are bad.

I turned and asked Kyle for the time—I never wore a watch, I always knew what time it was, within a few minutes—and he said it was nearly ten as I had thought. I'd better get going. I put my mug in a rubber tub and blotted my lips with a napkin and put on gloves and pushed the door out into the wind. My unprotected face felt the bitter cold. I hurried toward the office, looking toward the corner where no one, of course, waited. That was a fantasy, all in my head.

I laughed at my attempt to weasel my way into remote viewing. I lost myself in my thoughts and didn't notice the cold again until I was at the building, opening the outer door. Returning to the office triggered a territorial claim. I wanted to be part of the group. The loss of my old community was growing easier to endure but I wanted that bunch, waiting upstairs in their cheap rented space, to be my new tribe.

I wanted to work with Dasein Inc. I wanted my name on a business card. I wanted to explore this strange world. I wanted, as always, to be special.

I walked upstairs to the office, using the railing for support. I didn't know if I had permission to walk in unannounced so I knocked and Joe's voice said, "Come in."

I opened the door, and there they were, a quasi-friendly team ready to interrogate me, waiting with welcoming smiles. A paranoid thought: Were they a honeypot? Was the enterprise legitimate? Had Joe come to the bar because he knew I'd be there?

I dismissed the idea. Why would the agency do that, after they turned me inside out and found nothing? Come on, I told myself, don't indulge yourself. Take the event at face value. Joe and I happened to meet. That was all. Synchronicity, perhaps, but not a set-up.

I greeted my former peers with a smile.

I felt like Lolita climbing into Humbert Humbert's bed when she learned her mother was dead. Like the grieving nymphet, you see ... I had nowhere else to go.

Interlude

"Richard, if we could do what those guys can do, they would never have sent me to the moon in a tin lizzie."

- Captain Edgar Mitchell, Apollo 14 astronaut,
to me, in conversation

Chapter 5
TMI

"The lady or the tiger?" Hal said. "Which door did you just open?"

I smiled. "The lady, of course."

"Is that a koan?" Joe said, getting up and coming around the long table to shake my hand. "Good to see you, Nick."

I hadn't seen Hal in several years. Twenty pounds more, was my guess, and a lot less hair. Might be better to be all bald. He still had that white mustache and eyebrows that were too thick. The twinkle in his eyes was what I remembered from long talks about the invisible world. Hal straddled multiple environments, some of them shared with the rest of us. I never dreamed he would be one of my guides. I would have to decide if he was merely eccentric or flat-out nuts.

He rose and came lumbering around the table.

"You old Celt!" I said. I grabbed him in a hug. He was bigger, yes, but still a great armful of warmth and affection. I couldn't get my arms around.

"How the hell have you been, Hal?"

"Good enough," he said. "Could be worse."

"Hello again," Sylvia said, not getting up. "How was the coffee?"

"It was really quite good," I said. "Glad it's not a Starbucks. Nice barista, great ground chocolate, a nice vibe."

"Where'd you go, Jordan's?" Joe asked.

"Yes."

"Our home away from home," Joe said. "Besides the coffee, the brie and turkey wrap is great."

"The scones," Hal said. "Try the maple scones."

"We ought to get started," Sylvia said. "I have a noon appointment."

So that was that. I prefer a little more small talk before getting to work. It's like stroking one another with our antennae, palping for connection. I wondered if Sylvia was a Swede. Swedes call it kallprat or dodprat, cold talk or dead talk, futile and worthless.

"Sit down," Joe said, "let's keep it informal."

We sat in metal chairs around the long table. I was surprised there was so much paper in small piles instead of files on laptops and pads.

"We'll start with the business plan. Sylvia?"

She opened a folder and read from the first of many many pages....

"Sure, it's boring. But Sylvia knows what she's doing, Nick. We need a brain like hers. She's our holdfast in the world of practicality."

"I get it, Joe. We used to use Myers Briggs to have a balanced staff. Remember how Wally assembled his team?"

Joe laughed. "Yeah. Everyone was an INTJ. But seriously, Nick,

Syl runs through minefields for us. Hal and I can't do that. She's good at what she does. She's patient and strategic and knows the ropes. She knows how to calm a client's fears when he comes into crazytown."

"I won't argue with that," I said. "I'm not looking for a playmate, just a good colleague."

"She could have vetoed you, Nick. She didn't. She's just cautious. She takes this project to heart."

"Which is good. OK, so tell me more. What do I do next?"

"We'd like you to talk to Brian Metzger. He's agreed to help you see the bigger picture. He works with us in an ad hoc way. He has a lot of experience. He's in town this week. We've got some reading we want you to do, too. It's about time."

"It is," I said. "I'm more than ready to get going."

Joe laughed. "No," he said. "No, I mean it's *about* time. We have reading we want you to do about time–*about* time."

"Oh," I repeated." About time. Yeah, I guess you said that before."

"That's right," he was still smiling. "All we know is, time isn't what we thought. Einstein gave us a new way to look at it, but he didn't go far enough. There's spooky action not only at a distance but into the future too. Apparently entanglement happens in time as well as space. Remember what I said before?"

"Somewhat. I have to keep going over it. Impossible thoughts are hard to keep thinking."

"I understand. We want you to get enough experience to know that results aren't confined to the present. There's drift from the past ... and the future too. The future exists before ... well, before it does, by our old ways of thinking. If you get results that confirm what I'm saying, you'll see what I mean. Your learning curve will steepen. We want you to expand your understanding, not just view targets for clients."

"We're going beyond Einstein?"

Joe shrugged. "We're certainly going to try. Reality does. Where else is there to go except beyond whatever came before? He was pretty smart, but he wasn't the last word." He laughed." This is breakthrough stuff.... Did you see the movie *Chinatown*, Polanski's classic? I can't believe it's fifty years old. He's cancelled by a lot of people, but the movie is still great."

"I agree. It's a classic.

"It's a good metaphor: 'It's Chinatown, Jake.' Keep that in mind. Remember what Noah Cross said? You may think you know what you're dealing with, but believe me, you don't."

I smiled."I don't? With all my experience?"

Joe smiled back. "It's Chinatown, Nick. It's Chinatown."

That conversation stayed with me because it suggested I didn't understand the bigger game they were playing. Learning if I was a good remote viewer was one thing, but allowing the realities that burst from the experience to catalyze a new way of thinking was another.

I began to think that the ability to grasp the parameters of the bigger box into which viewing took us might be the real mission of the company, followed by teaching clients to act on that deeper knowledge for themselves. In my best days at the agency, that's what I did, in a way: I saw patterns others couldn't see, told them what they were, then taught them how to see them. I didn't want people only to see what I saw but to know how I got there. In my own way, I saw "the future" before it arrived. If we acted from the future back into the present, we prevailed. The mission statement Sylvia read to me was the usual list of platitudes, but the real mission might be different: to enable clients to think differently and outflank competitors.

My conversation with Brian Metzger did not contradict that inference, but it did confuse me a little more. The guy was all about UFOs.

Brian Metzger worked in a nondescript building that looked like a normal office. Most buildings inside the beltway look like a post office, and in DC, none can be bigger than the monument, of course. Designed to confuse the enemy, one said, and the enemy is us. From a drone, it looks like a bureaucrat's wet dream. That office is where you meet him on normal business. His clandestine work is done in a bunker in the nearby Virginia hills. There is an entire world down there, a refuge kept in good order in case the government has to duck during a disaster. I didn't know how Metzger figured in, but I knew that FEMA, the alleged custodian of the Blue Ridge site, was only half the story. I was not welcome there. I dared not be seen on video at either place. Brian had to come to me.

He suggested the home of "a friend," a house in northwest Evanston. The owners were in the Caribbean and their home was a neutral spot. Mike Stonehill, the home's owner, was an executive at a well-known insurance firm and his wife Carol was the president of a small college. Both positions raised red flags. I had been recruited, after all, by a professor in my green and salad days. Spotters were paid a bounty for every scalp. And if Stonehill was a friend of Brian's, he likely played in the Great Game. Spies don't have friends outside of work. We have to be suspicious of colleagues who want to be friends at work too. I learned later that there was an office at Mike's insurance firm that transferred information to the agency. We had a lot of insurance firms in our stable. Individuals and businesses alike gave them everything, financial data, medical histories, everything, and they sent it to us. Tinker to

Evers to don't-take-a-Chance.

The front door was open and Brian was waiting in an easy chair in the living room when I arrived.

"Pretty nice," I said, gesturing with my head toward the overstuffed chairs and tables and lamps, a gray-maroon decor with pale winter light washing out the color. The drapes were open on a garden where everything looked dead. I stood at the window looking out at nothing in particular and felt the chill of the glass with the backs of my fingers. I get colder quicker in the winter and hotter in the summer now that I'm older. My thermoregulating device is not as efficient.

They must have had a dog, judging by the mess on the grass.

"The Stonehills are friends. They're healthy and can still travel wherever they want. They're in that sweet spot, Nick, before it all comes tumbling down."

"Is your life tumbling down, Brian?"

"It's ragged at the edges, that's for sure."

"What's that you're eating, almonds?

Brian had found a bowl of nuts, addictive and irresistible, and he was munching them as we spoke. When he led me downstairs, the Wedgwood bowl of almonds was in one hand and the other ferried nuts to his mouth, one by one by one.

"Yep," he said. "It's the salt that does it. Want one?"

I passed.

"You want a beer from the ice box?"

To refer to the fridge as an ice box betrayed his age. But that was no surprise. Brian was in his seventies and looked it. He gave me a beer from the "icebox" downstairs. The rec room had a large wall-mounted screen across from a leather sofa and two chairs angled at the screen from the sides. Brian explored the room in cursory fashion, not expecting anything, knowing the house had been vetted for bugs.

He sat in one of the deep soft chairs and found a button on the side that raised his legs. I hadn't noticed the boots he wore, nor his olive green pants, making him look like a plump pea in a floral-patterned pod. I took the other chair which was angled toward him and let me see his face clearly in the light of a floor lamp.

He looked his age. Ragged at the edges, as he said. How did that affect his work? I studied his face in the light, blotchy with age spots, friable skin that bruised easily. His hands showed bruising on the backs. We seem to shrinkwrap as we age no matter how much we work out.

"Joe asked me to tell you some things to expect. It'll be important for when you view. Wearing your tinfoil hat?"

"Always. I carry a spare, too."

"I'm serious. I don't want to sound melodramatic, but once you go down this path, it's hard to go back. This is some very weird shit."

"That's what Joe says."

"For good reason. You're signed an NDA, remember?"

"Of course I do."

"You're ready, then?"

"Sure. What's the story?"

"You knew I worked with Joe, right?" I nodded. "Way back when. We learned not to jump to conclusions. Let the data tell you the story. Remote viewing requires the same patience. I was recruited for viewing by a psychology prof named Bill Braud. He taught in Houston then, and I knew a guy who knew a guy who knew Bill.

Braud wrote an academic paper on "psi conducive states" for a journal. According to his work, he thought I might be a good fit. The program was called Scanate back then. I had a long learning curve. Most viewers do. Many give up or wash out. Some can't handle what happens when they do the work for a while."

"Like what? What do you mean?"

"We'll get to that in due time. For now, stay with what I'm saying."

"Go ahead," I said. Curiouser than ever.

"At first, the impressions you receive are disconnected. Over time they build into a gestalt. They're like stars at first, points of light in the void, so you might think you see a bull or a bear but you can't see the fainter data until your eyes are used to the dark. Mostly you see blank spaces between points of light but they're not really blank. Over time, you see with greater subtlety, your brain learns to cooperate. The bull or bear turns into a twisting dragon or whatever. You learn how to become more conscious of what you filtered out. It's like replacing the Hubble with the James Webb. You see more than you think, but not consciously at first. Part of the game is training the unconscious to show you what it knows. The more you practice, the deeper down you go like you're diving beyond the reef. The streams of information are like thermoclines. The deeper you go, the fainter the traces, but the more important they become. If it were easy, anyone could do it. You have to stay with it, get used to the dim light until the darkness is the light. Then you hang in the void, passive but aware, letting the information come to you.

"Our brains see patterns in randomness so you have to question yourself constantly: who am I to think that? What makes me think that? If you guess too quickly, you're wrong. If you jump too fast you have to unwind the spool and go back to the beginning. If you jump to a conclusion, it stays in your mind like you're watching a movie that the brain thinks is real. That becomes a benchmark. The first interpretations can occlude your ability to see clearly. You have to have a beginner's mind. That's the optimal state. You have to notice if you start analyzing what you see. You have to detach and return to a state of unknowing. Your mind always prefers what it thought it knew, not new facts. Your mind is like a parent putting a kid to bed. Parents don't care if a bedtime story is true as long as it puts the kid to sleep. Our brains repeat familiar comforting narratives and don't give a rat's ass for the truth."

"Brian, was it you who saved Gene Nieman's life?"

He smiled. "Hell, Nick, that was quite a while ago. That just happened to happen. We helped some friends patch a few holes but kept some we needed. I was testing those backdoor paths, making sure we could use them without being detected, and I happened to see some communications. I wasn't looking for them, just testing the method, but there they were, and yes, we got in easily without being seen, and yes, Nieman was in trouble. I let him know. That was all."

"They say, if you hadn't warned him, he might have been a star on the wall."

Brian shrugged."They should know. They know everything, don't they?"

"Wasn't that around the time a cryptographer was shot in the face on a DC street? Police never followed up."

"Sometimes they do as little as possible, like Jake Gittes said. They're good at that."

"I heard that related to the Nieman thing. A double agent was involved?"

Brian shrugged."I don't know anything about that."

OK. I wouldn't learn anything more. Not knowing, never

knowing, not minding not knowing, like before. It felt like the good old bad old days.

He ate another nut, and another, and then started eating two and three at a time. At that rate, the bowl would be empty in a few minutes. "So what do you know," he asked, "about UFOs?"

"UFOs? Only what I hear. But I thought we're discussing remote viewing."

"We are. But not in the way you think. Let's take an orthogonal route. " He smiled. "Tell me what you know about UFOs."

"It's what I believe, not what I know. It's all hearsay. I believe they've been here for a long time. I believe they're a security threat just by being so far ahead of us. I think they wag their fingers in our faces if we get aggressive, like the time they turned off the avionics in the jet above Tehran or played tag over DC back in '52. They mostly make the point that way, but a few of our guys have been hurt, even killed. Mostly, though, demonstrations of power. Then there's all those stories about showing up at bases along the northern tier. Minot was a doozy. Malmstrom too, and Pease, near that famous abduction. Alleged abduction, I should say."

"You can say abduction."

"Oh? Okay. So I hear stories and file everything in my agnostic folder. ... By the way, can we still call them UFOs? Not UAPs?"

"I like the old name. I know it presumes they're unidentified, and objects, and that they fly. None of those are quite right but it's good enough. We think at least four different civilizations have been visiting. We called them all 'aliens' like Native Americans called invaders 'Europeans' until they learned the differences. They're physical objects, yes, but they're not aerodynamic the way we think of it. They move through water or into space as easily as in the atmosphere. They sometimes seem to fold in and out of spacetime. But what does that mean? I don't know. Nobody knows. And here's something for you to mull over: they're bigger inside than they look from the outside. They curve spacetime so strongly, we think, that it forms bags–Wheeler called them bags of gold–that have a small surface area but a large volume inside."

"John Wheeler? The guy who coined the terms *black hole* and *wormhole*?"

"Yes. That guy. And last but not least, our definition of 'physical' is not exact. Energy and mass are information. If you think about it, Nick, all we ever detect is information. Otherwise we couldn't see it or work with it, could we?"

"How so?"

"We'll get to that. Stick with the basic reality: Remote viewing is about information. And so, it seems, are UFOs. The point I want to make, Nick, is the methodology for exploring UFOs is similar to thinking about remote viewing. UFOs are mind-boggling technology, and anything that advanced is intrinsically a threat, as you said. We had to hide what we knew from enemies so we had to hide it from the people we protect. Information anywhere is information everywhere, the way the world works now.

"Starting in the forties, UFOs played games in our air space, surveilled installations and nuclear facilities, and we couldn't control what they did, but we could control the narrative. We had to make the people who saw them sound nuts. The resources we devoted to layers upon layers of disinformation tells you how big this is. We had to keep the stories confusing, and the visitors were confusing too. Every pattern we thought we saw turned out to be wrong. They intended that, we think. But good people, military, pilots, plain people out at night, kept seeing them. There were plenty of physical effects too, on trees and people and cars. There was plenty of weird shit, like people and cars levitating, and tractor beams, and all that woo woo stuff. Except it really happened. We had to make people embarrassed to speak about it or risk their reputations. All the while, UFOs appeared here and there to a few at a time, building the case over decades for the fact of their presence. They let us spin it any way we liked. Either they didn't care or it played to their game or it was all part of an experiment to see how we reacted or all of the above. We sometimes probe defenses with spoofed radar, and they did that too. There was no context for understanding what they wanted. The mind of an alien really is alien. Even now, we don't know what we're dealing with. Some think big questions like their identities or their ultimate rationale or the knowledge behind their technologies are totally unknowable and maybe always will be.

"On top of that, people in power will do anything to keep it. That's the first law of survival. Everything else is second. The top brass could not control the phenom but they could control the mind of society. That, as you well know, is our special gift. We are designers of the furniture inside that doll's house.

"Despite all that, what we knew to be true about UFOs challenged what we thought about the universe. Remote viewing did the same. We use the word 'universe' to mean whatever we say it means. Most people use the word to mean "everything" or "very big." Hundreds of light years across a single galactic cluster is easy to say, but can we grasp what it means? We're barely out of the tide pools. We evolved way out here in a spiral arm of a typical galaxy long after older societies flared into being. Some may have burned out by now, but some hooked up with others in confederations. Have you ever read a story called, 'Species, Lost in Apple-eating Time?'"

"No. Never heard of it.

"Read it. It'll take just a few minutes but it lays it all out. It's in some obscure collection of short stories."

"Brian, what do you—all of you involved with all this—want to get out of this?"

"The future, Mister Cerk! The future!"

The almonds were all gone and he used his fingers, moistened, to sticky-pick the remaining salt and lick it from his digits. I saw tracks of his finger-licking swiping on the sides of the bowl. The tips of his fingers gleamed in the lamp light and so did his lips, his tongue licking side to side to get all the salt.

"I'll be honest, Brian. I'm not sure what we're talking about."

He wasn't smiling any more. "We have to give you parts of the story one by one until you can see the big picture. We've been into both domains, UFOs and remote viewing, for a long time. You might have heard rumors but you didn't know what was true. You weren't read in and you had no need to know. Those were the rules. Well, Nick, at Dasein, we make the rules."

"Brian, are you on staff at Dasein? Have you retired from the agency? What's your status?"

"Don't worry about that. It's not important. I work with Dasein as I'm needed." He felt inside the bowl just in case, maybe there was one more nut, then left the bowl on the floor. "You want to know what got me interested in UFOs in the first place?"

"Sure. Can I take notes, by the way?"

"No. I prefer that you don't. Okay?"

I shrugged.

"Nick, I had an experience myself years ago so I knew that UFOs were real. I don't mean sprites or ball lightning or our own advanced technology or meteors or Venus, I mean the real deal. It was quite some time ago. I was in the Caribbean, working at a tracking site. My partner and I were walking back to quarters and taking a short cut over some dunes. We had to watch our footing in the sliding sands, so I was looking down. It was late, after midnight, when suddenly the whole damn place lit up as bright as if it was noon. It was like the sun had suddenly come up. We looked up for the source of the light and it was three very large discs maneuvering in a sort of start-stop fashion. You could see panel lines in them and dimples and opaque sections—it was very very bright, so you had to squint—and this part was crazy, all the sounds we had been hearing, the ocean, breaking waves, palm fronds rustling above us, all that vanished. Suddenly there wasn't a single sound. We were rapt, watching the acrobatics in the sky. I have no idea how long that lasted. Toward the end they stopped moving and hovered, they just hung there, motionless. Then they shot over the horizon in a tight formation, they must have gone from zero to a thousand in a flash or they folded out of space time ...."

"Wait a minute, Brian," I said. "You say things like 'folded out of spacetime.' What does that mean?"

"It means they might fold in and out of spacetime. I don't know how else to say it. Sometimes they seem to go impossibly fast, faster than our eyes can track, but sometimes they blur and smear into streaks of light. It seems like they're folding into another dimension."

"Or something."

"Yes. Or something. Anyway, once they were gone, sounds came back, the waves, the wind, everything. We went back up to the barracks and talked about it. We decided we weren't going to report it because we were in the military and who knows what they would do. I knew someone who reported an encounter and next thing I knew, he was off to the North Pole. He was traumatized by the event, but they wouldn't let him talk about it. It gnawed at him until he had to tell someone and it happened to be me. You know how it gets when there's only the two of you, and it gets late, and suddenly you're saying things that you ordinarily don't. That's what happened. The next day he was sorry he did. He asked me to forget he had said anything."

"What did he tell you?"

Brian was silent for a moment, mulling over his options. "There was a wave of sightings then, all over the country. There were op eds and articles and stories in the real news. But you know the drill. Wait it out, some celeb has a scandal, and everyone moves on. Oh what a pretty butterfly."

"But what did he say?"

"He said he watched a glowing UFO come low over the sky behind the family farm. He was home on leave, his father had had surgery and his mother was a wreck, and he went out for a smoke. Without a sound, this object passed over his head and landed behind the barn. He remembered the bright light behind the barn illuminating the mist, and then a cop came along the road and pulled up and they watched together and talked. The cop had followed it across town–Antigo Wisconsin, I think it was, not a very big place–and stopped when he saw Tom. Tom asked if he was going to go down and see what it was. The cop said, you nuts? No way! Then after a while it lifted straight up, hovered for a moment once it was off the ground, and shot off like a streak of light. Before it shot off, they could see windows or portholes. They were sure they saw movement inside.

"But get this. The next morning he went down there to see if anything was disturbed. There was a circle of broken branches about thirty feet across and grass pressed flat on the ground. But ... how well do you know cattle?"

"Not very well."

"Well, they had a small herd, and Nick, cattle know about barbed wire. They're not stupid animals. But something scared the living shit out of the cows and they piled right through the barbed wire and tore themselves all to bits and they had to put down the whole herd."

"So what's going on? What do we know and when did we know it?"

Brian laughed. "You know better than that, Nick. Cover stories on this are ten layers deep. You'll never know so leave it alone.

"So I knew that UFOs were real. I didn't know what they were, but that they were, I had no doubt. I was sure they were classified way above top secret. We couldn't ignore them and we couldn't scare the hell out of everyone. Nick, my marriage ended when my wife and I saw one at the same time and she couldn't handle it. The last straw, on top of a bunch of others things, as it always is, things we couldn't fix."

"Can you outline their agendas, then? In a superficial way?"

"I'll get to that later."

More holding back. I was growing impatient with hints and innuendoes which confused me even more.

"OK, Brian, I heard things like we were targeting the dark side of the moon. Some said they were looking for aliens. Pyramids. Ancient cities. I know we had something else in mind."

"Of course. Levinson was part of that. Halloran too. When the crazies spread those stories, we keep them in circulation."

"The bigger the lie, the easier it is to promulgate."

"The moon is strategic. The Chinese are on the dark side, looking for minerals, planning routes to the asteroids, planning for operational bases. We can't let them have the whole moon."

I tried to put two and two together and get something besides five. "Did some remote viewers contact aliens or UFOs?"

Brian uncrossed his legs and rubbed the residue from the almonds into the carpet with his foot, leaving a smudge the size of the toe of his boot. He clasped his hands behind his head and looked toward the ceiling. I didn't know if he was going to answer, but after a long pause, he said:

"There's a bunch of ways to approach it. Let me start with this: no matter how you mean it, UFOs are time machines. Let's agree that they're extraterrestrial...."

"For argument's sake."

He laughed. "Nick, what else could they be? Seventy years ago that's what the Air Force concluded. The estimate of the situation, all copies of which have conveniently disappeared. But we know Hynek read it, and Ruppelt. Guys like Al Chop knew it and said so. They weren't Russian, they weren't ours, they did things none of us knew how to do.

"Anyway, Nick, that makes them time machines of some kind. It wouldn't be efficient to travel around space and take thousands of years to go from star to star. So the fact that they are able to do that makes them time machines. They do something that accelerates their vehicles, and I don't mean the little two-person jobs that lots of people have seen, I mean the big ships that hang off the coast, out in space, like that mother-ship near Alaska. Big as two aircraft carriers, they said. The Japanese pilot Terauchi got pretty excited, and that FAA guy, Callahan,was pissed as hell when they told him to say it never happened and confiscated tons of data about the event. He went rogue and confirmed the details. Dick Haines went to Japan later to testify on the pilot's behalf when they stuck him in a desk job. Terauchi had over 10,000 hours flying time, he wasn't a novice. Haines told them what thousands of other pilots had seen and the pilot was reinstated. Anyway, big ships like that do not just cruise along for generations. They must accelerate–you know what acceleration really is, right?"

"I know we say it's the same as gravity," I said. "Einstein's principle of equivalence. An accelerated reference frame is equivalent to a gravitational field. Do I remember that right?"

I could see my hand-written notes from Skolnick's physics course.

"You do. So when I say 'accelerate their craft,' I mean they're changing their relationship to gravity which seems to vanish in fact as it did from Einstein's equations. It's not anti-gravity. That was the wrong path to explore. And it's impossible, based on what we know. In science fiction, yes, but in reality, no. They must come closer to the speed of light, closer than we know how to get. So obviously, spacetime has properties we haven't discovered, but they have, and they use them to ... they don't bypass things, they don't go around ... or through ... matter ... mass ... they ride imaginary lines on a spacetime grid like a sky diver in the wind. We can't even begin to get at it unless we know what time is, and that's one thing you've been told to explore, right?"

"Yes."

"And if you persist in remote viewing, you'll encounter UFOs or 'non-earthly intelligence' too. It can't be helped. So I'm telling you this to prepare you for when that happens. You will likely encounter UFOs. And yes, others have."

"What can you say about those encounters?"

Brian sighed. "Not too much. I can't speak to rumors you heard without adding details and I can't. I am simply suggesting, based on our experience, that you might have encounters like that. Do with it what you will. But right now, Nick, your task is to learn the discipline–cultivate the right state of mind for remote viewing, and incidentally, for evaluating UFO reports. You'll encounter hair-standing-up-on-the-back-of-the-neck sorts of things in both areas. Stay with the data, be specific, say what you see, and you'll be fine."

"Brian, I tried telling someone about remote viewing and he said, 'That's the kind of thing I would not believe in even if it existed.' You hear the same about UFOs. They can't be, therefore they aren't."

"Ignore the closed minds of the ignorencia. Be a warrior, Nick. Be mindful and vigilant. Believe everything and nothing. That's all there is to it."

"That's all?" I stretched and yawned, not from boredom but from feeling overwhelmed. "Brian, all this may be way above my pay grade."

"That's true for all of us. That's why we do this as a team. None of us is as smart as all of us. Not long ago we questioned the existence of black holes. Now we know they're everywhere. We have pictures of black holes eating their neighbors. When they merge they create gravity waves, as Einstein said. And recently we found one that looked odd. Now get this: It wasn't a black hole. It was a wormhole. We saw the deeply curved spacetime of a black hole connecting to the steep peak of a white hole and they formed a kind of bridge. A bridge, Nick. A way of getting there from here."

"Was that published somewhere?"

"It was, but not out here. You have to read it in a scif. We saw a massive object that was positioned just right for gravitational lensing. It looked at first like a black hole, because that's what we expected to see. But it was different. It flared around the edges. That wasn't normal. We've located seven formerly designated 'black holes' that are really worm holes. You find one and you start finding them everywhere. Maybe the visitors use them to tunnel through the universe. They're not the tiny baby kind, they're big enough to be portals."

"I need to take a leak," I said.

As I stood there, Brian's ideas darted around my brain like bats. I tried to follow their twittering and darting but gave up. When I came out, Brian had gone upstairs in search of something else to eat. He called down, "You like olives?"

"No."

He came carefully down the stairs with a jar of green olives stuffed with pimientos in one hand and a tiny fork in the other, a napkin between his second and third fingers, He sat and removed the lid and held the jar between his thighs and speared an olive, the first of many rescued from the brine.

"OK, back to basics, Nick. You're almost up to step one."

"Great."

"I mean it. This is background for when you get to work. Remember, UFOs are time machines, one way or another. We might think years elapse between UFO waves but at the speeds they move, it may be weeks to them. During viewings, sometimes information from the past or future shows up. We keep repeating these things and hope to find a hypothesis that make sense of the anomalies. Like discovering the benzene ring after dreaming of a snake eating its tail."

Brian held out an olive on three tiny tines. "These are really good. Sure you don't want one?"

"I'm sure, yes."

"Nick, an attack on the Cole was described two days before it occurred. The viewer described it precisely, but how would anyone know, when it hadn't yet happened?"

When you have nothing to say, ask a question.

"Did you personally detect non-human intelligence during a viewing?"

He looked at the olives and ate one and then another and thought too long. That meant he was making something up.

"Let me put it this way: One time a UFO target was mixed in with other targets and I didn't know it. The targeting material was a newspaper clipping from an incident where a pilot claimed he was paced by a UFO. It was a night flight heading for Richmond Virginia. The story was in the Richmond Times-Dispatch. Other pilots saw the plane and the trailing UFO. People on the ground saw it too. That was all in the article, which was folded and double-wrapped in a thick envelope.

"The viewing felt different. I sat at the table a long time. I might have sounded drunk, mumbling disconnected words, the monitor transcribing everything. The incoming information took a long time, but at some point, I saw the whole. I felt like I was inside another's frame of reference. You know how two bubbles attach to each other? It felt like a smaller bubble–the airplane–was bulging into a larger one–the other craft. I detected the presence of two pilots in the commercial flight and a small group of others–aliens– in a UFO. I didn't know that at the time. My mind started adding an overlay, distorting the material. It was like a strobe with flickering points of view replacing one another. It made no sense until I read the article. The pilot said he saw beings–his words, not mine–inside their vehicle.

"See, as a rule, the target doesn't know you're there. But I felt they were aware of me. I was trying to stay steady, when BLAM! a explosive flash of blinding light knocked me out of my chair. The monitor hit the deck too. Next thing we both knew, we were on the floor, staring at each other. A search for more articles turned up a witness who saw the UFO take off at a tremendous speed. Radar on the ground said the same. Blip blip blip gone. Somehow the eruption blew us back into our own frames. Did I encounter aliens, to your question, Nick? Maybe, maybe not. Did I read the article afterward and interpret my experience through it? The experience was real to me but all I can do is report it. We weren't hurt, by the way, just bruised from hitting the ground."

Brian lowered the leg lift of his chair and with his feet firmly on the ground, leaned toward me, setting the olives on the floor.

"Don't knock over the olives," I said.

"I won't," he smiled. "Does that answer your question? One viewer thinks we're dealing with information overload when we tap into something so far beyond our knowledge base. He thinks that as brains gain complexity, they comprehend a lot more and advances accelerate. It took 30,000 years to discover fire but only a few years to learn how to build a pump laser. That guy thinks we're immersed in a broad spectrum noise band. There's noise emanating out of the core of the galaxy and it affects our ability to do remote viewing. We may not scale up yet to where we can deal with all that information. But maybe some aliens have, long ago, and when there's contact between us, the gap tries to close. It does that on its own, it seems. It wants us to connect with other sentient life. That can blow us right out of the frame of reference."

"Or something."

"Yes. Or something. So we can't deal with UFOs without thinking about the nature of consciousness and the nature of time. We can't deal with remote viewing without dealing with consciousness and time. The challenge is to ride those currents without going crazy. Search for a unifying theory that includes it all." Brian leaned and picked up the jar and screwed the lid on tight. He looked at the jar as if he had a fetish for olives.

"I think that's enough, don't you? For one afternoon?"

I followed him up the stairs. He jiggled the olives to try to make it look like he hadn't had so many. He replaced the jar and rinsed and dried the fork and put it back and I followed him through the living room and out into the bright cold day.

Interlude

"With the unknown, one is confronted with danger, discomfort, and care; the first instinct is to abolish these painful states. First principle: any explanation is better than none. Since at bottom it is merely a wish to be rid of oppressive representations, one is not too particular about the means of getting rid of them: the first representation that explains the unknown as familiar feels so good that one 'considers it true.' The proof of pleasure is a criterion of truth."

- Frederick Nietzsche, *Twilight of the Idols*

Chapter 6
Me Too

Valerie here.

Nick can edit as he likes, but I want to say what took place in my own words and hope he doesn't alter them too much. He'll show me the changes and I can object if it distorts my meaning. He'll add some philosophical riffs because that's what he does. He can't help it. But Nick agreed, I am the editor, and the editor, he said, has the final word.

I am finding that a relationship, if it's to last, had better include letting someone be the way they are. The serenity prayer is framed in my kitchen right near the calendar on the wall. (I framed the December picture too. It was taken on Michigan Avenue, white lights twinkling in the trees, in the freshly fallen snow. On a cold December evening, Nick and I etched our initials in frozen snow on the trunk of a honey locust tree. NC + VP. That was sheer fun, our cheeks stinging from the cold, eyes blurred by tears that made the lights in the trees flare with prismatic beauty. When we stood back to admire our work, *Gloria in Excelsis Deo* played from hidden speakers. Nick pointed out that neither pair of initials were correct. I don't care, I said. The tree knows what we mean. I etched our initials in tiny letters on the tree in the calendar picture too. When I see it, it sometimes makes me cry.)

Beyond our collaboration at work, we have learned to trust each other completely. He'll likely rewrite what I say in wordier ways with bigger words–he's the one who pretended to teach literature and writing, not me, during his long charade with Penny, so maybe he learned to write by pretending he could. I read about a man who practiced the piano in his head while in prison and he became a better player. I read about a golfer who played a course in his head every day as a POW and reduced his handicap. The brain doesn't know the difference, it seems.

I call this section "Me Too." My turn too.

I never expected the events that ensued after the "Christmas party" for clients and investors and friends of Dasein Inc. We called it a holiday party for obvious reasons, but there was a little fir tree and a dozen ornaments and a lighted star on top, all perched precariously on a table in the room you came into first from the hallway–with relief, I said, from the odor out there, and everybody laughed. I got a good discount on tapas from the Wild Rose, formerly the Barbican, and they arranged them around the tree on real plates (a 2-1 vote said no paper plates, with one abstention). The landlord promised to clean the hallway right after the holidays, so we had to wait it out, hurry past those godawful stains on the floor and get inside as quickly as we could. Inside it was cheerful and burbling with conversation. The turnout was good. People, including me, were really very curious. Music played in the background, Pachibel's canon, mistaken for a Christmas piece, played over and over again until it was inside our heads. The wassail was well-spiked to boost our moods on a cold gray day and make potential clients susceptible to marketing.

The party was Hal's idea. He wanted to make it Wiccan and druidical but Sylvia objected, saying she knew at least one client was a devout Evangelical and would likely be offended. Think of the evergreen tree as a precursor of Christmas, she advised, imagine we're all Celtic Reconstructionist Pagans like you and think it's about the solstice, just a few days late. Hal was pragmatic as well as steeped in Celtic lore, so he agreed. He left Christmas to the Christians, both nominal and genuine. His primitive faith was rewarded: the sun hit bottom right on time and days lengthened and his world marched toward Litha. (On midsummer's day he lit a trash fire in the alley behind the offices, wisely forsaking a bonfire, but he didn't dance around it, which he said would remind him of *Spinal Tap*.)

I had not met Pantaglia or Hal or Sylvia Warner before the party, but I heard a lot about them. I wanted to know Metzger too, based on what Nick said, but he wasn't there. Nick's new posse was not like the customers I met at the Barbican, which seemed so long ago; I wanted to know what Dasein really was, know what they really did, know what he was getting himself into. My formal education was limited, luckily, so my openness to new ideas had not been squashed. Orthodoxy has its place but it can kill creativity. Once people adopt a model, most never change their minds. My model came from my life: growing up in Iowa, handling customers at the phone bank and the Barbican, two different marriages, now living with Nick which expanded my world at the speed of light, and I surf the net and watch TV. Clickbait is silly but can still teach you a few things. You can know a sitcom is made up but it still feels like friends. *Friends* felt like friends, and *Cheers* was a good model for how to do my job at the bar. A lot of people know the characters on a series better than their friends. I guess social media works the same way. People believe what they read and think bots are people. Nick said they often paid bloggers to reinforce a point of view. They use AI to generate narratives and make them travel far and wide. Memes bounce like pinballs from flipper to flipper as clueless users click inside their bubbles, credulous and trusting and naive.

When I was eighteen, I moved to Chicago to go to school and worked in a call center, handling angry impatient people. That was pretty good training for life. Two years of junior college were a breeze–the criteria for admission to Wright was, are you breathing?–but after I transferred to Northeastern, a local four-year school, I decided to marry Alvin who had waited patiently back home. That was it for higher education. I returned to Des Moines and we were married at Plymouth Congregational with only our families in attendance. The minister was tall, solemn, and disinterested. He delivered a homily by rote.

Then my high school love was killed and I was in shock. Des Moines became a haunted house: eating dogs at Chili King or pork tenderloin at Porky's became unthinkable after that. I had been to those places with Alvin so many times. I moved back to Chicago so I'd never see the corner where Alvin left the road on his motorcycle, helmetless of course, hitting a tree and breaking open his head like a pumpkin. Now that I'm older, I know that we lose our innocence as people we love die. Until we're the one that disappears, life is one loss after another. I rebounded into a bad scene with a bad actor named Pilgrim until I escaped. I went to work at the Barbican and found a refuge. I worked long hours and lost myself in camaraderie with customers. Jake was a great boss. I learned from them all. I was an attractive female version of Billy Joel's piano man, is how I thought about myself; I helped them deal with loneliness, chatting or flirting or just being pleasant, warm, hospitable, perky, optimistic, hopeful, and consoling, whatever was needed in the moment. On karaoke nights, the microphone did smell like beer. I made an OK living as they put bread in my pocket and I was mostly content. When you don't know what you're missing, you can feel quite happy.

My work was in essence sales and that came naturally. Nick said I was naturally seductive. I thought of myself as just being me. Would you like some shrooms or fries with that? Another glass of wine perhaps? I drew the line at crazy drunk, we all did, but we were in business, after all. I was Jake's best pusher. I picked up signs of sadness or loneliness and responded automatically. How can I help? Is there something I can do? My hand gently on an arm, leaning a little to look into his eyes. What do you need? Let me be your teddy bear.

Nick laughed when he read that. He said the mayor in Chicago did the same. When he found out what someone really needed and gave it to them, enemies turned into allies and they posed for photos with smiles.

Nick noted that Penny and I both tended toward co-dependency, but I said, well then! you must need women like us, key-in-lock-like, right? Takes two to tangle and all that. Why else would you pick us? So his diagnosis boomeranged.

Tango. I meant tango.

Having bailed on a college education, I was free of tenured profs whose time went mostly into jockeying for power in teeny niches, and when they reached middle age, sleeping with students if they hadn't before. That was before it was deemed a power move and many a Ph. D. was granted thanks to a willingness to stay and play. The trick was to sleep with people who had as much to lose as you did. The governor next door was a master of that strategy. Nick said when he was vetted for Bush's cabinet and asked about his many trysts, beginning in the state house and going on for years, he said that he told Bush's people "all the names he could remember." Health and Human Services. Like everyone in government, he built ties to the industry and after he left "public service" he made a mint collecting on IOUs.

Nick was my portal into a million places I hadn't even imagined. That was a bonus on top of the way I felt when I was with him, in his arms, or basking in his love and appreciation, or talking over everything, or just sitting and reading with the volume on the TV off, waiting for a play in a game we could repeat if we wanted to see a TD. And we both loved having sex, straight up or with sauces and pickles. But I did notice, after a while, the runway was growing longer–the kind of thing one better not mention, knowing what we know about the ego, comma, male, subspecies Nick.

He did slow down as he aged in other ways as well. Especially after the pacemaker went in, he lived with his fate. Accelerated decrepitude, he said, using humor to blunt the blow and quoting a film as usual. I hadn't gotten to the change yet, so he thought I would always be who I was when we met. When two people connect, the man expects the woman will not change and the woman expects the man will, so both are disappointed. That wasn't quite the case with us, but it's not just a joke.

I understood men so much better than they thought. It's how I made a living, after all. When Nick read that, he said, "Aha! You do understand how you can lose yourself in a role"–still dealing with Penny's inability to admit she lost herself in her therapist role, codependent as she was, which he thought would help her understand why he lied so much, so long. Thirty-seven years in fact, building a false narrative to cover his real job. "You do have a hunch, don't you, why spies love being spies."

Ish, I said. Ish. A waitress does know a thing or two about building trust until customers tell her everything. I would have been a pretty good spy. It's all about seduction and deception, after all.

But I was telling you about the party and I had better get back to that. I do think digressions, pop-up memories, quiet asides, are often more interesting, but not everybody gets that the real story is found there as a rule. I prefer the detours, not the straight path. Nick said Jung told a student who asked about the most direct route to her life's goals, "The detours, my dear! The detours!" I think that makes sense.

Anyway, it was Joe P. who talked to me the most. I don't think he was hitting on me, or if he was, I refused to let it in, because life was complicated enough. He was pleasant and attentive, genuinely interested, I thought.

He answered my questions and filled me in on what remote viewing really was. I had never heard of it before Nick brought it up, and when Nick told me that's what they were going to do, I was skeptical at first. But the more it bounced around in my head, the more it connected with experiences I had myself, not clairvoyant or according to protocols, not on behalf of some agency, but what a normal human might call psychic. The paranormal is normal, Nick said, a neglected part of our psyches, which some cultures used to greater advantage. Hal told me later about Japanese "belly talk" and how aborigines use miwi, if I got it right. The Navajo, he said, know when to start a ritual, all at the same time. He said the supernatural is natural in the same way. I took my own experiences for granted, not as precursors of a possibility for joining Nick at work. I assumed everybody had them. We didn't talk about that stuff aloud, not in Des Moines. What would the neighbors think?

I wasn't a big or deep thinker, not like Nick and his crew, so I never explored what any of it meant for the universe. That was way beyond my pay grade. The universe, to me, was just what was out there, all around. But I know what I experienced, and it was more than synchronicity, as I learned to call it, one of the big words I learned along the way, and it wasn't a hoax. After doing some viewing, I was able to think impossible things with ease. I learned the unthinkable was thinkable, the impossible was possible, and I had to ramp up to keep pace with my experience. And then there was lunch with my new friend Jelli.

Let me give a few examples of what I took for granted.

The low-hanging fruit of telepathy is knowing who is calling when the cell phone rings, before you look. I hear the ring and know who it is. Much of the time. Most of the time? I don't know, I don't keep track. Much of the time, for sure. Or I am thinking of someone, then hear the phone, and it's them. Or I think about them a lot, then get a text. Cynics call it coincidence but I know better.

Or I know what someone's about to say, and then they say it. If it's only intuition, I'm good with that. If it connected to something we were discussing, that would make sense, but usually it's a brand new thing, something I couldn't have possibly known, but I did, I do, and I say it to myself, not out loud. Nick moves his lips when he talks to himself but I don't think I do. Sometimes, I am saying, it does happen, and it stands out when it does. The words form in my mind and then the other person says them. I think to myself, that's interesting. But I never say a word.

I didn't tell Nick when I was doing it, but when he was lost in thought, which was often, and I emphasize lost, I would calm myself with long deep breaths—no one taught me to do that, it just seemed right—and I would try to see inside my head as if on a blank screen what he was thinking. It was like sitting in a theater waiting for the movie to start before the light and color and Dolby came on. Then I would say, are you by any chance thinking of X or Y and often he was. I didn't compute a ratio of hits and misses, I just thought, well if it happens once, it's real. Once is interesting but twice means it's commonplace, like life in the universe, and it happened more than twice, also like life in the universe. When I told him, he suggested he might have said something aloud, which was sometimes true but not often. Sometimes I just saw his thoughts, or felt them, I experienced the content or the texture of his thinking, and I was often right. That's all I'm trying to say. I've read that couples over the years form that kind of close bond. They finish each other's sentences, they act like two bodies sharing a single brain. The boundaries dissolve and they link up.

The fact that I could do that, like I said, was no big deal. I thought everybody could. For me it was fun, a game I liked to play. The world is full of games and we play the ones we like. Dasein taught me to go to new levels, and you know what thrilled me most about that? Not that I could do it, not that I had a knack for remote viewing, but that Nick loved that I was better than him at what was supposed to be his thing. He was not only not threatened, he delighted in my success. I can't tell you how much that meant. Some men would have gone ballistic when that happened. Pilgrim would have punched me. My gifts did not threaten Nick at all and our teamness stayed intact.

That's one more reason why, despite Nick's quirks and irksome tics, I love that guy so much.

Before the phone even rang, I knew when my mother died. I just knew it. She hadn't been well but not near death, I didn't think, and I was wiping a glass at the Barbican when I felt this chill, call it dread, I had to catch my breath, and I said to Jake, "My mother's dead," and he thought I was simply telling him, not knowing it came to me in the moment, and twenty minutes later, I got the call. But there was something else. Just before that happened, I could swear my mother was there in the restaurant, ten feet away from the counter where I worked. I didn't see her materialize, I was looking at the glasses as I wiped them and put them in a row, entirely focused on the task, and when I turned from the bar toward the tables, there she was, and she looked at me with a sad sweet smile that told me she loved me and had to say good bye, and then she winked out. Just like that, she was there, and then she was gone. I think I saw her mostly from the waist up, I don't remember seeing legs, but I was focused on her face. I'll never forget her expression, full of love, knowing more than the rest of us who are still on this side of the veil.

And then she was gone. It was like someone turning off a light. A UFO sometimes disappears like that, I learned later. Like many anomalous events, it was hard to take in. It didn't connect to my usual experience so my thoughts didn't want to include it. I went on with my work as if nothing odd had taken place, and a while later, the cell phone rang and Phyllis Manley, a friend of my mother's, filled in the details of her death. My mother was watering plants and ... just died, she fell over into the impatiens, the half-full watering can beside her and a muddy puddle where it spilled. At least she died doing something she loved. Phyllis took over the garden until the house was sold and cared for it as best she could. "But I don't have your mother's green thumb," she said. "Her garden was always so nice. Even the day lilies were beautiful." (My mother still lived on 45th Place where I grew up and Phyllis lived next door. Her daughter Mary and I played dolls and jacks when we were kids.) Then I remembered the apparition and connected it to the call.

I never told Nick about that. I never told anyone.

It wasn't like the movie. I didn't see "dead people." I saw my mother, period, at the time she died. She appeared to me and said good-bye. Do whatever you like with that.

That sounds defensive, I know. Society does that to us, right? It's funny, isn't it? what our cultures do? We have no qualms talking about sex but tell someone a story like that or that you saw a UFO and people think you're nuts. So we keep ourselves from seeing what's right in front of our eyes, and after a while the agreement that such things don't happen becomes part of our beliefs and we stay with what we agree to see. I read about a woman who saw more colors than most people but they told her she couldn't so she didn't any more, until she learned there was some genetic thing that let some women do that, and then she saw them all the time, because she knew she could. Her paintings were magnificent.

Nick pushed me to think about this kind of stuff in a different, more philosophical way. I listened as hard as I could but with limited success. He said things like, we're systems and we connect to other systems, some that we see if they aren't too small or too big. Our bodies have a hundred trillion cells that are entangled with other people's cells. Self-consciousness is somehow distributed among all those cells, especially the brain, but not only the brain. We're not islands, we're interconnected, part of the main. Nick said we interact with so many people and things in so many dimensions, we are like Indra's jewels, facets reflecting facets, mirrors reflecting mirrors.

Words words words.

Dasein taught me that my consciousness, my me-ness, my identity, my energy field, expressed itself as an intention toward a target or a goal when I did remote viewing. We think at first we have to reach but it was more the opposite, we have to be alert but passive, quietly waiting but not pushing. That's why Nick laughed at his silly attempt at the coffee shop to reach out and touch someone. We have to let the connection manifest itself naturally. We have to be patient. It is always there, the target, the site, whatever it is, everything is always there. We create the things we see in space but they're out there, first. I can't explain how inner and outer get mixed up but they do. Time exists because we need it to sort things. Otherwise we would live in a blooming buzzing confusion.

I think that when we are viewing, or meditating, or thinking of something entirely else, we fall suddenly into an altered state where either time does not exist or it seems like it doesn't. I don't know the difference. Remote viewing is one way of allowing ourselves to experience our larger selves in relationship to everything else. We're alone but alone together. We're like mitochondria that were once independent but now crank out ATP inside cells. The cells determine the ultimate purpose. We are like cells that thought they were independent and realize they are part of a body. Hal said he thinks of us all as apertures the universe uses to become aware of itself. It looks out through them and in at itself at the same time. That inner/outer deal once again.

We increase our clairvoyant ability through practice, and the more we do it, the better we get—but like Nick said, names like clairvoyance, psychometry, telepathy, dissolve. The bottom line is, we can go anywhere in spacetime, gliding down world lines that draw themselves ahead of our steps or maybe at the same time, if "same time" means anything, an obsolete way to think of simultaneity. The point is, we're always "there." It's only a matter of going, as Lawrence said, pointing toward Aqaba in one of Nick's favorite movies.

That was my experience, anyway, as rewritten in fancy prose by helpful hubby Nick. My hubby in effect. Nick adds metaphors and links to films or books. I don't think that way but I said okay, it's your book, and if you think that reaches readers, nothing's lost. I can do metaphors too: like the Velveteen rabbit, we become real through relationships.

How was that?

We are a society of one mind.

That's Nick, saying it his way, of course. So I let Nick doctor up my prose, but I also got better at saying things as I grew in understanding. Nick urged me not to hold back. "You understand a lot more than you think," he said. "It's a matter of finding the right words to say it." I came to believe he was right. Pilgrim told me I was stupid, so I thought I was, and it took time to heal from his abuse. Nick thought I had a very big brain. He thought my way of seeing things, the way I experienced my life, was a real gift. Or maybe he said that because he was feeling randy.

When I went into that deep timeless state, it was like I swam out from the beach and over a reef with myriads of colorful fishes and beautiful corals. I wanted to stay in the ocean when I first went snorkeling and I wanted to stay in that state where my ego, my sense of self, dissolved. In that highly focused condition, I wasn't attached to things that made me anxious or afraid. I felt free. I got good, I got damn good, and became aware, I am trying to say, of who we really are. It's none of the things we're taught as kids. It's something else entirely.

I do wish I could say it more clearly. Language illuminates a lot but it also makes up the bars of our cage. We can make distinctions–creativity, I think, is a matter of making distinctions– but they're never fine enough. No matter how many words we know, they're surrounded by a cloud of unknowing, all the things we don't know how to say. Nick's interpretations of my experiences are based on what I tell him but I'm the one who sits in a darkened room, making sketches. I'm the one who knocks. I respond to impressions until I can build a bigger picture, based on scribbles that seem unintelligible. Sometimes there's distortion. Often I fail and my notes are useless. That's why God made shredders.

"Consciousness"–boy, I never used that word before, and now I use it all the time. I think it's how we create and picture the world. It is axiomatic, reflexive, an emergent property it seems, and without something to compare it with, we think what we see is the real deal. Remote viewing suggests that non-local consciousness is real. Time and space, spacetime, is the frame, entanglement the means, but after doing this a while, I was pretty sure that entanglement is not just pairs of atoms but a matrix of connections that scales up to systems of systems, as Nick thought. The One Big System is a tangle we can't unravel. We would have to step outside of it to see it whole and that's not possible. We are inside it, we are inside ourselves (ourSelf). We chase galaxies that race away and tumble over the edge of the horizon. What we can't see is so much bigger than what we can. It doesn't do it justice, calling it the universe. We don't know what's beyond that horizon. Some try to define it with math but there's got to be a better way to say it, something a normal human might understand.

Nick tidies up these paragraphs and makes them philosophical.

Thank you, dear. I leave that part to you. We're a good tag team. As I said, I am not a very deep thinker. I just know what happened to me. I try to tell the truth. My intuition is the best tool I have, and it works for me, so I use it. I would not make a good engineer. I don't think in that structured way. But I make customers happy. I made them happy at the Barbican and I make them happy at Dasein too, judging by my evaluations. I make Nick happy too.

But all this talk about remote viewing and what it might mean, that came after the party and after I signed on.

Back to the party.

Joe Pantaglia finished his intro to their business model, then moved on to talk to a client. As he did, Sylvia who had been eclipsed by his large body made a pivot from the food table toward where he had been standing. She had a huge buffalo shrimp on a small plate and celery and ranch and a glass of white wine in her other hand. She set down the drink and dipped the shrimp and ate it without getting sauce on her fingers or chin. Very neat, she was, and, I suspected, maybe a bit anal. It's the little things that reveal who we are.

"So you live with Nick," she said, implying something with her tone but I didn't know what. She was smiling in a way, but it wasn't really a smile. She took a second bite of the shrimp and chewed until she could speak again without spitting bits of shrimp.

She wore a gray suit with a high white blouse with a costume brooch and her hair was sort of shaped but she wasn't wearing makeup and although she wore heels, you could tell that was a concession, not a habit, the way she kept shifting back and forth from foot to foot, even though the two inch stacks would not have bothered most women. Later in the evening, the shoes went off. It must have been her age, I thought, or bunions, or arthritis. Her neck and her hands were tells, you can't hide that, unless you do a load of procedures. Not doing "work" makes a statement too about what you think matters. She was, I guessed, late fifties, maybe?

I wore low-heeled waitress shoes which I knew from experience would get me through the night. I also wore slick maroon slacks and a shiny pink blouse and my hair was swept forward and framed my face nicely. I had recently added coloring to help my shiny brunette hair stay shiny and brunette but I don't think you can tell. My hair looks the way it always has, to me at least.

I think from our thirties to our fifties, women just get better. Twenties, we look like kids. Sixties and up, we start to look old. Our experience, our character, shows in our faces in that nice mid-range before the teeter totter tilts.

I wondered if Sylvia was interested in me. Nothing she said, just a vibe. I decided not, the vibe I sensed was a need to be in control, but that's a different need, not the same as needing me. Once I knew her history, her career in a white male military world, her behavior was understandable. She had to learn to raise her hand a million times and keep it up, and raise her voice, and repeat herself a lot. Clearing her throat loudly just didn't do it. When a man took her suggestion and acted as if it was his, she called him out. "I just said that," she would say, and she had to say it again, and again, until their sullen silence said okay, Sylvia, enough! we get it. Let's move on.

"Yes I do," I said (live with Nick), and I left it at that.

'He has some gifts that we think will add to our organization," she said, "now that we know he's under control, more or less. Not gonna blow no whistle on us."

"We're all under control more or less," I said. "Some days more, some less. And no, that's unlikely to happen again. Unless you torture someone."

She gave me credit for that one. "True enough. We'll count on you, Valerie, to keep him sane and sensible. We'll count on Nick to keep you around. It sounds like you're good for him. So you're important to us, too."

"Thanks," I said. "I hope everything works out." The shrimp disappeared like the tail of a mouse into the mouth of a snake. "This whole thing fascinates me," I said. "You all have balls, I will say that."

She smiled, sincerely (I think), then someone who had been hanging around at her elbow, close enough to say "I'm next" with his pushy presence, moved closer in and asked her something about some business thing and I turned to let them talk and poured more wine and, seeing his opportunity, Hal McCutcheon trundled over, saying hey, hello there, Valerie Patchett. Welcome to our bizarro world.

He did look a little like Santa Claus, as Nick had said, jovial and bright-eyed and twinkling, but that was deceptive. Yes, he was big and his hair was white and he had a big white beard, but that was it. He wasn't into elves but he did insist that faeries were real, and he told me that gnomes were not only real but all over the place. He showed me later a page of gnome sightings, dozens of pictures of the little guys, and he brought to work a plaster cast of the footprint of a Sasquatch with whorls in the toes like ours. "Read the good accounts," he said, "and make up your own mind." Eccentric, one might say, but still into the game and astute when he was focused. You wouldn't know from his demeanor that he had killed a few people—of necessity, Nick said—and lived with it comfortably. He was devoted to the agency, and the country, and his Celtic heritage, the folklore of which he knew cold. Over a long professional career, he had done good, Nick said. I'll leave it to Hal to provide details, if he likes. So I came to respect him highly, and I enjoyed his stories about Sasquatch and gnomes and fairies. Angels, space brothers, native Americans, what's the diff? A lot of people believe in discarnate entities, call them what you like.

Ramtha, Seth, they're all made-up names for wispy metaphysics personified as special friends, making channelers special too, and selling lots of books.

"Nick says you two go way back," I said.

"We do. He was a good worker and open to non-standard m.o.s. He also had an appreciation for the legends of the Celts and how we saw the world. Not everyone has that."

I nodded, but I didn't know what he meant. "Tell me more about that," is a good way to respond when someone mentions stuff you don't know. Most older men are delighted when a younger woman asks them to tell her things and they get right to it. Hal was no exception.

I won't repeat what the next twenty minutes of Celtic legend-telling added to my knowledge. You can look it up. I will say, though, I bet I could pass a pop quiz on the Morrigan or the Legend of the Banshee. The Morrigan captured my imagination. When I was deep into development and operating frequently, someone had to have my back, not only in the viewing room, but out there on site when bilocation happened. You could lose yourself projecting into the target or someone else's mind and the silver cord might break. That would not be trivial. When that almost happened to me, it was, I chose to think, the Morrigan who stepped up. She/they were cavalry, coming around the bend to save my skin.

One can do worse than having a goddess in the posse.

Interesting as Hal and Sylvia were, Joe provided the memorable content. He had the meats, you might say, and as the party continued, with people changing partners like a barn dance, we connected again and he told me stories that he said were no longer classified about things remote viewers did. As I listened, I could not fully believe what I was hearing. If what he said was true, the world he described was not the one I lived in, with firm boundaries around people's lives. The nature of time itself was the biggest shocker. I always thought I knew what time was, because it was like a moving stream and we all swam in the currents, even if they took us far from shore. Sometimes the stream went fast and sometimes it slowed and sometimes you got stuck in an eddy. I realized I used the word "time" as if I knew what it meant, when in fact I had no idea what I was talking about. "I'm out of time?" "I have no time?" What did we mean by that? One metaphor led to another but it was all poetry. Or—when physicists tried to write about time—it was incomprehensible math with lots of Greek letters. The cognoscenti shrugged when we asked for explanations in plain words. All they said was, "Do the math."

"That's really interesting," I said, after he told me of going after a particular person and not only finding his stomping grounds but describing him in detail, where he was, who he talked to, what he was doing. He added that the computer guys can do the same, which often provided confirmation. I could understand the computer bit, with our far reach into everybody everywhere that Nick described at length, but how can you sit in a room thousands of miles away and access an image of a guy well enough to "get" his identity just like that? And know what he was up to? Were these stories real, I wondered, or was Dasein a bigger scam than Enron or Theranos?

"So you have a target and you go there—"

"No," Joe said. "You don't *go* anywhere. Or if you do, you go inside, you go down, you go into the silence. Everything is there, it's always there, but we make so much noise, we can't hear it."

I was intrigued. I was baffled.

"I would love to try it some time," I said. "Remote viewing, that is. See how it feels. So I know what you're really talking about." I hadn't planned to say that; it just popped out.

Joe tapped Hal and told him what I said.

"Really?" Hal said. "Why?"

"I have a hunch I might be able to do it. I'm curious, is all."

Joe looked thoughtful, then shrugged. "We've nothing to lose by letting you try," he said. "Why not? Come in sometime and see. Do you agree, Hal?"

"Sure," Hal said. "Go for it, girl."

"If nothing else, you'll have a better notion of what Nick is up to. He is your hubby, after all."

"Partner," I said. "Nick is my partner."

"Oh," Joe said. "Okay. Partner."

"But it is like we're married," I said, not wanting to leave the wrong impression. Then I said to both our surprises: "I love Nick like I've never loved anyone. I didn't know I could."

Joe didn't know what to say. I was embarassed too, but what I said was true. I was all in.

Joe smiled, "Well, I can't say that, but I do respect him."

Then Sylvia dinged a glass until people settled down and we poured more wine and we all listened to the principals make a few statements about their appreciation for everyone who came, and the value of the work, and their gratitude for everything, and please ask anything you like.

Some wanted to know the odds. What's the likelihood of a useful hit? The long replies from Sylvia and Joe suggested they couldn't really say. It depends on your criteria, Joe explained. What's considered a hit? We measure success by what did you need to know. Does the information contribute to your bottom line? Do you profit from our work?

Do we pay for a viewing per se or for results?

As a rule, one pays for the viewing. Our overhead is limited but we do have expenses. And if we don't deliver, we won't be in business very long.

Is it all strictly confidential?

Yes.

OK, said a guy with a grin, say all this is real. How do you prevent a competitor from using his own remote viewer to view our viewing and learn what we learn? What prevents *his* competitor from viewing the viewer who's viewing the viewing?"

Everybody laughed. Who's on first, what's on second. Very funny, one thinks–but then one thinks a little more. Hey, wait–that's a serious question.

Nobody replied. They left it alone but later, Joe admitted, he wished they had addressed it, not in a public setting like that, but anticipating what might happen. You try to imagine all possible scenarios, he said. but sometimes you miss one or two. There was a report that named aerial terrorism as a possibility in 1995 and suggested airlines might be used to crash into buildings. We had it, but you can't plan for everything, and it would have cost a fortune to do everything to stop it in advance, same as shoring up the levees in New Orleans before Katrina. They were told the levees couldn't handle a category 5 but they didn't have a spare billion bucks and rolled the dice. So naturally, it happened.

It happened to us too. A viewer viewed a viewing. It wasn't very funny.

Can you give us an example of a successful viewing?

"We can't violate the confidentiality of clients," Joe said, "but I can give you examples that are no longer classified. Some of what we did back at the agency. Is that OK?"

Sure it is.

The three took turns telling compelling stories. The crashed plane that Carter blabbed about. The Typhoon class submarine, a significant hit. The states of mind of enemies discerned at a distance. Noriega. Terrorists in hiding. The plans of Russians inside the Kremlin. Stories about McMoneagle, stories about Swann.

Then Hal got into the question of time.

"Have you had enough to drink?" he asked.

Nodding and chuckling, wiping lips. Refilling glasses.

"Do you remember the attack in the Gulf? When the Iraqis used Excocets?"

Most said yes.

"A viewer described the attack in detail a day before it happened. It hadn't happened yet, we thought it was a fail. But it wasn't. It was early, is all." He let that sink in. "That was precognition. The viewer described the damage and casualties and the perps the day before it happened. When we compared his report with the event, it was solid.

"When we began doing this, we would ID a target using three dimensions of space. Now we work in four dimensions. Sometimes we access an event in the past, sometimes in the future. In one case, it was the far distant past; one of the viewers accessed the Battle of Hastings. He described stepping through a mess of bloody guts. He didn't know where he had been sent, but his report fit. He described the weapons correctly."

The silence when he finished was pretty thick. Wheels in people's heads spun like Stuxnet-damaged centrifuges. Gears clashed, clanging, and flew into the sky.

"OK, those tales are mind-benders, but how will that help us?"

"A good question," Joe said. "You can target competitors' plans and know their intentions in advance. It all depends on the frame of reference. We work now in five dimensions and see time and space from a higher point of view. Then, like all good intelligence agents, we confirm what we see."

"Then why not get intelligence through standard ways and skip all this?"

"You can do competitive intelligence in all the standard ways. But viewing provides more data. Sometimes it reaches things we would never see.

"Look (sometimes Joe sounded like Obama, all professor-like and starchy, always saying look like he was talking to children), we focus on the task. You want results. But there's something underlying this entire project that's maybe more important. Your way of thinking will change. You'll see things others don't see. The context of how you look at things will evolve.

"I know it sounds crazy but relativity sounded nuts and it took years to be understood. You'll expand your understanding in ways that blow up your beliefs. You'll see doors where you once saw walls. You'll go through the looking glass."

"The what?"

Hal laughed. "It's from a story. The point is, you become ubermenschen. I don't know the woman-word, but you know what I mean."

Someone made a silly joke to break the tension. "You mean the Oberübermenschen." It wasn't funny but everyone laughed. German is seldom funny even when grammatical, which that wasn't.

Hal chimed in. "We know this seems like an extraordinary way of knowing and it is, but once we know that this is how it is, it's like a child learning to read. The world is filled with super-charged meaning."

My head was spinning. They weren't bending spoons, they were bending minds. But that's what they had intended to do—make cracks that would let in the light. There are cracks in everything, Cohen sang. That *is* how the light gets in.

I looked over at Nick and he looked at me. We didn't need to say a word.

Our lives had changed forever.

Interlude

September 25, 1947

From: Lt. General Nathan Twining

To: Commanding General of the Army Air Forces; Brig. General George Schulgen

Subject: Air Materiel Command Opinion Concerning "Flying Discs"

"The phenomenon reported is something real and not visionary or fictitious."

and

"The UFO phenomenon is characterized by the constant flow of reports from 150 countries. Most important, we have many reports from highly responsible people. You finally get to the point where you say that something strange is going on, and I can't keep calling all these people liars. If there are independent witnesses, you have quite a job proving that they all hallucinated."

- J. Allen Hynek, scientific advisor to UFO studies undertaken by the U. S. Air Force under three projects: Project Sign (1947–1949), Project Grudge (1949–1951) and Project Blue Book (1952–1969) and founder of the Center for UFO Studies

Chapter 7
Something Strange is Going On

"**I** was surprised by your call," Jelli said, leaving the menu closed and looking down at her hands. Her nails were shaped and polished pale mauve, her hands soft and smooth, but she kept them clasped to keep from trembling. Her nervousness was obvious and I felt sympathetic. "I told Brad we'd never talk to you guys again. Who in their right mind would want to deal with us after what happened?"

"Brad doesn't handle your ... episodes ... very well, does he?"

"He gets scared. He's embarassed. He told me not to discuss it unless I'm talking to a therapist. Then he told me not to see a therapist. You have to understand about Brad. He grew up in Edina Minnesota. They're not like people here, or anywhere else, unless it's Norway or Sweden. I've sat for twenty minutes listening to Edinans trot out their pedigrees, how long they've been there, how long their parents were there, their grandparents, on and on. It makes them comfortable to circle their xenophobic wagons."

"Is it really like that?"

Jelli laughed. "I once asked where a small town was that this guy was talking about and he looked at me with hostility, and I mean hostility. He finally said, you know where Hibbing is, don't you? I didn't, all I knew was that Bob Dylan grew up there and got out of town as fast as he could. He shook his head as if I were an idiot. "It's near Hibbing," he said. They know about things inside the state but they don't care about much outside. They talk about the Vikings, fishing, hockey, the Twins, how much they don't mind winter.

"Brad doesn't like it when I 'prattle,' as he calls it. He means talk about things. Share feelings. It's a Nordic culture, Valerie, they think smalltalk is wasting time, not getting to know someone."

"They can't be that insular."

"If you share something personal, your work or where you went to school, they think you're arrogant instead of trying to engage. They don't want you to know them, and they don't want to know you. If you ask where they went to school, they think you mean high school. They grow up with friends from pre-K on and don't want more. They're just not interested in other people. Brad came to church and the coffee hour as a favor to me."

"They don't want friends?"

"As a rule, not new ones. They'll smile and be polite, but they just don't care. They may invite you to their house but it never happens. That passive aggressive thing is no joke. If they invite you to their cabin on the lake. you'd better not pack."

"The lake? They're all on one lake? You mean Lake Superior?"

"No," Jelli laughed again. "They never name the lake, it's always 'the lake.' There are thousands. That way you'll never find them. They would turn to stone if they saw you on the front porch."

"You're exaggerating, right?"

"Nope. If they move away, they often move back, or want to, like Brad. There're more people there who grew up in the state than anywhere but Louisiana. Moving to Chicago was a jolt for Brad. He hates it here. He hates that people say what they think, he hates how loud people are. Honking in traffic makes him crazy. Up there, you seldom hear a beep on the street. I learned that when we were behind a guy at a light, but he didn't go when the light changed. Brad was driving and just sat there. "Honk!" I said, thinking he was daydreaming. He was annoyed. "He'll figure it out," he said. "There's no need to be rude."

I smiled and shook my head.

Jelli laughed. "They apologize for everything. You hit someone with your grocery cart and they say 'sorry' right away. It's how they avoid conflict."

"You make it sound difficult for outsiders."

"Ex-pats like me, transplants, move in thinking it's like where they left. We thought state boundaries were lines on a map. They treat them like walls. It's the way we are, Brad says, without apology or understanding what it does to to someone to move there and deal with that. I lived there for six months and had enough. Brad came with me because we're a couple, but … I don't know if he can make it here. Or if we'll make it as a couple, honestly."

"I don't mean to be rude, but Jell: why are you still together?"

"My work is here. I like my work. I like the big city. I grew up here. I moved there for Brad and he's giving Chicago a try for me. Look, when you hook up, who knows what's coming? Sex and ethnic food was the basis of our relationship."

"So when you went to Minnesota, did you make any friends at all?"

"Other transplants. We find one another. Valerie, listen: we had been there a week and were in a coffee shop and a guy in the next booth could tell I was from out of town. He leaned over and asked had I made any friends yet. I said no. He laughed and said, come back in five years, you know what you'll say? The same thing.

"I thought he was kidding. But he wasn't. I met ex-pats who had been there for ten years and didn't really know a single native." She shrugged. "I apologize for TMI, but I do like to talk about things, real things. It helps me process feelings, right? Brad doesn't do that. I didn't even tell him I was meeting you for lunch. He would have guessed why. I didn't need that conversation."

"Are all the men like that?"

"They don't talk much. They think sitting in an ice-house in silence for hours is a good time. There are jokes about stuff like that but they contain a lot of truth. I made a joke once, that men up there were like totem poles, tall and solemn and silent. I thought it was funny but no one laughed. That's another thing, the lack of a sense of humor. They're pretty literal. I tried making jokes, thinking it would ease the conversation, but almost always, no one laughed."

I shook my head. "I love engaging with people. All my work has included that. Customers energized me. The way you describe it feels like solitary confinement."

"I can tell you more stories, but that's enough. Anyway, I had to move." She scooted in her chair and leaned over the table. "But I want to know why you called. I'm glad you did, but—why? I assumed you wanted to know what was happening, right?"

"Are you ready to order?" said the waitperson who had quietly waited while Jelli talked, pad in hand, pen in hand.

"Give us another minute," Jelli said.

"Of course," said the wait-person, used to waiting. She retired to a waiting nook.

I tried to cross my legs but had to push back from the table. I wore wool slacks and ankle-length boots but I was still chilly from the walk to the cafe. I hadn't expected the wind to be so biting. You hunch in your head like a turtle and walk real fast.

I felt in my pockets to be sure I hadn't lost my gloves. I'd need them walking back.

"I was curious," I said. "You're interesting. That episode was interesting, whatever it was." I laughed. "I guess that's not very Minnesotan."

"No, that would be considered rude." She turned and looked toward the street through the window of the cafe. "But we're not in Minnesota. Listen to all that honking." She laughed. "Anyway, ask whatever you like."

The wait-person returned and Jelli opened the menu and settled on soup and a half sandwich. I knew what I wanted and ordered something easy. I wanted to eat without having to think about it, and I'm glad I did. It took energy to focus on what Jelli said next. I did not want tedious chewing to distract me from paying attention.

"Are you comfortable discussing what happened?" I asked. "You don't have to."

"I have to talk to someone about it. But it's pretty wild, Valerie, pretty weird." She was hesitant and wary, looking for misgivings in my expression. "Are you sure you're game?"

"Sure. What have we got to lose? I assumed it was something medical. Neurological perhaps."

She smiled. My openness, warmth, neutrality, were helpful, I think. And she sure wanted to talk, that was clear.

Still, she sat for a bit more, not looking me in the eye. It was a pretty long runway before she finally took off.

"I guess it is neurological somehow. But not the way you'd think. ... Valerie, do you believe in UFOs?"

I shrugged. "I wouldn't say 'believe.' I can't say what they are or what they're doing, but Nick says they're real, that inside the agencies a lot of people know. It's seriously hush-hush. They've tried to figure them out but they haven't done it yet. Nick said we've known they were here for at least 75 years but he thinks they've been coming for a lot longer than that. He said he heard about high-intensity magnetic field research to try to facilitate the same kind of propulsion but he didn't think it worked. He said if you want to know what's happening, look at patents. Nick said a guy named Pais got a bunch of them and they spent hundreds of thousands of dollars on his High Energy Electromagnetic Field Generator (HEEMFG) experiments. But that's just hearsay."

"The agencies? He really was a spy?"

"He really was."

"Huh. Interesting. So you're used to keeping secrets, if he told you about his work."

"I pretty much am," I said. "If you're asking me to keep this between us, that's not an issue."

"Okay. Good. Okay. So let me tell you what happened." She sipped soup noiselessly and rested her spoon on the under-plate. "I had what you can call an encounter with a UFO. I can't tell you the whole story because I don't know the whole story. I only know fragments. Memories are missing. Some recur now and then but how do I know they're real? I do remember a lot of it, though. They did things I don't understand. No anal probe," she laughed, "but things with … probes, wands, I don't know what. They certainly examined me. There were panels with flashing lights and graspers that came out of the walls and took samples. They took fluid too but I don't want to go there. Some was embarrassing. They didn't seem to care. They had a job to do, is what I think, and they did it with efficiency, from their point of view. During all that, I felt like I was property, not a person."

When someone begins a story with stuff like that, it can be hard to listen closely. We hear it, but we can't quite believe it. I saw that on lots of faces, myself, once I began remote viewing, when I told clients how it worked. Their mouths would say uh-huh but their faces said I was crazy.

"Start at the beginning. Just tell me what you remember if you can."

She picked up her spoon and ate more soup. She used it for a break before revisiting the event.

"This was a couple of months ago. I wanted to go for a drive and headed into the country. We had been scouting out a new apartment and Brad had to meet someone about work. I wanted to feel the flatlands around me and leave the strip malls behind. I wanted to know I was here and not in Minnesota. Both states are pretty flat, but you know where you are when you've lived in a place a long time. The Indian names are different, too. So I drove out of the city until I saw nothing but farms. Then I took back roads. When you haven't a destination, it doesn't matter what roads you take. I like the old houses and the farms and the feel of the landscape in winter. I drove until I noticed it was growing dark and time to turn around. I turned what I thought were the right directions but kept running into lakes that made me curve this way and that so I didn't know where I was. I didn't have my phone so I couldn't use waze. After I hit another dead end I found myself next to a park and a lake and it was so pretty, I stopped to enjoy it. I watched the moon rise over the lake. The wind had died down. The surface of the water was absolutely flat. Not a ripple or a current. I lowered the window and inhaled the cold air and I felt at peace. I was happy to be back in the area. The birds had all flown south so it was very very still. The sky grew darker and the moon smaller as it rose from the horizon and I lost myself in the moment.

"The car was idling in neutral and the radio was playing an oldie so it made me nostalgic. I could see the distant lights of homes across the lake–there was even a green light at the end of a dock– and I knew I'd have to find my way back to a highway and get back for dinner but I didn't want to leave. It just felt so peaceful.

"Then I saw what I thought was a star over the water. It was quite bright but it got a lot brighter as I watched, not like a normal star, bigger and bigger. I thought it must be an airplane with landing lights on, coming toward a small field, or a helicopter, maybe a drone. The light got bigger until I could see that it was an object, not just a light, and it came lower and suddenly made like a leap and was right there in front of me. Like it jumped instead of flew. Suddenly it was right there. The radio crackled with static and then it went dead. The car died. Planes don't make that happen. Planes don't move like that; I mean, one minute it was way out over the lake and next I knew, it was right there, big as a house and so bright I couldn't look at it directly. As it got close, I saw lights flashing around its rim like a theater marquee, green and white and red, I think, moving fast, real real fast. The brain doesn't know what to think in a moment like that, so it doesn't think at all, it goes on hold, and then ... I went into a kind of trance like at the church. I think it was the same kind of thing except at the church it didn't last long. Its like there's a tunnel and I'm looking down it from one end. I sense a presence far off in the distance. You don't know when it will happen. I was aware of being there with you guys but like in a dream. I felt like a patient etherized upon a table, as some poet said. I couldn't move. It was like I was paralyzed. I wanted to move but couldn't. They did that, I think. The next thing I remember, a beam of light that looked like a dense medley of colors but dazzling white at the same time came out of the craft. It was like it was solid. It didn't look natural. That's weird, right? I don't know how to describe it. It came toward me and suddenly I was inside the light. I don't remember leaving the car, but I must have, because all at once I was outside the car and in that strange beam of light and moving toward the hovering craft. I call it a craft for lack of a better word. ... Valerie? Are you with me?"

I nodded. "I'm fascinated. Please go on."

"So I was inside this light and at the same time, it was inside me, inside my head. I know that doesn't make sense, but that's how it felt. And I moved right through the wall and into the vehicle. How? Who knows? It was dimmer inside. It had a distinctive smell but I can't say what it was. I was aware of what was happening but I still couldn't move. Then a voice in my head said, don't be afraid. We won't hurt you. Val, I swear it was a voice in my head, not me thinking the words. The voice calmed me down. What are you doing? I said in my head–I could tell when it was me, thinking thoughts, not the voice. You call it telepathy, the voice said. Then it repeated, don't be afraid. We won't hurt you. I still couldn't move, but I wasn't frightened anymore. I was suspended in that light like when I make a jello mold, there's a pear inside the jello, but this time I was the pear. I thought the light was some kind of laser. But that isn't how a laser works. It's some kind of technology, I thought. That was the closest I could get to thinking what it was."

"Wow," I said. "So you were onboard some kind of a craft and still in a trance?"

"Yes. I was thinking, hearing what they said, aware of myself. But they were in control."

"Jelli, telepathy is real. I know that from experience."

"It sure felt real to me. I felt like they plugged into me. You know the feeling you get when someone is staring at you? Or you know your dog is looking at you from across the room? I felt I was being looked at. I felt like they could see right into my mind, into my thoughts."

"They built some kind of bridge, mind to mind? Lake a mind meld?"

"Maybe. I don't know. I remember thinking, where are they from? Where do we come from anyway? Maybe they engineered us. They said, these were their words, 'we spawn consciousness.' What do you do with that? A phrase like that sits in your lap like a brick. When I asked later, after the exam, where are you from? they sort of laughed. It felt like a laugh, anyway. 'It wouldn't mean anything to you. You wouldn't understand.' I thought, try me, and they said, "Parsecs and parsecs and parsecs. They flashed an image in my mind of a cluster of stars and I tried to draw it afterward but so many patterns match, it didn't help at all. Somewhere in the universe, far far away, is all I could think."

"Do you trust these memories?"

Jelli shrugged. "They feel like memories. I think they were playing with me when they said that. I saw this movie *Bladerunner* and I thought, maybe they implanted memories like they did with replicants. When they were examining me, I asked why they were doing that, and they said, we want to see how you are now. We want to know how you evolved."

"Could you see them? Do you know what they looked like?"

"I could when I was on the table. Did I mention that? I found myself on a table. I remember how cold it felt. I either turned my head or moved my eyes to see who was doing what. The table was about the height of their heads. Their heads were bigger than ours. They were maybe five feet tall, maybe less. Their eyes were the thing. I can't forget those eyes. They seemed to penetrate straight into my brain. They were large and black and shiny. When one of them used what I called s scraper, I saw three long fingers on each hand. I remember that. The skin was grayish-white and the fingers were long and tapering. If we looked like they did, we'd think we were anemic. It might have been the light, though. I would guess with those big eyes they were like nocturnal animals. Maybe that's why it was dim. Once I touched a hand and it was damp and clammy. So they were like us in a way, but different, too. 'There aren't many like you,' they said. So maybe we are special, like we keep telling ourselves. But I don't know what they meant by that."

I thought I was keeping up but when she finished that description, I realized I had started to drift. My brain kept pushing her story away, but it must have been affecting me: I felt a tear on my cheek. I felt like I did at the end of *ET*. I felt like I did when she gave Jason the final rose.

"I don't know why this is getting to me. I think it's the implications of what you're saying. If it happens twice, it's everywhere. Wherever life can happen, it does happen. There are hundreds of millions of galaxies, they say, that might be teeming with life. Maybe matter is just the medium in which life emerges. It oozes into being, out of the elements, or maybe like you said, it was spawned."

Her eyes moistened too. "Valerie, thank you so much for listening. I haven't talked it through with anyone and Brad doesn't want to hear it."

"I'm feeling everything you're saying, Jell. I'm not just listening. I'm taking in what it means."

We had both finished eating, the wait-woman brought us our checks when we passed on dessert, and then came a bigger surprise. While waiting for the credit cards to be returned for signatures and tips—I always tip a lot, having been in the life—Jelli froze for a moment as she had at the church. It didn't last long but her eyes glazed and she didn't speak. A few minutes later, she shivered like a dog coming out of the water, blinked and looked away.

"That's how it happens," I said, more a statement than a question.

"Yes," she said. "That's how it happens."

"Are you in touch with them when it does?"

Jelli shrugged. "I don't know." She gathered herself together. "I think I might be. I don't know. Maybe it's a side effect."

I sensed that she was all out of story for the day.

"There's more, isn't there?" I said.

"There is," she said. "Let's save it for another time."

I waited but she meant it. She was done.

We left together and stood for a moment in the vestibule, looking out at the cold gray day. We added our hats and gloves and scarves and zipped our coats. We could hear the wind and the door rattling and suddenly the street I saw through the glass on which my breath condensed became a symbol of all the streets on all the planets everywhere. The road meant civilization: the world was in a grain of sand, the cosmos in a city street. I visualized the crisscrossing paths of millions of migrations, looking like string in a game of cat's cradle. Odysseys of life went every which way, filling every niche, until like loops of a fractal seeking an attractor the paths became denser and denser and blotted everything out.

I hadn't been just listening. I had been wide open to the meaning of her narrative. Her experience became my experience. I imagined countless species, shedding identities when they met and inventing new names for themselves. I rode the arrow of time to the end when it all came together.

Is everything that happens purposeless? Or is there an upward call? I thought of old Doctor Bennison at Plymouth Congregational, preaching in his wobbly voice. He came down on the side of design, but then, that was his job. Being a professional religious, he said the only word that applies, the only one, he repeated, thumping the pulpit and raising his voice, is love. I was a little girl and he scared the hell out of me. The way he said it didn't sound like love at all.

That was an astonishing vision for me, a regular sort of person, a graduate of Roosevelt High, a bartender, a waitress, a call center phone drone. As I listened to Jelli's story, time dilated, my eyes widening to behold a universe brimming with life. The whirligig of time spun like a pinwheel, throwing off sparks.

How long that "moment" lasted, I don't know. Everything around me disappeared until I came back to myself. When I did, I must have laughed because Jelli touched my arm and I snapped back to attention. It was my turn to see someone stare at me as if she was normal and I was the odd duck.

"What did I miss?" Jelli said. "What's so funny?"

"Nothing," I said. "I was lost for a moment. Thinking of what you said."

We were once more two chilly women waiting in the vestibule before we went our separate ways.

My mind that night as I tried to ride the dying flames of the fading day to sleep rang like a clanging bell. When I finally fell asleep, I dreamed that the future was already past. I dreamed of bridges crossed in all directions by myriads of beings in the light of a thousand suns.

They changed Jelli by bringing her aboard, then Jelli changed me, opening me to the truth of her experience. The knowledge that we're not alone is spreading like a pandemic. I was one more channel in a network of millions. Everyone who saw a UFO and told someone else became a repeater. Consciousness was spawned. Before we went to the moon and sent probes and robots all over the neighborhood, we were prepped for the shocks and changes that keep us sane. The readiness was all.

I tried to make sense of it all when I told Nick what happened. He said it sounded like a conversion experience. Whatever it was, I lived at a different level after that. I felt like Algernon, the mouse. Valerie Patchett 2.0.

Sitting at the end of our love seat, my legs in a curl beneath me, my hands animating my words, Nick sitting on the other end a few feet away, I retold Jelli's story in my own words. That deepened the impact of the event. We repeat stories to etch them more deeply into our brains. I guess churches repeat pericopes week after week like alarm clocks trying to puncture lifedeep sleep.

Trying to tell people about remote viewing is like that too. I so want you to understand what its like to be given that gift and the grace to sustain it, enhance it, use it to the max. When I do remote viewing, when I settle into the darkness, when I extend my antennae into the void, there is a prickling on my skin as fragments of the target, traces of buildings, places, people, whatever I am viewing, come into view and I narrow my perspective and fix on the destination. My mind condenses to a point and my hand sketches what I see on a pad in my lap. I resist the temptation to analyze the images. It's a balancing act and if I fall back into my normal self-awareness, the session is over. But when it works, it is so great, it is such a high. The experience delivers freedom, fulfillment, bliss. Once I began, I couldn't get enough. I became addicted. Dasein was a pusher and I was hooked on virtual crack.

Jelli and I were on parallel tracks as we waited in the vestibule. I didn't want to release the connection we made. I had thought we were simply meeting for lunch and shared instead her discovery of a universe. The brevity of our communion did not diminish its depth. We were bonded forever.

We gave each other hugs and then, together, pushed out the heavy door into the cold wind and went our separate ways.

Interlude

"The illiterate of the future are not those who can't read or write, but those who can't learn, unlearn, and relearn."

- Alvin Toffler, *Future Shock*

Chapter 8

Sorting Out the Pieces

V alerie again.

The readiness is all.

So that was a hell of a lunch.

I want to be sure you understand how I was affected so I'll try different metaphors. Nick says that's a good way to convey challenging ideas. If one doesn't work, try another. When you finish this book, I want you to be changed by what you learn, as I have been by all these experiences.

Jelli's experience went straight into my brain. I realized that alien visitation was a meme that over most of a century had infected our collective consciousness. Some ask naively, Why don't they communicate? Brian said they did, they have. Everybody knows what "an alien" is. Everyone can draw a "flying saucer." The meme exploded in our minds like ping pong balls on mousetraps showing how a chain reaction happened in some old film I saw in school. Like seeing the earth from the moon, thousands of UFO reports from all the countries in the world altered how we think of ourselves, the planet, the cosmos, everything. We know we aren't alone, we aren't the top of the food chain, and if we're the apple of some God's eye, we know the tree is loaded with other apples.

Even if you don't really know that, you know that you do. Be honest.

They disclosed their presence in a way that interfered as little as possible with our cultures. They showed up in obscure rural places late at night. They appeared to a few at a time. If there was a pattern to the appearances, we couldn't figure it out. We knew only that there was a cultural intrusion on a global scale. Hey! Look! Over here! We look and see an saucer and then, with a streak of light, it looks like a star again in a matter of seconds.

The combination of Jelli's story and remote viewing was mind-blowing. The widening of my field of vision made everything seem larger as if I magnified the font on a screen. I was dazzled and excited. My interior was less like a castle, more like a disco dance under a turning glitter ball. My mind was a merry-go-round of activity, thinking of things I saw during viewings, wondering how I saw them. The more I did, the more I knew. I lived between two worlds. In one I went grocery shopping, stopped to buy stamps, and took walks until I was too cold. In the other, I explored the mysterious domain of spacetime which offered itself in cryptic ways. There are hidden variables, I was told, where unbroken wholeness exists. Diversity and separateness emerge from unitive consciousness but we don't know how to say it. I mean, hidden means hidden, doesn't it? Hal made me read Schrodinger who said that consciousness is a singular of which the plural is unknown. If it's unknown to a guy like that, you had better believe it's an unknown to me.

The better I got at remote viewing, the more they had me do. Sometimes it was stressful. I was sometimes excited and sometimes exhausted. In my giddy exhilaration when things went well, I didn't notice that the work took a toll. Nick noticed, but when you're on a roll, it's hard to hear even the most well-intended spouse. He quoted some shrink, that excitement is anxiety plus oxygen, and maybe I didn't give it enough gas. Sometimes he was more clever than helpful.

I took my NDA seriously, more or less. When I tell the execs at Dasein or a friend like Jelli that I won't say a word, I mean of course beyond my spouse-like Nick. People do need to talk and I was no different. When you're a bartender, you're like a priest for people who don't have a priest. People say what's really on their minds. I listened to every imaginable thing. I asked Bill Webb if that was his experience, and he said, yes, but. But? I said. But once he left the ministry, he said, he was surprised that people were much more open. When they knew they were talking to a clergyman, they filtered what they said, lest they be judged or embarrassed. His collar invited projections. He hadn't known how much people censored themselves until he shed the uniform. It was ironic, he smiled, because a major motivation for entering the ministry was to engage with others in deeper ways.

I went to Bill to try to sort things out. I needed to talk to someone other than Nick to clarify what I was feeling. After talking to Jelli, I made an appointment to see him. I don't remember exactly when, just that it was, sometime before. After and before get very confusing when you live in circles and loops and links. Memory and time are not linear, I keep trying to say. Takes a long time to sink in, doesn't it?

Nick had conversations with Bill Webb too.

When he told him how it felt to leave the agency, especially with former colleagues attacking him for being honest, Bill said he felt the same way after he left the ministry.

Once he was free to talk about how it really was behind the costumes and the curtain, his peers resented his excitement at taking new paths and drummed him out of the club he'd already left. Bill and Nick had both deeply internalized the personas of a priest, in Bill's case, and a professional spy in Nick's. The commitments that led both into their roles were indelible. Both were young, naive, and convinced of their righteousness when they enlisted, but as James Baldwin said, "The price one pays for pursuing any profession or calling is an intimate knowledge of its ugly side." They lived with two realities, the reasons they signed up and the toll it took to do the real work. Bill was a priest forever and Nick was never free of how he had been molded by the agency.

Bill succeeded in his career. He read a book he found at a used book store, *How to Become a Bishop Without Being Religious.* The cynical, funny but true account, written by a cleric at the peak of his profession, was a blueprint for success in the most worldly way. Bill was in his first parish when he read it, pastoring a small group clinging to the hope that they would grow by cloning others like themselves. The book had clear advice: get out as soon as you can. He did. He migrated to St. Sisyphus, a good move since the previous rector had driven away a lot of members and Bill knew how to build it back into a thriving parish.

That worldly wisdom about how to climb the ladder was golden. But he never became cynical about the deeper truths he learned. The people who allegedly came for his advice, he discovered, served him as much as he served them. They revealed capacities for resilience, elasticity, dignity and heroism when the worst that the world can do was dumped on their heads. They taught him, he said, how to be a more fully human being. Those lessons never left him.

Yet the work wore him down and diluted the potency of his "conversion experience." The narrowness of small minds made his vocation feel more and more constrained. He felt more and more like a "professional Christian,"paid not to articulate the shared ethos of the community, but to carry their sins like a sacrificial lamb while they went to Cancun for Christmas and he did extra services for the few who remained, the least and the last and the lost. It hadn't helped that as he wrestled with his decision, the bishop, a narcissistic bully, added to his stress. The Bishop managed his own stress, it turned out, by having sex with his assistant, an attractive woman named Carolyn Leary. The bishop thought he could get away with affairs because he knew so many who had. But times had changed. Leary lawyered up and offered a deal: If he made up a reason to resign and paid what she asked, she wouldn't tell. He could walk. They shook hands and he signed ("here … here … and here") and moved out of town. He wrote a farewell letter, saying he resigned due to arthritis.

Bill's cognitive dissonance increased until one morning, he woke up with a deep peaceful feeling and knew he was done. He freed himself of the internal constraints of doctrine, dogma, and discipline that had bound his soul like barbed wire and moved into a new life, a wider life more akin to the one he sought when he entered the ministry.

"I was suffocating," he said. "I looked at other positions, but that wasn't the answer. I was offered good positions and realized that none of them would work. A geographic cure wouldn't work. So here I am. I wake up every morning eager to get into the day. I took the high road out. A lot of the guys who blow out of the water want to get out but don't know how so they adopt a self-defeating strategy as I think that bishop did. I was told by a therapist who treated clergy for depression that they wished that they could do what I had done but their self esteem was in the pits and they couldn't think of something else to do. They wore their golden handcuffs as if they were badges of righteousness and honor.

The last time Nick went to Bill's study, he told me with some sadness, the cleric's face was tinted by the light of a table lamp with a crimson shade from which golden tassels hung. Autumn was over. Winter had fallen like a curtain of ice across the landscape. The winter wasn't beautiful yet, just cold. Inside the office, it was warm and cozy, and after the staff left, there was no noise from the hallway. It was a refuge Nick had come to value.

Bill and Nick were real friends. Both had to feel a way into another life so they shared strategies. The back-slapping self-congratulations at the agency never allowed the kind of friendship Nick had with Bill. Inside the cloistered life, they laughed a lot, used dark humor to lighten stress and bonded of mutual necessity, they drank to excess until the wee hours, but they had to keep one another at arm's length. A duplicitous colleague could ruin one's career. Nat was the only real friend Nick had at work and that was because they broke the rules. Now Nat was gone. Bill said clergy were similarly wary of backstabbing colleagues. Passive aggression was the M.O. because they had to pretend they never felt anger. Some adopted smiles that felt like their faces would break. Sniping and nasty gossip ruled the day. It could be a very lonely job.

In Bill's study, the bond between Bill and Nick grew strong. He said he didn't want to leave and feel the icy wind on his face like a whip, but when he wasn't with me, he felt my presence pull him like a magnet. I had become his psychic home. In the deep midwinter, we hollowed out cozy caves inside each other's souls and went into hibernation.

Nick sometimes had difficulty staying on track. PTSD was a constant threat, not recalling images but putting him back in that room. His developed defenses and let his thoughts drift to obscure the grim recollections. Bill was patient when he had to repeat himself but at Dasein, Joe often droned on and on and Nick thought of other things until one day Joe said, You do that a lot, Nick, you disappear. No, he explained, I was thinking. Your voice is a soporific. You could soothe a colicky baby to sleep.

Joe didn't like that but Nick didn't care. He had to deal with his own ghosts, what he did in Poland and the impacts of remote viewing. That's what I was trying to say, what those impacts did. We never knew what we would encounter during a viewing. I told Joe I was stressed but he seemed indifferent to how it was affecting me. I noticed he was doing less and less viewing and supervising more. I challenged him on that and he said he was the CEO and that was his decision.

On top of that, the unexpected lore of UFOs, that the presence of the "visitors" had been covered up for years, was more than distracting. What I learned was exciting at first but over time became frightening. Sometimes the universe bared its teeth. They are not all benign, you know.

The world was piling on.

Valerie again.

I liked Bill Webb. After he left the ministry, every time Nick and I saw him socially he had a different woman on his arm. We had him in for dinner a few times and he always brought a different one, younger than the last. I had no high ground on that score so I kept my mouth shut. I know some thought I was a trophy wife, but that was BS. I was a mature woman in love with the man I was lucky to find at just the right time.

I did ask Bill about the growing collection of one-night darlings with good natured playfulness, and he said, "Free at last, Val, free at last, thank God almighty, free at last."

Anyway, Nick and I told each other everything. I had signed an NDA, sure, we had to to work at Dasein, but my fingers were crossed behind my back. In my head, I mean. They didn't remote view my head when I signed the agreement.

Nick came in late one afternoon and he didn't look happy. He unzipped his parka and removed his knit cap and looked in the hallway mirror to see if his hair was mussed. I could see, even in the fading light of late afternoon, it definitely was. His hair was thinning, and I think he let it lengthen to pretend there was more than there was. He had asked his barber recently if it was all gray. The barber paused and looked it over and said, No, there's plenty of white. That was not what Nick wanted to hear. A few patches of gleaming skin shone through the thicker hair. It was like the illusion of the vase and the face, which one do you see. Nick focused on the hair, not the bald.

He went to the bathroom to brush it and splash his face with cold water, as if he was just waking up. Maybe, in a way, he felt like he was. I could feel the weight of his day as he came back into the living room. His center of gravity was low.

"From the way you look," I said, "it wasn't all giggles and bliss at Dasein Inc."

He went into the kitchen to mix a negroni. I heard him swirl the ice, then he came through the door sipping it, and when he sat, he took a great big gulp.

"Yep," he said, "not a good day. I read the horoscope this morning and it said, Aries, you can't be good at everything. Treat negative feedback as what you need to work on." He half-smiled. "For once it was right. How was your day?"

"I met Jelli for lunch. I wanted to know more about that episode she had."

"And did you?"

"I sure did. She apparently had an encounter with a UFO. A real abduction-type deal. I also had an incredible experience at the cafe."

Sitting at the end of our love seat, my legs in a curl beneath me, my hands animating my words, Nick sitting on the other end, a few feet away, I retold Jelli's story in my own words.

I told him what I could remember and he tried to listen closely but was clearly preoccupied by whatever had happened. When he chooses to listen, he really listens. When he does that, I feel like he's really with me. I also know this guy pretty well by now, and I know that finding me at home, lamps lighted and our snuggery intact, compared to when he lived alone and had to come back to an empty dark apartment on a cold gray day, would often make him amorous. How I responded would determine what we did. I kept my expression serious and sober, not playful, not eager for that at all, staying on topic. UFOs. Transporter beams. Telepathic communication.

As a rule, UFO-talk doesn't lead to sex.

"Have you heard stories like Jelli's? At the agency, I mean?"

He sipped his negroni thoughtfully. He didn't drink a lot and wanted it to count when he did. He said the agency had a pretty boozy breath, all in all.

"We talked about them but I wasn't in any of the real programs. I knew they existed, that we did our best to monitor what was happening. We wanted to know how they work. Whoever got there first would rule the world. We also used the useful idiots to disinform, cover up projects, and generally fuck with the public.

"It's hard enough to do CI when we're all from the same planet. It's impossible when you have no clue who or what they are. I heard that we picked up pieces of craft that crashed, but we couldn't replicate the alloys. We scanned them, I heard, and could see how the atoms were arranged, but that's not the same as making them. Even if we could, we wouldn't know how the alloys interact with the crew and their uniforms. Von Braun said we didn't know what we were up against. He and his mentor, Hermann Oberth, were both baffled. So we talked about it, yes, but we were ignorant of what was going on behind closed doors. If we weren't read into the programs, we didn't know squat.

"Getting back to Jelli—sure, we heard stories like hers. There are thousands of stories and they get boring. A luminous object comes down and weird shit happens. Or someone sees humanoids in a two-seater cockpit. We didn't need to keep collecting details to confirm what we already know. They let those reports go into a civilian data base. They pile up without critical examination and there's no investigation, so meaningful research is impossible. It bleeds off the fanatics and gives them something to do."

I let out my breath which I hadn't known I was holding.

"Okay then," I said."Wow. Well, I can see that the agencies, the military, had to have agendas. But when it happens to you—like it did to Jelli—it's not just interesting data. It has a huge impact on a person, and when she told me her story, it had a huge effect on me. Your pals were debunking credible reports, you're saying, for seventy-five years. That traumatized people even more, you made them afraid to speak. Did anyone care?"

"That was a problem," Nick said, "but it couldn't be helped. Innocent people are always collateral damage. That's just what's so."

Even now, despite what he's gone through, Nick can sound like a company man. It goes so deep. In that mode, he forgets how normal people think. Individuals might care about consequences or act on the nudging of a conscience but not organizations. An organization, regardless of its stated agenda, does not have a conscience. It has no soul. When Nick talks like that, I need to determine which Nick I'm talking to.

"Well, what happened to Jelli had an impact, Nick, and on me too. These encounters change people. I was changed by listening to her."

That made him pause. "I hear you, hon. But it doesn't change how power people act. Insiders have a get-out-of-jail-free card. They live in a different world. And don't forget, we did a lot of good. Has another plane crashed into a building? No one back here asks the price."

"You also did a lot of bad. You were like gods. You emptied yourself of your divinity and became a human being and paid a price for doing it."

He thought about that for a long time. "You can say it that way, yes, I guess I did. I got crucified."

He didn't sound like a company man when he slipped back into himself. His voice changed. He sounded like a human being.

That was the guy I loved.

We both sighed, which made us laugh.

"Anyway ... you were saying, your day at Dasein wasn't the best."

"No. I may have washed out as a remote viewer. It's that simple."

I looked at him with concern. "What happened?"

"You know I've been doing runs. Joe was training me, and sometimes Hal, and I thought I was getting better. I made a serious attempt today with a target and it was dead wrong. Not even close. I was viewing a square block in Milwaukee and I was sure I was getting data from the place. The building I sketched came into view pretty quickly with plenty of details. But when we looked at the site, nothing was there. It was nothing but a parking lot.

"Val, I don't think I have the knack. I'll try again, they want me to keep trying but also to be more customer-facing. That means working with Sylvia, which is not going to be fun. They could have cut me loose, and I'm glad they didn't, but it's disappointing. It's deflating. Obviously, if my performance doesn't improve ...."

He finished his drink. Then he went and made another. When he returned, he said, "You haven't said much recently about your own viewings, Val. I know you were getting good results. I know you've been working long hours."

"Well—yes, I am."

"Okay. So ...?"

"I'm getting good results. They increased my work with clients. I do come home more tired and don't want to talk about it much. But I'm getting better and better, so it's not a surprise they want me to do more."

"Val, that's great to hear, as long as you can manage it." He wasn't just saying it. He meant it, and I got it. I hadn't realized how anxious I was about talking about my success. I was afraid my success might feel like I undermined him somehow, since he was the one they approached and I had tagged along. I didn't want to lose what we had. But I had to be myself as well. I couldn't surrender my hard-won growth but I knew that competition can poison a relationship. I felt so relieved. Telling him was a huge test, and he passed.

I looked at Nick with gratitude. Our future was intact.

Neither had to say a word.

He looked at me and smiled. I smiled back.

"Yes," I said. "Let's."

Interlude

"The moment has no time."

- Leonardo Da Vinci

"According to theoretical physicist Carlo Rovelli, time is an illusion: our naive perception of its flow doesn't correspond to physical reality. Indeed, Rovelli argues that much more is illusory, including Isaac Newton's picture of a universally ticking clock. Even Einstein's relativistic space-time — an elastic manifold that contorts so that local times differ depending on one's relative speed or proximity to a mass — is just an effective simplification.

Rovelli posits that reality is just a complex network of events onto which we project sequences of past, present and future...."

- *The Order of Time*, Carlo Rovelli,
reviewed by Andrew Jaffe (16 April 2018)

Chapter 9
And Then What?

"And then what?" Nick said. "That's a question I learned to ask at the agency. If I choose a course of action, what's likely to come next? What's likely to follow? I don't have to do full-on scenario planning to see viable options."

I looked up from whisking the pudding in the green ceramic bowl at the kitchen counter, debating whether or not to add real pistachios. Delicious and nutritious but highly caloric. Nick was in the doorway, but I wasn't sure what he was referring to.

"What exactly are we discussing?"

"The feeling I had about my last viewing. They said they surveyed the site and it's nothing but a parking lot. The elaborate building I described was nowhere in evidence. There are two buildings across the street, a hotel to the east and apartments to the south. Both buildings are trite modern, one tall, one short. That's not what I glimpsed. I saw a weird maze of hallways and stairways and I even heard music—very faintly, but it was definitely music."

I smiled. "What kind? I never heard music during a viewing."

"I could swear it sounded like Cobain. Crazy, right? Early stuff, I decided after googling their list. It wasn't hard core grunge, it came from a small room with a tiny crowd, maybe a dozen. In Milwaukee no less."

"That doesn't sound like Nirvana, Nick. Their crowds were huge. Did they even play Milwaukee?"

"I haven't checked that out yet. But that's what I heard. Or thought I did. It was faint, it faded but came back. I could swear it was them."

"Who else did you hear?" I smiled. " Smashing Pumpkins? Green Day?"

"Maybe. I don't know. The music was a strange mix, a cacophony; there might have been others, but Cobain is who I thought I heard."

"And you saw a building?"

"I did. And as long as I'm saying how crazy it was, I saw an image of a unicorn. A black and white unicorn. A drawing, like, not a real animal."

"I'm glad you didn't view a real unicorn, Nick. That's where I draw the line."

"The building was weird. It was like a maze, seemingly endless hallways, rickety staircases going every which way, a maze of twisty passages."

"Did you play Colossal Cave? Did you see a goblin?"

"Don't be sarcastic. It really was a twisty maze. I tried to move through hallways to find the music, I could hear it, but I couldn't find it. The layout was confusing. Some hallways were normal but some were real narrow. My point of view was like I was floating. The stairs were ridiculous. It was like an Escher etching. You wouldn't know where a hallway would come out. It made no sense. I've never seen a building like that."

I focused on whisking the thickening pudding. But I had to say something.

"It's not easy," I suggested, trying to be helpful, "separating what we think from what we're detecting. Once we decide what we think it is, we reinforce the decision by believing it. Then we see it even more. Don't you think?"

"Yes, I know that's how it works, but ... like I said, then what? A diplomat from the UK, Catherine Ashton, wrote a book with that title that illuminated how they make decisions. If we do this, she said, then what? We should always be asking that question."

"She sounds like the voice of experience. I imagine that's not acted on as much as we'd like."

"That's right. I am sure at the agency we failed to do that plenty of times. We often made a decision and then acted, without that kind of reflection."

"I asked myself that question when we met." I smiled. "If we go ahead with this ... then what?"

Nick smiled. "This is what. Together in the kitchen whisking the pudding and talking about everything. I love how we're doing this thing, the more we do it."

"This thing." I smiled. "A good name for cohabiting. Yes, 'this thing' is working, isn't it?"

I tapped the spoon on the edge of the pyrex bowl, then offered it to Nick to lick. He took it and when he finished there was pudding on his chin. I nuzzled it, kissed it off. It tickled him, and he laughed.

"I think it is," he said. "Anyway, if I ignore my feelings about a viewing they called a dud ... then what? I would always doubt myself. I want to see for myself. Then, whichever way it goes, I can move on. I need closure."

"So you want to drive to Milwaukee and–where is it exactly?"

"The corner of Juneau and Third. They call it Old World Third."

"You want to go today? Right now?"

"Why not? It's Saturday and the weather's pretty mild for this time of year. I think in the forties. Let's go. We can stop along the way for lunch."

I washed off the spoon and put the pudding in the fridge and washed my hands and kissed him on the nose and said, "OK, mister anxiety. It's a good excuse to take a ride. Let's go play."

"Jesus!" Nick said. "It's Saturday. Where is the traffic coming from?"

We had driven out to 94 on a stop-and-start surface street, but that wasn't the problem. Once we went up the ramp, we hit a mass of traffic that, when it moved at all, barely crawled north. Honkers abused the drivers ahead who extended as far as one could see, as if their noise would make the traffic move faster.

"I'm glad we kept the Prius," I said. "Even if we run out of gas, we can inch ahead on the battery alone."

"Let's hope we don't have to do that. Okay, it's moving now."

It was but not for long. He accelerated, thinking we had broken free, but the Prius shrieked STOP! as the car engaged its brakes and stopped just in time, a foot or two from the bumper that would have crumpled to the tune of a thousand bucks. I started to suggest a strategy for managing the traffic but decided not to help. If I had, Nick would have one more problem.

We made the toll gate in just over an hour. Traffic feeding in from the right made the bottleneck worse. We arrived at last at the money machine and Nick threw change into its mouth and it raised the gate. Nick shot through and the traffic flow increased until it was nearly at speed.

We reached the state line a couple of hours after we left.

"Welcome to Wisconsin," Nick said. "Jesus, what an ordeal."

"Road trips are not all they're cracked up to be," I said with a light-hearted laugh. "But here we are. It's pretty boring but–look, there's a pretty hill–oops, you passed it."

"It's the least scenic part of the state. But we didn't come for the view."

"No. We came to set your mind at ease, one way or another."

They must have had more snow up there. The fields were furrowed black and white, the trees along the highway leafless and stiff. I could hear the wind through the window even when I closed it all the way. The glass felt cold to the touch. The landscape looked desolate.

"It's almost lunch time," Nick said. "My guess is noon. What is it exactly?"

I looked at the dash. "Not bad. Twelve twelve."

"Ready to stop?"

"As long as it isn't fast food."

I asked the cell phone to find nearby restaurants. The Texas Road House was just ahead. On weekends they opened for lunch at eleven. "Want to try it?"

"Sure," he said. "Bar food is okay."

We cruised off the interstate and turned into the parking lot after making a few turns and a u-turn or two when we hit a curb or median. "Watch out for that ice," I said. "It looks rock-hard."

"I see it, Val."

"I wasn't sure. I was just trying to be helpful."

He found the roadhouse parking lot and we parked away from the door. The cold wind coming over the fields stung my forehead and I held the collar of my coat closed with one numbing hand. We hurried into the restaurant, grateful for its warmth.

The Texas theme was overdone, but the smell of peanuts permeated the place and Nick loved eating peanuts from their shells. Pouring handfuls from a jar was no fun and they never tasted as good. He said it reminded him of going to Cub games.

We sat in a booth. The place raised memories for me of the Barbican. There were menus on the table and condiments and napkins in a holder, just like my old home den. There the comparison stopped: the Barbican was a retreat in the city for office workers and lonely souls, while this was a stop on an interstate with hotels, strip malls, farms and suburbs all around.

A perky lass in gingham and a stetson hat appeared with water and a big bowl of peanuts.

"I'm Rosie," she said. "I'm your server." Her sweet voice and a large cross hanging from a chain advertised her religious commitment. Nick thinks a cross dangling like that is meant to draw a guy's eyes to cleavage.

Nick was feeling mischievous. I could tell from his playful smile, his need to make life interesting. He said he felt like Henry Hill at the end of the movie, feeling like a schnook. He did silly things at times to perk himself up.

"That's a beautiful cross," he said. "You're a real Christian, aren't you?"

Rosie bought it straight up.

"I am," she beamed. "I'm an Evangelical. You are too. I can feel it."

"You have the gift of discernment," he said, mirroring her smile. "When did you become a Christian?"

"I was seventeen," she said, "ten years ago at the Second Baptist

Church here in Kenosha. Pastor Bunche baptized me. He's gone now, but everybody loved him. I've never been the same."

"That's wonderful," Nick said. "I was baptized at Falcon Ridge, that big church on the North Shore, one cold autumn morning. The waves in the lake were fierce. I'll never forget it either."

Their eyebeams crossed. They were two of the faithful, gathered together, one in the booth making it a game, the other sincere and smiling. That's how he did it at his former work, creating a bridge across which information would subsequently flow. Even before Nick finished the peanuts, Rosie brought a second bowl and set it down with a "here you are." By the time our sandwiches arrived, shell casings were all around us. Footsteps on the wooden floor crackled with breaking shells. When we finished and Nick computed a tip, she said, "Wait right here" and went and returned with a huge paper bag filled with more peanuts. "I see how much you like them. You take these."

"Thank you so much," said Nick, taking the bag of contraband. Like exchanging data on a back street.

When we were back in the car, I said, "'You're backsliding, Nick. You played that innocent girl just for fun."

"Well, yes," he said, and then he said, "so what's the harm? The day needed color. I had no idea she'd give me extra peanuts. That was a bonus."

I shook my head. "The thing is, you slid back into using a false persona to manipulate her, and you said you would stop. You said you would practice being honest, acting normal. Aren't you a little guilty? You didn't need the peanuts. We can afford all the peanuts you want."

He turned the car back onto the highway. "You are right, sir," he said, which he taught me was what Ed McMahon always said to Johnny Carson. His references to TV shows were often to things before my time.

He got serious then. "I get it, Val, but I do miss the life." He sighed. "It's childish, I know. But habits run deep, and it was fun, and it was harmless." He set the bag on the console between us. "Would you like a peanut?"

"Not in the car," I said. "it would make a mess." And with that, I moved the bag to the floor at my feet where he couldn't reach it unless he was willing to crash. He wanted another peanut, but not *that* much.

When he looked back on his work, Nick said, it was often for peanuts. A lot of the time, he said, we exaggerated the importance of what we did. When you ran a disinformation campaign, you never knew how well it worked. We didn't do too many crazy things like in books and movies, but we exaggerated quite a bit. I think we wanted to be a little more important than we were. Combine that with insularity, working behind a one way mirror, and we often forgot that none of us knew the big picture. We shared secrets, but only with others cleared to know. Even when former secrets were slated for declassification, it would take centuries to do them all, since every phrase has to be checked for links to sources and methods. All of us were in the dark, including keepers of the light.

"But don't the people on top see it all?"

Nick chuckled. "When you prepare the PDB–condensing, editing, getting it all to fit on a single page–so much is left out that by the time the final copy is in their hands, the briefing is distorted. Nuance is sacrificed every time it's rewritten. On top of that, you might get a president who thinks that other opinions are not worth knowing.

"I am making the point," he said, "that much of the time, we worked for peanuts and didn't even know it. Same as if I ate peanuts in the car. It would make a mess."

"And I like the car to be neat and clean."

"Indeed," he says, "I know you do. Directors want the agencies to look clean too."

We were downtown by then, off the interstate, looking at street signs as we cruised down Third Street. As we guessed, there were older buildings as the name of the street implied, intended to create a nineteenth century vibe. We found Juneau and swung around the corner to park on the street. We sat for a moment and enjoyed nothing happening.

Now, here's a funny thing: I had noticed that our boundaries were becoming more porous. The longer we were together, the more we made up a third person. We didn't know who was thinking what. That happened as we sat in the car. We were twisted together like a kinked hose.

I was in that state, happy as a clam, and I had to shake myself back into the gal called Val, looking out the window of the parked car along a fence around a big parking lot. To the left was the Moderne, the tall building Nick was shown in street view photos, and if I turned around and looked a little more north, there was the hotel, an Aloft, part of a national chain. They were Mutt and Jeff, the only two buildings at the site, just as Nick was told.

How did he miss that parking lot? Information came from a specific space-time site, and that's what we see remotely. We see it now. The past the future and the present are here now. Everything exists now. Who knows what that means? I'll never have the answers that I want. Hal said life is like walking into a movie after it began and leaving before it ends.

All that monkeymind chatter danced in my mind but without relevance to our quest. Apart from those thoughts, all I saw from the car was a parking lot surrounded by a fence on which were plastered signs about buildings a developer hoped to build.

"We might as well get out and look around," I said.... handing the narration back to Nick.

Val put the peanuts on the floor of the back seat, even more beyond my reach, and zipped her coat and put on gloves and pulled down her knitted hat until it covered her ears and most of her forehead. I got out and locked the Prius with a click of the fob.

We walked over to the fence and looked out on the empty stalls. There was no game at the Forum across the street so the gate was locked. Parking lots around a downtown area are signs of a city trying to be bigger than it is. The fence around the parking lot had signs about "building the future together," which is what signs say when there's not much going on.

We walked around the block and returned to where we parked. There was no way to pretend there was anything but a parking lot where I thought I had seen an unusual building. I thought I heard the words, "I can't escape every night," repeated in a course voice. Standing there with Val, I heard nothing.

Val looked at me with concern, a look I knew well. Ever since I broke down and sobbed in her arms and confessed the terrible things I did, she was wary of what might happen if I slid into that broken state again. She didn't know if I had emptied the closet of monsters, and I didn't either. I scared myself as much as I scared her.

When I told a colleague I thought it was futile to hope we might end torture, he said eliminating lawful slavery took hundreds of years. All we can do, he said, is tell the truth and hope for a better future.

"I'm afraid it's just a parking lot," Val said. "There's no building here, Nick."

"I see that," I said.

The wind had died down and we walked along the fence reading the signs. There were few people on the street. It was too cool for shoppers to be strolling. I saw only one person, a figure in the distance walking toward us, staring at his cell phone as he walked. He wore a red white and blue hoodie–a red hood matched his red sneakers, white across the middle, blue around the belly.

"Careful," I said when he came near, speaking loudly to penetrate his trance. "The sidewalk's broken in front of you. Don't trip."

He paused and looked up. He stopped and removed the buds.

"Were you talking to me?"

"You're walking toward the sidewalk where it buckled," I said. "I was afraid you wouldn't notice."

"Oh, right," he said. "Thanks for the alert."

"No problem. … You live around here?"

"A few blocks away, across the river," he said. "Juneau Village." He was standing a few feet away and turned so the filtered light illuminated my face to a greater degree. "Why? You looking for a place to live?"

"No," I said. "It's a long story, but bottom line, we were checking out this corner. Has it always been a parking lot? I thought there was a building here."

"There was, but they tore it down. It had lots of problems, fires, drugs, revolving tenants, but there were a lot of great memories in that crazy place. So no, now, obviously, it's a parking lot, but there was a building here. It was actually three buildings connected by hallways and stairways and passageways, it was like the fun house at an amusement park. The rooms were rented to every imaginable counterculture gig there was back then. It was a great place to hear new bands. A lot of them played at the Unicorn before they were famous. Lots of beer and pot and hard drugs. I went there a bunch of times."

Valerie and I were more than listening.

"Tell us more," Val said. "What bands played here?"

"A lot of local Milwaukee bands, I'm sure you never heard of them. But some came through before they got big. Smashing Pumpkins, Green Day, Nirvana–"

"Nirvana? Really?"

He laughed. "I know a hundred people who say they were there that night, but there weren't more than dozen. It was raining like hell and hardly anyone came. No one knew who they were. They didn't know who they were yet. I think they were on the Blaech tour. I knew all the songs. Perry and I used to sing them around the house. Perry was my partner then. He died of AIDS a long time ago.

"Some of the local bands were great. Ever hear of Soda?"

"No."

"I liked them a lot."

"The Bleach album," Nick repeated. "Was one of the songs about a girl?"

The guy looked surprised. "It was. It was called "About a Girl," in fact. Cobain wrote it for his girl friend, Tracy Menander, but she didn't even know it until after he was dead. Apparently he never told her he had."

Nick couldn't help leading the witness.

"Was there a line like, I can't escape you every night?"

The guy thought for a bit. "Something like that. No, wait. I think it was, I can't date you every night. Was that it?"

"Yes! That's it!" Nick said. "That's what I heard. Valerie, I swear, that's the line I heard."

"You watch it on YouTube? I think their stuff is online."

Nick dissembled, naturally. "I must have. YouTube."

"Of course I was younger. Right after college. What a great place it was, the Sydney Hih building, squares of colors on the front and inside like a maze. You could seriously get lost. If a building was a Kafka story, Sidney Hih was it. There was lots of nostalgia after they tore it down. They said for redevelopment, but you can see what that meant."

"When was it demolished?"

"Oh jeez, let me think." He looked off into his past. "About twenty years ago? This is 2023, it would have been twenty years ago. It was a real shame. They paved paradise and made it a parking lot."

I was seeing with my mind's eye the sketch I made during the session. His description fit, but I wanted to be sure. I wanted to compare the way the building looked and what I had seen.

"Man, I hadn't thought about the Sydney Hih for a long time. I used to go to the Golden Draft, the first gay bar in the city. I went to Betty's for beads, she had every kind of bead you can think. We used to go to a great restaurant called the Fertile Earth. They were the first place to ban smoking in Milwaukee."

He smiled. "I can smell the smells. I remember everything."

"So do I," Nick said. "So do I." Then—"Valerie? Let's go see."

I thanked him and we hurried toward the car.

"Can we stop for custard? They have really good custard stands."

"If it's on the way, sure. Hey, thanks," I called to the guy as he walked away. "Thanks for filling us in."

"No problem," he said, turning around and walking slowly backwards. "My name is Todd by the way. Thanks for the memories."

"We're Natalie and Ned," I said.

"See you around, Natalie and Ned."

We got into the car as Valerie searched for the nearest custard stand on her phone. "You can't help it, can you?"

"Actually, I can," I said."That was a joke, just for you."

"Tee hee," she said. "Here's one on the way out of town. The flavor of the day is Chocolate Madness."

"Tell me how to get there."

The robovoice on her cell directed us to a custard stand called Kopps and the rich creamy stuff was genuinely wonderful. There were chunks of chewy chocolate in the creamy chocolate custard and pieces of chocolate on top. I ate fast and headed out of town as Valerie made her double scoop last until we were on the highway heading south. She always ate ice cream in a cup so she wouldn't drip.

"Don't you wish we had this stuff in Chicago?"

"Sure. Custard is good. Pork chops are good."

All I could think about was getting back to my drawing of a strange building with multi-colored squares on the front and a maze of twisty passages.

"Easy on the gas," Val said. "I don't want our insurance to jump because of a ticket."

I stayed in the left lane. It was made for heavy-footed scofflaws and I was a need-to-know machine, revved up to the level of a primal scream. We made it home in record time and did not see a single cop.

Interlude

"Reality is that which, when you stop believing in it, does not go away."

- Philip K. Dick, *Valis*

Chapter 10
The Twilight Zone

V alerie here, mostly. Telling the truth as best I can.

The twilight zone–that's what I called it, despite the lack of a musical cue. The room was dim and sometimes before viewing I applied a warm compress over my eyes and lay down and let the darkness become comforting. There was no light through my eyelids as there would be if I were in bright sunlight. I sometimes fell asleep but was somehow aware of it and brought myself back into wakefulness. I had to be focused, alert, fully present. I had to set aside the mundane matters of the workaday world and enter the twilight zone.

Preparation for the protocol *was* the protocol. The protocol was a portal into a liminal world, I was taught by Hal McCutcheon. He thought that twilight itself was a portal too, a curtain that rose before darkness fell, when marginal creatures appeared and dimensional realities disclosed themselves. He totally believed that. He also believed that fairies and gnomes were real, reports of their mischief viridical. We see them in shadows, they look like shadows at first, he said, then they laugh or move or disappear. They play games with us, they deceive us, they lie, they're worse than the aliens, who at least have agendas. Fairies and gnomes just like to fuck with us.

Hal told me to study writing with Alan Moore. He has a course on the BBC. So I did. Moore likened creativity to doing real magic. He said that when artists, writers, composers, impose their consciousness on the world it alters it in the process–both their consciousness and the world. That's magic, and in a similar way, remote viewing is too. During a viewing, our consciousness engages with and manipulates the physical world. Consciousness is dangerously pointed like a spear, directed by our intentions, and when we abandon the materialistic paradigms that govern us these days, when we learn that clairvoyance and telepathy are real, and psychometry and telekinesis too, we align our lives with those facts. Consciousness expands to include those realities. It's like Dorothy lands in Munchkinland and the film turns from black-and-white to color. The world does become more magical. The more we experience psi, the more it happens. We don't control it, we can't make it happen, but like other kinds of creative work, we can tend it, nurture it, wait for it to manifest. We can't foresee when any particular electron will make a quantum leap, but they do. We can't foresee when we'll receive a message in a dream or know that someone is knocking from afar. We're shamans, Hal said. The so-called material world is elastic and so is our extended self-awareness. When they grapple with each other, something new always comes. Our brains' plasticity works on our behalf.

I didn't know what a shaman was. I didn't know I was an esper. To my knowledge, no shaman ever came to the Barbican for a drink, no one on a barstool ever brought up consciousness, or remote viewing, or anything like that. Sometimes I knew who would walk in the door, even if they had no regular pattern, but I never said anything about it. I told you about my mother's death, what happened then. But growing up in Des Moines, I didn't know a single shaman, or wizard, or seer, at least not by those names. There was a Warren Gill on our street who was certainly unusual, we skipped his house when we went trick-or-treating, but we were taught not to ask personal questions so we called him The Duck, the Odd Duck, and walked on the other side of the street. I used to play jacks on the sidewalk in front of his house when my mother was watering our lawn and I couldn't play in the spray and if the door creaked open, I picked up my jacks and ball and ran. When I was twelve he died after a stroke and the Bowers bought the house from the estate. Then it was just a normal house with a mother and a father, a boy and a girl, and a dog and a cat, straight out of Wichita Kansas. Billy Bower said the place was haunted by Warren Gill's ghost. His sister Harriet told him after they grew up that she was making the noises, not a ghost. Everybody knew it but him but he was so committed to his story that he stayed with it. He asked his sister if she had done the poltergeist stuff too. The what? she said. Uh-huh, he smirked. Point taken. Case closed.

Hal said a shaman is just a person who found out how to do what I was being trained to do and knows that they can do it. Knowing that they can is critical because then you can choose to do it instead of it just happening to happen. Shamans move between two worlds, and the trick is knowing how to come back. Otherwise they're considered crazy, living only in a world that no one else can reach. You gotta keep that silver cord unbroken.

If you bilocate and fuse with the site you're viewing, it can be dangerous. You can lose yourself and get stuck. You can't detach easily and have to be retrieved by a control team and brought back to where everyone else lives. When that happened, after I was home again, I got really frightened. The ability to lose yourself in remote viewing is a double-edged sword.

Hal thought we all had the potential to learn how to expand our capabilities or access something called an Akashic record. Once you know that the boundaries between us are porous, the categories of psi dissolve into just one. We may be fetching data from some one else's brain, now or in the past or even from their future self, or we may be lifting impressions like fingerprints that adhere in a specific site in space-time or saturate a place with intense emotion after some traumatic event. Where is the information coming from? Nobody really knows.

I scribbled notes as he spoke and read them again later. My vocabulary grew by leaps and bounds, even if I didn't understand everything he said.

I know you heard some of this before. I have to keep repeating it to myself until I believe it's real. I want you to know how much I grew as I pursued this magical mystery tour but it didn't come easy and it didn't come fast. It took time to grasp that what was happening was real. I'll leave the fiction to Nick. I am telling you facts.

Before I discovered it for myself, Hal said that some places were sacred and some were evil. I mean it, he said, thinking my expression betrayed doubt. You might enter an emotional field and find yourself experiencing perfect peace. I'm thinking of the ruins of an abbey in the north of England, he said. The minute I crossed the threshold, a deep serenity absorbed me. Even the birds nesting in open windows under a bright blue sky were enchanting. I felt the same at Iona. I left a tour group and went into an anchor hold, a small door with the written injunction, "Hold Fast." I stooped to go into a tiny room and looked out through a window, squinting at a St. John's cross and the main building near the sea. I didn't know at the time how deeply I was absorbing the tranquillity of the place. When I heard the group getting ready to leave, I didn't want to go, but I had to.

"I think of it every day," he said. "But my path led to the agency and then to this old office, and I have to honor the path. If the path includes sorrow as well as joy, so be it. All paths do."

I never knew how to take the more arcane aspects of his narratives, so I mostly listened and took notes. I didn't judge, I let him talk. My work at the Barbican had been good practice. My job was to nod and pour another drink.

Hal pointed toward one of the windows in the office. I looked out through the dirty glass at the low clouds.

"Do you see like a blue stripe in the sky?" he said.

I looked harder. "Nope. Just low clouds."

"Hmmph," he said. "Well, never mind. And don't forget, you were the one who asked to be included, that night at the reception. You asked if you could try it out. I think you were led by a guiding spirit. Way leads on to way. Now you can't unring the bell. Right?"

"I guess."

"No guess, Valerie. Know." He laughed again. "You broke out of the paradigm that said this isn't possible. Other cultures know all about this. They communicate by thought over long distances or create thought forms to retrieve what they need. If you see a thought forms racing by, get out of the way. In the Himalayas I could see them coming. We backed ourselves into thinking we live exclusively in a material world. We decided that consciousness is inside the brain and the brain inside a head and that was that. Most folks don't know who they are. As Deckard said, how can they not know who they are? Of course, he didn't know who he was either."

I shrugged. I hoped I looked thoughtful. "I have no idea, Hal," I said. "I imagine I don't know who I am, either."

"Wise woman," he grinned. "Knowing that is halfway there."

My teachers, my mentors, my guides, led me into that twilight zone. I was an eager learner. Once we do successful remote viewing, our astonishment segues into confident belief in our abilities. We see a little more into the heart of a mysterious universe. They told me that would happen, and it did. My former beliefs are still useful for talking to others, letting me speak their language, but now I know that everything is connected. Joe said physicists know that stuff isn't stuff. If it's anything, it's thought, defined by symbols, language, math. Math is a map of the invisible world, he said, a huge tautological set of equivalence and transformations. Symbols are nothing but modules of meaning that we turn into tools. The more symbols we can jigger, the more we see. It's like when English exploded from tens of thousands of words to more than a million when printing was invented. You could see and say much more. Mean much more. Which implies that the universe is meaningful, even if we'll never know the meaning.

To know we live in a meaningful universe is the same as being free. Then again, the opposite is the same as being free, too.

I can't believe I am saying these things. Living with Nick, working with Joe and Hal, being taught by Brian, doing remote viewing, reflecting on it afterward, has taken me a long way from waiting tables at the Barbican.

Nick and I look into each other's eyes when we wake up and say, thank you for being there. We say thank you again to whoever might be listening, in case someone is.

I may sound balmy but please understand, this is very weird shit that's been happening. Sure, we may be delusional, Nick says with a laugh. We may be like Don Quixote. So let's mount up and ride, lances lowered, righting wrongs, doing good, armed with a powerful delusion. Doesn't everyone live like that? We don't need medals. Our work is its own reward. Let so-called heroes like Geoff Miller brag about his DSM. We know better, and if there's anything left of his soul, so does he.

Speaking for myself, he says as he turns and looks into my eyes and I melt and we hold hands like teens tumbling into love, I am just one starfish that you threw back into the sea. You gave me a second chance. I am so glad I met you, Val. I am so grateful for everything.

So we ride our momentum like we're riding a kayak in a torrent of white water, giggling at the bends and turns, going where the water goes, not even thinking it might not last.

I (Nick) reviewed the historical record of remote viewing. Protocols have varied over time. The first viewings used latitude and longitude to define the site of the target. No one knew why that worked, since numbers on maps should not lead to specific places, but they did. Then we discovered that we didn't even need them. Proctors merely had to write out the intended destination and one's consciousness rose like a drone, whirring into full functionality, hovered for a moment, then took off. Intentionality was the engine, the means of discovering the right direction, then the means of the strike on the right target.

I hold a folded paper in a sealed envelope in my hands. I don't put it to my forehead the way Johnny Carson did when dressed in his swami costume as Carnack the Magnificent. I just let it be there, in my hands in my lap, and I center in on a destination. Sometimes it doesn't come into focus and the whole thing is cancelled. But some of the time, something shows up and the fun begins.

Twilight descends, as Valerie said. The twilight is in my mind, a faint bluish glow that comes from within. I wait for something to happen, leaning into the task, patient but expectant. It's like sitting in a theater waiting for the play to begin. The lights go down, someone coughs a final time, there's a rustling of scenery, and then the curtain rises and actors come on stage. In my case, what came on stage–my mind like a proscenium arch, a geometric space–was a glimmer of an image, just a line, then two at an angle with no context to explain them. I see lines, dots and spirals. I tell myself to wait, not to push. The twilight is the ground, the lines the beginning of a figure. I have no idea what it is, but my right hand knows its task: holding a pencil, it begins to sketch what I see on a pad as structure emerges. Once that happens, it intensifies my ability to see more clearly, with more definition, the process governed by its own internal dynamics. A control is in the room, at least one, watching. They seldom interfere and fade into the background. After a while there is just me, hanging in the darkness. The vista expands and I see what I intend to find. The forms that emerge become a portal, a passageway between two worlds. Information is procured. The medium is the message, and I am the medium.

My sketch becomes two dimensional and sometimes three. Sometimes I shade perspective or depth with the side of the lead. Mostly I stay with basics, a general impression, the way it feels, and I exclude as best I can the part of me that likes to know what's happening. Keep analysis at bay. Stay with "right brain" impressions and let the prefrontal cortex wait its turn. I feel myself slide into the world I am entering and struggle to stay steady, stay on track, as I see the target at its site.

I assumed I was always in the present when I viewed. If something from the future or the past showed up, it was impossible to distinguish. Then ... as I drew, and sketched, and paid close attention to the manifesting shapes, when we checked it out... what I saw did not fit what I was taught about the world.

I directed my attention to what was written on the slip, the corner of Juneau and Old World Third in downtown Milwaukee. The lines tilted as I sketched, becoming a stairway and then one more and a third and a fourth. They went in different directions and defined the canvas, as it were, sitting on the easel in my mind. Then it got even stranger. An image of a unicorn in black and white began to flicker in and out and faint music played in the background, barely heard, but I picked up enough of an oft-repeated line to believe later that it fit a line from "About a Girl," an early Nirvana song that departed from their grunge plunge. It had a somewhat lilting tune, although it was sung with the same course voice as all the rest, and I have a hunch I heard it because it had a strong emotional field. His girlfriend learned he had written it after he pulled the trigger and was found with the gun on his chest and a bloody wound. I think strong emotions supercharge an event, especially love and anger and grief and fear, but we can't prove it. I think those feelings are embedded deeply in some targets. I think when people die, the same emotions alert the ones they love and they get the message. Sometimes they see an apparition.

Clients could care less: clients only care about results and how they can outplay, outwit, and outlast a competitor. One colleague accessed the scene of a murder. He freaked when he reported out. The client didn't care. All he wanted to know was, can you see the wound? Describe it to me, please. Can you see the shooter? That's what I need to know.

I had no client for the Milwaukee session. It was a dry run to see how I was doing. As I said, they judged it a complete failure because checking the scene after the viewing showed only a parking lot. That's all we saw too, when we went to check it out, but then serendipity, synchronicity, or both, brought a stranger down the street to tell us about the Sydney Hih.

Then I remembered what else I had seen. A facade with squares of colors, a building like a harlequin, different and kitschy and fun. My viewings were in black and white but I colored the squares afterward, like the Close Encounters guy building models of Devils Tower. Itches like that have to be scratched.

We returned to Chicago and the office and I hurried up the stairs. "Easy!" Valerie said. "Remember your heart!"

I didn't care. I had trouble with the key because I was so anxious but I managed to unlock the door and went to the files where my drawing had been stashed in a folder with name and date and coded ID. I opened it on the table under the bright fluorescent light and there it was: an image of the Sydney Hih.

This is how it looked:

We googled pics of the building itself and they perfectly matched. I had seen the Sydney Hih, as it was, two decades earlier. Before it was razed.

"Valerie," I said. "Valerie! I saw what was there in the past, not what's there now. How the hell does an image from twenty years ago make itself available?"

Val was amazed and genuinely thrilled. "This is fabulous!" she said. "Not only because you didn't fail at all but ... what does this say about ... what does this mean in terms of ..."

She didn't know how to say it and neither did I.

"Didn't I tell you what Metzger said?"

"Yes, but I don't remember. Tell me again."

"He said time isn't what we thought. He said Einstein didn't go far enough. There's spooky action not only at a distance but into the future too. Apparently entanglement happens in time as well as space. The future exists before ... before it does. We simply have to find it. So what the hell is it? Is it still the 'future?' Does everything exist in multiple dimensions?"

"It's mind blowing, Nick. Did you do those colors during the viewing?"

"No, I put them in afterward. I wanted to remember what I saw."

The shades were up on the windows and the twilight was deepening, snowflakes beginning to flutter, catching the last of the light as gusts of wind blew them about the empty street. I thought my head might explode, it was so loaded with realization, trying to grasp the truth of my own experience.

Past and present and future, all of them now. All is always now.

That was a sensible thing to think, but at the time, all I could think was, holy fuck! Holy motherfucking fuck!

"I know," Val said. "I'm reeling, Nick, it's making me dizzy."

We needed a better way to say it. Our exasperated stuttering was an incoherent gesture toward grasping the inscrutable. I had to believe in my experience, what it said about time, what Brian said, that information and intense emotion adhered somehow (but to what?), leaving traces in spacetime at nodes that we graph in four dimensions, then add a fifth so we can slide along the axes with a broader frame of reference.

I was being rocked in the cradle of a mystery, deeply perplexing multi-dimensional maps of a world more baffling than I could understand. My brain gave up. I went back to mumbling, holy fuck, holy motherfucking fuck.

Valerie again.

Have you noticed? We are speaking more and more, me and Nick, out of that third person we have created by interacting, then blending, then becoming one-ish.

Valerie's my middle name, the name I prefer. I hated the name they gave me and made them stop using it. I refused to answer when they called and they came around when I never gave in. At the age of eight, I became Valerie, Valerie Patchett.

That name is written on a post-it note and pasted to my nose. But on the other side, inside my head looking out through my face, I don't know who I am. My identity is in flux; identities are like waves cresting before breaking and flowing over the sand, flowers of foam flowing back into the sea. My identity blinks in and out like what we still call "particles" as if they're little bits of stuff, as if they're things, as if they're anything but what they are, or so I am told, fields that change into this or that "thing" when we look. I am Valerie 1.0 in the morning and Valerie 2.0 by noon. I am Valerie-Nick by twilight and by the time I go to bed, I don't know who the hell I am.

Jelli's story disoriented me. I think it's like being weightless in space for the first time. Over time it becomes a familiar feeling of floating. Jelli's words delivered the event to my psyche and it became my experience. Narratives work the same way as remote viewing. If the doorways of perception are wide open, what we read becomes our experience. What we hear in a conversation becomes part of our lives. Lines from books and movies become part of our vocabulary. We absorb them and quote them without thinking. We don't even notice that our points of reference are to fiction much of the time. Our shared hallucinatory world is built of words and images, symbols and icons, memories true and false.

It wasn't the trip I signed up for, but once you're on the train, there's no going back. And to tell you the truth, I love what I'm learning, and I love learning who I am and who I am not. I am lashed to the mast, hearing the siren call and longing to break free. When you feel the tight binding keeping you safe in the pain of your ecstasy, vibrating to the siren call like a tuning fork to a shrill note, you can bear it. But if the bough breaks, down will come baby, cradle and all. That reality was hidden in the bushes, waiting for me to amble past like little brunette riding hood, oblivious of the wolf.

Naivete is rewarding. I love the party to which I've been invited, a costume ball where I dance in the long-toed shoes of a clown. If I pay attention, I think I can hear the music of the spheres. That's on good days, of course. The bad ones are something else.

Jelli told me more of her story when we met again for lunch. I sure liked her grit. She told her captors she wouldn't be a lab rat and wanted to know what they were doing. To her surprise, they responded.

"'You are not merely a specimen," said the voice in her head. "We want your planet to fulfill its promise.We want you to overcome yourselves, but we can't make you do it.

"You are a specimen too, of course, but we try to be humane, as you call it. All of your virtues are self-referential. We do not think of you as property, although we can see why you might think we do. The link that you feel is not a leash. Think of it as a tunnel of love."

Jelli paused for a long while, looking at her empty plate. She finally said, "I *think* that's what he said. I may have imagined it or read it in a book."

"Channelers draw on aspects of themselves, but think it comes from discarnate entities. Maybe the shock of your experience made you hear those words like a voice in your head. Maybe it's you all along."

"Maybe. I have no way of knowing. I hope talking it through will help me sort it out."

"What else happened? You ended last time in the middle."

"Remember I said there was a table?"

"I do. Yes."

"They told me to get on it. I figured they'd make me do it if I didn't comply so I climbed up and lay down on my back. I knew I was helpless. That's when I felt one of the hands. It had three long fingers and the skin was pasty, a washed-out greenish white, hard to tell in the dim light. It felt damp and clammy. It reminded me of holding a frog."

Jelli instinctively knew to save energy by doing as they asked. When Nick was discussing interrogation tactics, he said that captives learn to save energy when they know they're going to be tortured. He said they often went limp and sat meekly on the chair while they attached the electrodes. He said a psychologist was often there who said he knew when someone was lying and that's when he applied pain. That conditioned terrorists to associate lies with pain, he claimed. He also said, when they told the truth, he knew that too. He thought he had x-ray vision and was the smartest guy in the world. It gave him permission to press that button. When the shit hit the fan, that bastard had the balls to say, "we were only following orders," blaming Bush, Rice, and Cheney. Later he had to settle for a plea deal when he was sued for torturing a guy to death. No one else was ever sued. He still did all right: his company was paid eighty million dollars for its work. Alfreda the Dark Queen opened a beauty business afterward.

Jelli remembered one thing, then another, just like Nick. Neither reported events in the sequence in which they occurred because neither could. Jelli said she felt restraints across her body and then she couldn't remember what came next. The large-eyed large-headed crew had milled around her, and then, everything went black.

I listened so closely, I felt like I was in the ship. I felt like I was with Nick when he went through his EITs. Dr. Guzman said I had secondary trauma. By our third therapy session, he revised his diagnosis and said I was traumatized, period.

It makes me depressed to know what Nick did. Everything he said got into my head. I had nightmares too. When he remembers something, some buried detail, he feels compelled to say it. His memories became mine. I try not to look into the abyss. I listen and try to help him move forward. That obligation comes with the relationship. I never dreamed it would torment me too, that dark world he lived in until he couldn't stand it. On top of that, there was Jelli and the aliens, the things she said they did. And on top of that, the crazy-making world of remote viewing. My ability to compartmentalize was seriously compromised. The boundaries between my different states of mind became more and more porous.

Bill Webb agreed that I showed signs of trauma. He said I listen so closely to Nick that I can't distinguish him from me. Webb said he had the same issue when he did counseling; he was always confusing others for himself. He felt their emotions as if they were his own and had to untangle afterward. He was like a medical student thinking they had whatever disease they studied. He loved his work, and I loved mine, and I was glad I could be there for Jelli and Nick, but there were unforeseen consequences. That's all I'm saying.

All blessings are mixed.

That's all I'm saying. All blessings are mixed.

One of my clients wanted to know if a competitor was selling a product in certain foreign countries. Had the guy paid bribes? Can you see his transactions well enough to know?

"I need to know who he's talking to," he said. "I need proof that he's breaking the law. Can you help me with that?"

Joe and I sat in the office and he explained how we worked. It was always on contingency, with a lawyer-like retainer up front. We promised our best effort and the full fruits of our efforts, not the results they wanted. No one could promise that, any more than marketers know what does and doesn't work. Joe would have liked to explain the underlying dynamics so clients understood why the data might be elusive. He wanted to explain that what we saw wasn't "out there" but "in here," inside a field of consciousness more properly understood, that we were all insiders. But if he did that, clients would walk out. They weren't philosophers. They were practical people. So we kept it simple. "We see things," Joe said, "that most people can't believe," and left it at that.

In that particular case, everyone was pleased. I saw enough to tell the client that yes, money was transferred illegally, I told him who and when and where. He paid his bill promptly so I guess he got what he wanted.

We didn't know what clients did with the information. That wasn't our concern. But that one was happy and apparently told others what we had done. Word of mouth marketing.

Despite the NDAs they signed, clients blabbed. That was fine with us, even if the stories were exaggerated as they spread from one to another like a game of telephone.

Sometimes I just did the work and thought nothing more about it. The bigger important issues, that's what Joe and I and Hal and Nick and sometimes Brian, talked about for hours. We explored every aspect of the work, including our responses, how we felt afterward, side effects if any. But that didn't get us any closer to answers. We understood that, but that's not why we talked. We had to reinforce our belief in our work, its reality, its value. Exploring UFOs, Brian made clear, required the same kind of effort. The data ran counter to our deepest beliefs. You don't just shake a paradigm that everyone believes, that you believed without even thinking. To counter a paradigm takes a lot of energy. Denial tries to protect us. If it has a mission statement, it's "don't upset this person."

Good old denial. You can't blame it for trying.

Interlude

"The major advances in civilizations are processes that all but wreck the societies in which they occur."

- Alfred North Whitehead

Chapter 11
Memories ... You're Talking About Memories

"How about that tapas bar?" Jelli suggested. "The Wild Rose. I heard it's a cool place."

She meant, of course, the successor to the Barbican, and that was not what I needed. The memories that swirled in the musty air of that place would cloud my thinking and keep me from listening closely. I needed a neutral site.

"Too recent. My old place," I said. "Can we go to a diner? The Chicago Diner has a decent menu."

"Sure," she said. "I'll go to the Rose another time, maybe with Brad, when he comes back."

"How is Brad?" I asked. He wasn't in the picture much.

"I'll tell you at lunch," she said, and so she did.

We chose a booth with a wall behind and an aisle to the kitchen. The wait-people going to and fro were not much of a bother, and the noise from the kitchen was minimal. We could hear faintly the distant sizzle when fries were dropped in fat and now and then a louder conversation rose above the noise of a fan, the chitchat in the kitchen, and traffic noise when someone opened the door. It was all a cushion of familiar city-sounds for her otherworldly tale, the background noise of big city life.

"The pumpkin pancakes sound delicious," Jelli said, reading an insert clipped to the main menu. "They must be an October thing. I hope they still have them."

They did, Patti said, our twenty-something waitress. "We keep them on the menu til Christmas. They're big around Thanksgiving. They're my favorite, especially with the pumpkin syrup. We make it ourselves."

Her pitch made Jelli salivate. It didn't work for me—I don't like pancakes for lunch—but it worked for Jelli.

"I'll have a tall stack. And coffee," Jelli said.

Patti smiled and, after taking our order, returned with Jelli's coffee. Be careful, she warned, it's very hot, setting it down with care. The aroma of the fresh coffee got me, and I ordered one too. I was sleepy and wanted to be alert.

Jelli sipped it slowly until it cooled. Her pancakes came with two scrambled eggs and a side of potatoes. I ate a salad and freshly baked bread. I ate it plain, without butter or the little package of grape jelly. The butter pats were cold and wouldn't spread anyway. I had to shift in my seat when my knee kept bumping something on the table.

"Brad is fishing," Jelli said.

"In this weather? Really?"

Jelli laughed. "You don't know Minnesotans. They push these big shanties onto the ice and hack out a hole. The joke is, two guys can go in there and spend all day and neither says a word and they both have a great time."

I smiled. "Lots of Minnesota jokes."

"Yes, but they aren't really jokes. They usually have a lot of truth, and like the Wobegon stories, they're often passive aggressive. Every year Brad and his school chums go up north to a frozen lake as soon as the ice is thick enough. One of them, Mike Blomquist, has a cabin near Rainy Lake and parks the fish house there between winters. He calls it an ice hut. Rainy Lake is one of the first to freeze."

"Where is it?"

"Near International Falls. The lake is mostly in Canada, about two thirds I think, but you can fish the whole thing. It's nearly twelve hours to drive up but Brad says he finds it relaxing to head north. The more north he goes, the more at home he feels." Jelli made herself smile. "We really are different, like I said."

"How long will he be gone?"

"As long as he can," she said. "He feels like himself up there. They drink beer and hang out and cook the fish they catch. It's quite cozy in the hut. He says the sky is blazing with thousands of stars, not like here where you might see a dozen stars on a clear night. He lies out as long as he can until he's too cold, all wrapped up in his sleeping bag which he hauls onto the ice. It's fine with me. I prefer it to his moping around down here, complaining about the city."

We were quiet for a bit. How could they possibly stay together? It depended, I guessed, on what they each really wanted. I thought of Nat Herman and his wife Miriam. Both needed a lot of distance and alone time and didn't mind how little they shared of their real lives. It didn't feel like a loss to them. As long as both people want the same thing, whether its a lot of space or a lot of togetherness, it works; if one changes and wants more or less of either, then the ties can fray.

Miriam definitely loved Nat. When he dropped dead installing a TV, thanks to a faulty device in his heart, she exacted what revenge she could. Nick said she wanted to kill the CEO and whoever else had skipped due diligence when they bought the company that made the killer device. He didn't tell me at the time, wanting not to worry me. He said Nat trained her to use his Luger. He was gone a lot and wanted to know she could put a bullet into an intruder's head from twenty feet. It would have been easy to go to that dinner at their club, make her way through tables until she was behind him, and blow his head off. She dreamed of doing it but settled for exposing him in front of his country club friends. She realized, no matter what she might do, it wouldn't bring Nat back. Nor change the way Syntactic did business.

Nick helped her avoid a life behind bars. He avenged in a sane way what Syntactic had done to his partner, Miles Archer-like.

Nat often went out to his home-made observatory and looked at stars late into the night. He had favorite galaxies and clusters of stars and used a good Dobsonian scope. They would have found how much time Nick and I spent together to be cloying. When we both found work at Dasein, we were thrilled. We couldn't believe our good fortune.

Nick and I did our viewing apart but loved talking about the work. We hesitated to do that at first but our need broke through the flimsy fence of the NDAs and my fear that he couldn't handle my success. We built a shared context out of continuing astonishment at how well it worked. It's one thing to read about that stuff–Hal had me read *Extraordinary Knowing* by Elizabeth Myers and Upton Sinclair's *Mental Radio*–and another to have the experience time after time. We had to keep pinching ourselves to remember it was true. When I told Hal about my mother's appearance when she was dying, he referred me to *Human Personality and its Survival of Bodily Death* and *Phantasms of the Living*. I leafed through those big books when he told me to read them. Those tomes demanded a real commitment. I read reviews on Amazon instead.

Sorry I digressed.

Jelli bounced back and forth between her time on the craft and raving about her pancakes, between her memories and her obvious struggle to believe in her own experience. She poured on the syrup and ate with relish. The sound of my munching crunched in my ears so I finished my salad quickly, then patiently waited for more of her story. Too much iceberg lettuce makes for loud sounds and less nutrition. How can something made mostly of water make such loud sounds?

She ate all four pancakes and ordered more coffee. I rested my chin on my folded hands and created the space for her to begin. Whenever you're ready, my body language said.

"You want to know more of the story, right?"

"I do," I said. "It's fascinating."

"OK, so–Valerie, who are they? I've read a bunch of stuff since then, I got pretty compulsive, wanting to understand. A lot of it does not make sense. The internet chatter is crazy. I try to ignore the silliness and remember the details of my own experience."

"Like what?"

"Like when the vehicle came down and hovered over the water, I saw human-like figures through windows or portholes, whatever they were. I don't think I said that before. There were lights that went around the rim real real fast like lights on a theater marquee. They were red and white and green, I think, but they moved so fast they blurred. The effect was hypnotic. You know how they all looked up at the mother ship in *Close Encounters*? That's how I felt. That's how I must have looked.

"There were definitely windows and I definitely saw shadowy figures lighted from behind. I felt like they could see my thoughts.

I read an article the other day, that Elon Musk and the Facebook guy–"

"Zuckerberg."

"Yes. Zuckerberg. They're working on using computers to translate thoughts into words and put them directly onto a monitor. I read that our brains won't be like we think, inside our heads, a private space, they'll be open books for anyone to read. The aliens do that already, I think. I have no idea how."

"We do reveal quite a bit now," I said. "Nick told me how quickly they can know everything about a person with a single click. All of our relationships are mapped out to some huge number. Everyone we talk to, everything we've written, everything we've read, everything we've done."

"But how do the aliens do it? How do they put words into our heads? How do they know our language? They have bigger heads and must have bigger brains with more folds and lobes. They must see and know more things."

"One of our viewers, Hal McCutcheon," I said, "thinks that as species evolve, they can access higher and higher levels of information. He thinks we're all transceivers. He thinks information streams from the center of the universe. Our brains are like step down transformers, lowering the voltage to a level we can apprehend without getting fried. Hal says books, once we invented printing, were like repeaters, amplifying signals, extending their reach. Making us a hive mind. He says our digital media are like that too."

"That's pretty profound, Valerie. I never thought of it that way."

I smiled. "Working at Dasein is like being in a seminar. Some nights we order pizza and sit around for hours, talking about this stuff."

"I'd get a headache."

"I love it. I think it's exciting. There are drawbacks, though. The more we share our experience and agree on what we know is real, the more distant we become from ordinary people. The world, Hal says, can only handle so many mystics. You can imagine the looks I get if I talk about this stuff. "

Jelli snorted. "Tell me about it. Try to tell people about your time on a UFO."

"I'm sure," I said. "But I don't want to get off track. You said you sort of floated into the craft. Was that a real memory?"

Jelli shrugged. "How can I tell? There's no one to ask. I think so. No, cancel that, yes it was. I know it was. It's confusing. Maybe they put some of these memories into my brain but they feel real to me.

"I keep wondering, why did they pick me? I was just sitting in my car, minding my own business. When I was a little girl, I had an ant farm, I didn't pick out an ant and talk to it."

"You were at the right place at the right time. Maybe like eagles looking for a fish, when they see one, they dive. You were probably prey."

"There's another wrinkle, though.They wanted to get data from me, obviously, but they also want me to do something."

"What do they want you to do?"

"They want me to share my experience, share what I learned. They didn't say so in so many words, but I came away thinking about everything differently. A guy I read named Haines who worked at NASA and collected thousands of reports from pilots said we go through a kind of initiation. He didn't say to what, but that's his hunch. They didn't give me a to-do list but I got the sense that I'm supposed to tell people what we're doing to the earth. I never thought that way before. That's one more thing that nettles Brad.

Are you getting religious? he asked, by which he means, am I going off the rails? I think they want people to know what we're doing to ourselves. They want us to realize we're not as smart as we think. And they want people like me to sound the alarm."

"That is what religions do, Jell. Recruit, indoctrinate, teach and spread the word."

She smiled apologetically. "See, if I could be precise, I would be, Val. But it's vague. At the same time, I know more deeply than ever, I can't just live like I did, for myself alone. I have what you might call a mission now. I admit I'm a little obsessed. I think about this all the time."

"So are you supposed to spread a particular message?"

"Not exactly. It's more a way of thinking about everything and sharing what I think. Besides you, I only told Brad and he told me not to mention it again. He told me to forget it. Yeah, right." She shook her head. "I keep going over details. It wasn't there and then it was. That's a fact. It was rounded, with windows. It was whitish silver, like paint on a new car. I felt someone staring at me and I saw figures in windows with big heads and big eyes. I was afraid. I thought, 'please leave me alone.' The voice said: 'We won't hurt you. Don't be afraid.' I know that happened. Those are facts.

"I was mesmerized. When I first saw it, it was farther away, about a block away, and slowly came close. Maybe half a block away, it made a jump and then it was right there, filling the windshield and so bright I had to squint. I remember that distinctly. We can't hop through space like that. Next thing I knew, I was paralyzed and outside the car, floating through the wall into the craft. I didn't even question it. You can't tell something that's happening that it can't be happening, can you?"

"No," I smiled. "Reality won't go away just because you refuse to believe it."

"I went through the wall. It was dim inside, They were waiting. Those are facts. If they aren't aliens, Valerie, what are they?"

"Brian Metzger said they knew seventy-five years ago it wasn't us and it wasn't the Russians, so it had to be extraterrestrials. A lot of people knew it, in other countries too, he said."

"Who is Brian Metzger?"

"He's one of our associates, I don't know his exact status, he just comes and goes. He knows an incredible amount about UFOs. I think he's been part of the organized effort to try to understand, or engage with them, or reverse engineer the way they move, or all of the above."

Jelli said uh-huh, uh-huh, waiting for me to finish so she could continue. A little obsessed indeed.

"So I asked where they were from and they said I wouldn't understand. I don't know if they meant another galaxy, another planet, or what. Maybe they're wanderers linked by communications and a shared sense of history. Have they left a home planet for good or do they go back for R&R? Have they escaped a threat of annihilation, like their star going nova? Or are they more like us, curious about everything, needing to see the other side of the mountain? I asked about all that and they just said, those questions are irrelevant to our task."

"But why are they doing this now?"

"Let me tell you what happened, Val. It may provide a clue."

"I'm all ears, Jell."

She ordered another cup of coffee. I would have been jumping out of my seat if I had that much. But it didn't seem to bother her.

My foot was falling asleep and I had to move it around. My back felt stiff. I wiggled a bit and felt more attentive.

I noticed that her hands weren't trembling now.

"When I blacked out, they did tests. I don't know what they were, any more than when they draw blood at the doctor. When I found myself awake again, the restraints had been removed, but no one was around. Maybe they went to tell others to come see me, like on SNL, which was a very funny skit. Peek-a-boo, peek-a-boo. She's very funny, I'm sorry she left the show. Anyway, I slid over the edge and plopped onto my feet and stood there for a minute, leaning back against the table. I didn't feel dizzy like after an anesthetic. I felt clear-headed, and in fact, a sore back I had that morning was gone. I felt good.

"So I wandered down a hallway and it was like a maze. Do they manipulate space? Inside seemed so much larger than what I saw from the car. Or was I transferred to a bigger ship? I went down the hallway and up a ramp to a deck. There was a big screen that practically filled the whole wall and a chair that faced it and controls of some kind. I didn't dare touch any buttons. For all I knew, I'd be ejected like on a plane. I stared at the screen with amazement.

"It was an array of stars, real bright, much brighter than they seem from earth. I could see different color stars—red, yellow, blue-white—but I didn't recognize constellations, not that I'm an expert, but I know the dippers and the bears, and we all know Orion. Orion is high in our skies now but it wasn't there, or the Pleiades. Those I know. I saw the Southern Cross when we went to Australia. I loved seeing it the first time. I woke up in the middle of the night and it was framed by a skylight in the ceiling of our room. On the screen, nothing was recognizable. I was captivated, thousands of stars, different colors and brightness. It was beautiful.

"Just then, one of them came onto the deck. He took me by the arm and I felt a hand again, clammy and moist, and he led me to a room where some kind of assembly was taking place. There were dozens of them there but I only saw them for a second. They fitted something over my head like a helmet and I couldn't see."

"Who did that? Where did they come from?"

"I don't know. It just happened. There were all these entities. I couldn't see how many or what was going on. The headpiece did something they wanted, read my brain or something, and they must have liked what they saw because there was a loud noise like they were all excited. They were looking at something I couldn't see and were happy with what they saw, I think, but that's just a guess. The scene was surreal. but I never felt threatened. I felt I was part of something I couldn't understand. But I was calm and happy. My brain was exploding with the knowledge of ... something, something more than I had ever known. I was suddenly deliriously happy to be alive in such a wonderful universe. And I knew, I absolutely knew, Val, that the universe teems with life. They're all over the place. We are so provincial, so arrogant. I mean, we just figured out how to go to the moon. A century ago we thought the Milky Way was the whole universe. God knows how far ahead of us they are.

"Anyway, one of them removed that thing from my head and led me back to what I call the examination room. Then the voice was back inside my head.

"Your planet is at risk. Your nuclear bombs are dangerous in ways you don't understand. You need the insects but you think of them as pests. You need to relate to life on your planet before you go adventuring.

"Then he said, there is an invisible engine, a framework, a form, that unifies expansion. You are beginning to say it in math."

"What do you mean, engine?"

"They said it's a 'manifestation of formal consideration,' whatever that means. It is a way of framing the finite number of possibilities that exist in a universe constrained by laws. It is necessary for cohesion. Meaning is intrinsic to existence, he said. Otherwise your genetic codes would be meaningless. Information can't be meaningful in a meaningless universe. We understand the rubrics and try to align ourselves with their implications."

"Are you saying there's a God?" Jelli said she asked.

"No. I am describing a phenomenon. Now," he said, "I am going to take your thoughts and lift them up to illuminate your mind."

"Val, it felt like time stopped. Or maybe they stopped my thoughts. An incredible brightness like cooling water filled my mind with soft light. I was aware, not of thinking, but of what my mind does when it thinks. I didn't experience the content of thinking, only the context. Does that make sense?"

"I'm afraid not." I tried to think what she might mean. "No, I'm sorry. I don't know what that means."

She shrugged and became quiet. She looked at her empty plate and resisted swiping syrup with a lickable finger. Then she looked into my eyes. They had an intensity I hadn't seen before.

"They showed me these things without using words. Their symbols tumbled into my brain."

"What do you mean? Which things?"

Her frustration showed at my inability to get her gist.

"I've been trying to tell you, Valerie. I'm doing the best I can."

I didn't press. Okay, I said to myself. She has no words for wordless thoughts. She knows but cannot speak of what she knows. I think I heard that before.

She looked away, looked back, then looked away again.

My seminar was done for the day.

"All blessings are mixed," Jelli said, the third time we met. She was alone. Brad had moved back to Edina and rented a condo. He invited her to share his life but only in the Twin Cities. She invited him to return to Chicago and he shook his head as if she just didn't understand. So they were at an impasse.

She said that Brad had been surprised that the Edina in which he grew up was not the one to which he returned. Things were changing. Old buildings were going down and bigger ones going up. Urbanization had the city council by the throat. Traffic was denser and some drivers—not natives, obviously—honked when traffic lights changed. The chorus of "sorry, sorry" was heard less often. Transplants and ex-pats moved in. Brad said you could tell who they were, they started conversations waiting in lines, chatted with people they didn't know. They asked personal questions, like what do you do for a living? More people said what they thought. By percentages, Edina was still Edina, few who grew up there moved away, but it didn't feel like it to Brad. It didn't take many new people to make it feel diverse, uncomfortable, and threatening.

"So there he is, and here I am," Jelli said, trying to brighten up. "And I have other news too. I have a new job."

"You do?" I said. "What?"

Jelli smiled. "Now, don't laugh, okay? Promise you won't laugh."

"I promise," I said.

"Well," she said. "I told you how I had changed. I saw an ad—"

But that's enough Jelli for now. My brain was buzzing. I mean, aliens, and remote viewing, and kinks in time and space, and Nick's flashbacks, and Hals' faeries, and Sylvia's tapping pencil as she crunched our numbers, and worrying about the nature of the universe, and coping with the side effects of viewing—I mean, jeez! I'm a Des Moines girl. I went skating in Greenwood Park, I ate pastries from Barbara's Bakery (and when I married Alvin, we had them provide a champagne cake), and here I was, not knowing what was real anymore. When I was a child, I knew what was real, and no one around me challenged what we believed. Now I was challenged every day. I felt giddy, nearly hysterical at times, trying to focus during viewings when they took me to places that frightened me. If I had been lashed to the mast while the sirens sang, the bindings were getting loose.

"It's all in your mind," Hal would say to comfort me. "It's not in the next room."

"It is in the next room," I said. "I'm learning that everything is in the next room *and* in my mind."

"Well, that's true," he said with a smile. "But then where else would anything be?"

When Jelli and I finished lunch, I needed to take a walk, despite the cold. I needed to steady my wobbly world.

The intense cold when I left the diner made me wince. I hunched and headed north head-down. I saw only the few feet on the walk ahead of my fast-moving feet.

I needed a different melody playing in my brain. I needed Nick but he was busy on a black off-the-books deal, searching for a lost pilot. If they found him in time and he was alive, they needed to get him out of there before the bad guys did. His rescue radio was busted and all the guy could do was sit and wait.

I didn't care if they found him or not. I mean, I did care, but given what I was dealing with, I needed to focus on myself, not some pilot I never knew. I needed my own rescue radio.

Interlude

"A scientist must be absolutely like a child. If he sees a thing, he must say that he sees it, even if it wasn't what he expected. Otherwise he will only see what he expects to see."

- Douglas Adams, *The Ultimate Hitchhiker's Guide to the Galaxy*

Chapter 12
Don't Ask, Don't Tell

You might have gathered from how I worked with customers at the Barbican, I was always curious—it's a mark of intelligence, right?—but I never pushed into conversations where I didn't belong. At Dasein there were lots of those. When Brian Metzger came by, he and Joe and Hal and sometimes Sylvia went into the conference room, the one we called the mini-scif, and I kept to my knitting. I was only in there a few times at first, but more and more often as I got better at viewing and my reports brought me into their world. We insulated the scif in an amateurish way because we trusted one another. Once in a while I was asked to come in to verify details. We always wanted a second source to verify what we thought we saw, and they knew how to get it. Joe in particular had so many links to colleagues at the agency, I wondered who he worked for, them or us. It went without saying that Brian was still a heavy hitter back there. I sure wasn't, but Nick's years of intelligence work had become part of the context for my thinking too. When I shared what I learned with Nick, he often added more details, and one day, when he said, "you've learned how we think," I knew I was finally spidey-fied. I was in the wilderness of mirrors enough to know that what I was seeing, wasn't what I was seeing. I was proud of my progress, but I knew it meant I could never go back to the happy place where I had lived before.

I was more anxious, too. That wasn't me at all. Not the old me, in any case. Maybe Valerie 2.0 was a mixed blessing too.

Hal said everyone had to think like a spy these days if they wanted to know what was going on. In the modern world, misinformation abounded and disinformation was everywhere so daily life required an intense level of due diligence. Most people do not have time or the level of critical thinking needed for that kind of analysis, so most people live with a hodgepodge of contradictory beliefs. I don't think I'm being cynical, only realistic.

One day they were all in there for hours, and Sylvia was flushed when she came out. She said good-bye, and Joe and Hal came out a few minutes later, whispering to each other, followed by Brian who hung back and let them leave before he said, "Valerie, you here for a bit? I'd like to talk to you."

"Sure," I said. "Let me text Nick and tell him I'll be late."

"If it's a problem—"

"No, no, it's fine. I'll tell him to postpone dinner. No problem, Brian."

Metzger was a very big man, a *very* big man, but he carried his weight well. He was Paul Bunyunesque and as solid as Jesse Ventura in his prime. He sat at the conference table and let out a long sigh. He took a pack of peanuts from his pocket, opened the end, and began nibbling.

"You OK, Brian?"

"Sure, I'm fine, I'm—"

Wait one minute. I am not sure when that conversation took place. We think in a linear way, so where it is in memory equates to when we think it was. We should know better, with memory building links and loops and moving images around. The conversation with Brian happened sometime after I began working at Dasein but I don't remember when. The important thing is, it helped me know why Brian knew so much about UFOs. I should have included this account in an earlier chapter, I guess, but it's not the only one that's "out of line, out of time." I think anxiety and stress made me forget to do that. I should have written it down instead of hoping I'd remember. It's no wonder how complicated things get, what with one thing leading to another.

Memory is not a historical timeline, but works by association. Nick said in his memoir that after his "event" his memories were jumbled. He confused one agency for another. Some memories disappeared and others came to the foreground. I think remote viewing and its traumas did something similar to me. The more I went into an altered state, the more I drifted out of the present even when I didn't try, finding myself straddling two streams of consciousness–the normal one that most people know and the deeper one which rumbled like a rock-filled meltwater stream under a glacier. The first mode was orderly like a set of slides in a powerpoint deck; the second gave past present and future equal weight, and each of them was "now." The more that happened, the more I could see that my customary timeline included dead-ends, cul de sacs, a number of U-turns, and some patently false events. I thought I was going crazy at first, but Nick laughed and quoted a book as usual. "If I am going crazy, it is all right with me," he said. I don't think that helped, but it was all he had. The blind leading the blind.

The point is, at some point, Brian asked me to stay and listen to his story. In retrospect, I think they all agreed that he should do that, for reasons I didn't know at the time.

"You were divorced, weren't you?" he asked.

"Sort of. I was widowed first, then I split from the second, but we were never married. Why?"

"You know we deal with some weird shit–"

"Yes. Very weird."

"But we don't know how it'll impact our relationships, do we?"

I waited.

"OK, that was a rhetorical question. Val, I think the work is affecting you. I think you're mildly traumatized. Nothing major, but it's clearly having an impact."

"Oh?"

"Nothing extreme, but you've gone through a lot of changes since you came here, don't you think?"

"Sure, but mostly for the better, I think. Nick agrees. He says there's always a price to pay for knowledge."

"Viewing can be traumatic. Rethinking how you think isn't trivial. Going in and out of the state conducive to viewing isn't trivial either. You're very empathetic, you pick up on emotions right away."

"I thought that was a good thing."

"It is. But when you encounter some of the darker events, the fact that you're so wide open can be a problem. That's all I'm saying. You develop cracks in your defenses where not only the light gets in. Everything gets in.

"I want you to be prepared for whatever you might encounter. You and Nick have a good thing going. I want you to keep it."

"You're scaring me, Brian."

"Just be aware of what this work can do to a relationship." He paused and looked sad. "I'm thinking of what happened to me. I'm trying to give you a head's up ... have you heard gossip about my wife—my former wife—Jan?"

"No I haven't. Not a word. What happened, Brian?"

"It wasn't about viewing per se. It was about a UFO. There is little doubt, Val, that you'll encounter one when viewing. Jan and I saw one together. We were there at the same time, that is, but had completely different responses. I had seen a display years ago so I knew they were real. Jan had no context for knowing what she saw. It knocked her for a loop." He sighed."Let me tell you the story, OK? A narrative can communicate so much better than discursive language."

"Sure," I said. "Tell me a story."

He relaxed into a story-telling slouch, finished the peanuts, and extended his legs, crossing them at the ankle. Then he began at the beginning and went on until he came to the end.

This is Brian's story.

"You know I've been involved with this UFO business, right?"

"It comes up a lot in your conversation."

"I worked in that area. I still ... stay in touch."

"You still go back there, is that what you're saying?"

"No, even if it's true, I can't confirm or deny it, Val."

"OK, I'll draw my own conclusions. Go ahead."

"I saw gun camera film from the early days and I read reports from qualified people, veteran pilots who were shocked by what they saw. When you think you're chasing lights and they suddenly go into formation around you and close in while you transmit an SOS that no one can answer, it has an impact, Val, especially when everyone is ordered to lie the next day at a press conference and deny what they saw. It's a cover story, of course, not a lie, for security reasons, good ones, too."

"But the decision to lie is yours. You're the ones who decide to cover it up."

"Of course. People don't vote on classified affairs. We call the shots.

"Today we can do some of the things the UFOs could do when they were first tracked, but we're way behind. Their technology is vastly more powerful than we thought. We can cloak our craft, we can be invisible, we can reflect radar, we can hover and shoot off at a high rate of speed, but we can't approach their top speeds and we don't know the source of their power. We sure don't know how to take those Gs.

"Val, we've known what they were doing since the 1940s. Not only here. The Danes had interceptors on continuous alert. The Russians, the French—hell, I won't go down the list. Take my word for it, everybody knew. Vanderburg knew, he said we can't laugh them off, he claimed over 300 reports that weren't in the papers from fliers with experience. Loedding was a top civilian guy and he said he saw more than 100 reports from airline pilots, test pilots and experienced officers. Hell, this was right after Kenneth Arnold started the whole thing going. I can go on and on, the cases are voluminous, so we knew for years this was all legit. No one can study the cases without coming to that conclusion. But we still can't do what they can do. And they won't tell us how."

I turned the chair around and sat with my chin on my hands to keep myself focused. It was late in the day and I was tired. I had done a viewing earlier that left me shaken up. I was seeing a cabin in the woods and the feeling was ... bad, but more than bad, it was downright evil. I don't know what else to call it. I stayed with the viewing by sheer grit until I had to stop.

"But that's all background," Brian said. "You want to read the history, get that book by Powell and Swords. My point is not that we've known for a long time that they were here. My point is what it can do to a person to encounter a UFO.

"So ... one summer night, my wife and I were having dinner with our friends, the Taylors. They're normal people and we never discuss anything real. I never told Jan, either, what I'm telling you now or what I did at work. That was our agreement. I liked being with the Taylors, it was like a vacation from work."

"What were you doing then?"

"I can't tell you the details. I was working with a guy named Selva."

"Did he know about UFOs? (I had Nick check and he certainly did. Not a surprise for a Vice Chair of the Joint Chiefs)."

"I'd have to ask. Anyway, the houses around us were mostly dark. We don't have streetlights or sidewalks in the village. There are ponds and a few lakes among the houses. Jan and I lived on Hidden Lake. It's across the road from our home.

"We had been married long enough to weather some bad patches. That was an OK time—I thought. I drove home and pulled into the driveway and parked and we walked out into the hot humid night. There were locusts, whatever they are, making a loud noise. I put my arm around Jan as we walked to the door. She was warm and perspiring and I held her as we walked.

"We forgot to turn on the porch light," she said.

"Mea culpa," I confessed. "I was in a hurry because we were late."

Before we went in, we walked past the house to the road. We could see the dark circle of Hidden Lake across the road surrounded by darker shadows of dense trees. I looked up at the sky which despite the heat and humidity was about as good as you get in the summer.

We didn't say anything. We just stood there, my arm around her, listening to the insects, looking up at the stars.

Then ... "What's that?" Jan said.

"What's what?"

"That." She pointed.

I followed her point and saw a star, brighter than most.

"It looks like a star," I said.

The star was shimmering, but pollution will do that too. This star, however, was super bright, brighter than Sirius. That couldn't be. Must be a planet. But Venus had set. Jupiter? Not in the sky that night.

"Why are you whispering?" Jan said.

"I don't know." But I didn't raise my voice. The star looked larger now. "Hey," I said. "What happened to the locusts?"

The noise was gone. The night was perfectly still.

Eerie as hell, I remember thinking.

"I don't know," Jan said, a tinge of fear in her voice.

There was no mistaking it now. The star was growing larger. Maybe it was a plane banking as it turned toward the airport or a helicopter except there was no noise. It looked the size of a nickel held out at arm's length. It was so white. The whitest white I had ever seen.

It's always a shock, I guess, when they show up. I just stood there and stared.

"What is it?" Jan whispered.

It was growing larger faster now. It looked distinctly like a disc and suddenly it was over the trees across the road, hovering above the lake. A reflection glowed in the water. It was definitely a luminous vehicle almost too bright to look at directly. I squinted or looked away. The trees around the lake were illuminated by the bright light as if were daylight. The trees were no longer shadowy but deep green.

It made no sound. I think I held my breath as I watched it tilt on end to an angle of maybe thirty degrees before it edged slowly into the water and entered the lake. I watched it slide through the surface of the water without a sound and disappear into the depths.

I walked across the road toward the lake. Jan didn't want to go but didn't want to be alone and hurried to catch up.

"What are you doing?" she demanded in a frightened whisper.

"Stay here if you want."

"I'm not going to stand here while you–"

I stopped at the water's edge. The water very gently stirred against the reeds at my feet. In the otherwise dark lake I could see a luminous oval in the depths. *Something* was under the water, glowing with its own light.

"What is it?" she whispered.

"I don't know. A UFO."

She didn't say a word.

I don't know how long we stood there. But suddenly the diffused glowing in the lake started to quiver and the water was disturbed as the edge of the craft emerged and it very slowly left the water at the same steep angle at which it entered. I remember thinking it should be forty five degrees, my engineer's brain said. But the angle was more like thirty degrees. Water cascaded from the sides as if not touching the thing itself. As if there was a plasma sheathing the craft. The water flowed off the object until the disc was no longer touching the surface. There was a pause, one minute it was hovering over the lake and the next it was gone. It shot off at a nearly impossible speed. I looked up and watched it get so high it looked like a star again in seconds. Then it was among the other stars and I couldn't tell anymore which point of light it was.

The locusts were loud again, sawing away. The surface of the lake was quiet. The water at my feet slowly gently moved against the reeds. There was no breeze at all.

I turned to see Jan staring up at the sky.

"Did you see that?"

"See what?"

"What it did. Whatever it was."

Jan was noncommittal. "That star, you mean? That bright star?""

"Jan, that wasn't a star. Stars don't go into the water."

I waited for something more but didn't get it. We crossed the road to our home and went in the front door.

"Honey! Wait!"

She was already climbing the stairs.

"I'm tired," she said. "I want to get ready for bed."

I hurried upstairs after her.

"I had no idea it was so late," she said. She was putting her shoes in the closet and undressing. "Did you realize it was two o'clock?"

"I'm going back outside."

She came out of the closet. "At this hour? Why?"

I went downstairs and crossed the road to the edge of the lake. The water was dark; whatever stars had been visible were hidden by mist. I heard a mosquito and slapped it. Stars appeared and disappeared in the haze or high clouds. I looked over the lake and could not see anything at all. I turned around. A few house lights burned through the trees, familiar sentries keeping watch. Trees houses lights.

Then I looked up at the sky again. Nothing there.

Jan was asleep when I returned, the bedroom dark. I sat up as long as I could, wanting to think, wanting to understand, but I fell asleep against the headboard, waking up at four, feeling stiff. Then I lay down beside my wife and fell asleep.

The next morning, she was dressed and making breakfast when I came downstairs.

"You leaving early?"

"I'm meeting with the Junior League committee about planning the luncheon. We're meeting at nine because Betty has to be somewhere."

"Oh," I said. "You look nice."

"Thank you. I might not be here when you come home. I have a late appointment with my trainer."

"OK," I said. I waited. "Can we talk about it now?"

She looked at me as if I spoke a foreign language, then went to get her purse. She left without another word and I heard her driving away.

I looked at the apple in my hand. It had the look of an apple that was looked at. I was unusually aware of the morning light through the kitchen window and how it illuminated the breakfast nook. The strawberry cookie jar looked like a work of art. The crumbs on the counter near the toaster looked like abstract art. Everything had gone up a notch in contrast or brightness as if someone fiddled with the controls while I was sleeping.

When I left, I paused in the driveway and looked around. The sun blazed on leaves and grass with inexplicable splendor. The sky was diamond bright and made me squint.

I remember parking in my usual space at work and saying hello to the guard at the door and punching in the code and pausing for the scan and taking the elevator upstairs to the office.

There's a bit of a backstory, Val. I was frustrated at work. One contractor in particular was a real bitch. The system is broken, see, and it just gets worse. Too many people have access to things they should never see. Things leak. I saw people in areas they should never have been in, and when I asked why, all I got were shrugs.

"I had a long term relationship with two contractors and one of them really fucked up. What he did put a spotlight on me. I remember standing at the office window, mulling over the implications, what it might mean for me. A glint of light in the sky caught my attention. I watched it become a sliver of bright sunlight, then a disc as it turned and finished a maneuver by becoming the familiar shape of a plane coming in for a landing.

"What's up?" My superior, a guy named John Kaster, leaned through the door and knocked at the same time.

"You tell me."

"I think you know, Brian. That guy from Booz Allen really screwed up."

"Uh-huh."

"He's damn well connected, Brian. He has friends on mahogany row. They know better, but something has to be done. He'll get a reprimand but you might have to take a transfer. Not a demotion, a sideways slide."

"That's what's up?"

"That's what's up."

He came into the office.

"Listen, Brian, I'm trying to help. We're trying to spin the narrative so you don't get screwed. We have your back."

"I understand."

"We'll have to move you to something. But I think you'll come out OK. We'll make it interesting."

"Thanks a lot."

"Listen," Kaster said. "The point is politics, period. We're trying to make it a win by moving you out of your slot. Just go along with a slap on the wrist."

The next day, I kept thinking of the UFO. You know, it's one thing to read reports but it's another to see one up close. It is otherworldly, and insanely powerful, beyond anything you knew. Or thought you knew.

Kaster asked me to meet with him that afternoon. Oddly enough, the subject of UFOs came up at lunch.

A legal named Jerry Castle had gone to an Air Show.

"They have a model of an old flying disc," he said.

"A flying saucer?" Merribeth Cummings perked up. "A real one?"

"Not really. They never got it to fly."

"Have you ever seen a flying saucer?" I asked generally, picking up my thick sandwich and squeezing it to keep everything in. It still dripped on my fingers, onto my plate.

Castle laughed. "After the fourth martini."

Merribeth said, "I saw a program about them on cable. It was nonsense."

"Eyewitness testimony is nonsense," Castle said. "Hell, in court you'd be amazed how people get things wrong. They fill in blanks, conflate events, add details. Yet they're sure they're telling the truth."

"Perception is everything," Merribeth said, "and by the way, changing perception is how we can improve the optics for the agency." That was her hobbyhorse, using consultants to reinvent ourselves or at least make it look as if we had. Her powerpoint slides had moving arrows, pop-up toons, even words. Her schemes didn't work but they were a good diversion from real work. She was young, full of ideas, and older men were easy to get onto her bandwagon.

After lunch, Merribeth and I walked down the hallway. She stopped me with her hand gently on my arm and drew me aside and whispered, "I saw a flying saucer once."

"I thought you said it was BS."

"You have to say that in public. I don't want people to think I'm crazy."

"What was it like?"

"It was years ago," she said. "We were on a country road in North Carolina. My husband was driving. It was late afternoon. We passed one of those power stations at an intersection. I saw this thing hovering over the station, tilted toward it like it was feeding on the energy. I know I couldn't have seen it. But I did. I know what I saw."

"What did it look like?"

"Well, if you asked a kid to draw a flying saucer, that's what it looked like. About thirty feet across, made of some kind of metal, with a little dome on top. Lights around the rim, going real fast."

"What did you do?"

"You know, that's the funny thing. I didn't do anything. I didn't say anything for five or ten minutes and then I told my husband. He said, what? Why didn't you say so? and we turned around and raced back but when we got there it was gone.

"Please don't mention it. Okay?"

"Of course not, Merribeth."

Later than night, I told Jan about our conversation.

"Why in the world would she bring that up? What if others heard you? What would they think?"

I sipped a gin-and-tonic and squeezed the slice of lime to add its juice to the drink. "I don't know. I don't really care."

"Brian, you don't want to get a reputation. You said, when those little scamps get together, they're worse than a sewing circle."

"I can't forget what we saw," I said. "I keep thinking about it."

She sipped her Prosecco. "What do you mean, what we saw? You and Merribeth?"

"That thing we saw when we came home."

She looked for a long time. Her eyes had something in them I had never seen before. If eyes are the windows to our souls, hers needed Windex.

"Brian, I don't know what you're talking about."

"When we came home from the Taylors," I said. "That thing that looked like a star but came down and went into the lake."

"What are you talking about?" Her voice was angry and, I thought, afraid. "We stayed too late and drank too much and when we got home we walked across the road and looked at the stars and went to bed."

It was my turn to stare. "Jan, I'm talking about that thing, whatever the hell it was, that came down out of the sky and went into the lake. We watched it, Jan, we stood there together and watched it."

"Maybe you were dreaming."

"Jan, that's – "

"No, Brian. No no no." She rose and went into the kitchen where the tossed salad was waiting for sliced chicken to be added. She kept talking through the door. "That's crazy. Things like that don't happen. And if they do they don't happen here. That's the kind of garbage you read in tabloids."

"That isn't what I'm talking about."

She came back into the doorway. Her face was obscured by the windowlight behind.

"Brian," she said, "listen to me. You're scaring me. Something's wrong. Something has *been* wrong. Between us. Haven't you noticed? You, the great analyst? You haven't noticed what's going on? The tension, the growing distance between us? What it's like for me to live with your secrets and your lies? Living at arm's length?"

The silence swelled until it filled the room. I looked for something to say but came up empty. The silence turned dark like a sudden thunderstorm. I think we kept talking and then we were shouting at each other and pretty soon we couldn't hear each other at all.

Then my wife burst into tears and ran from the room. As near as I can tell, she is still running.

Val, I'm a careful thinker. I see patterns. That's what I do for a living. When something happens that doesn't connect to what you think you know, you don't even see it. You don't let yourself see it. For Jan that experience went straight down the memory hole.

I had to move to another office. That was the official verdict. They knew I hadn't done anything wrong, but I had to be moved from the scene of the crime. That's how I moved into UFOs. I was transferred to a project I hadn't even known existed. The project has lots of moving parts and is layered in so many cover stories, no one knows what's real. But real it is, and that's where they put me. The lateral move looked like a slap on the wrist but that's not what it was. It was meant to look like that. They had the move planned for some time. Kaster did have my back, like he said. I learned we had been on UFOs since the early fifties. Once I was read in, I was amazed how big it was, how many tentacles went in so many different directions. There was research into so many things. We covered it up with debunking and ridicule and disinformation. The UFOs still came and went and we saw them all the time. We had data from witnesses and radar and sensors. But we didn't control the saucers. They kept coming in waves.

So there I was, inside black budget programs that researched UFOs. Some of the best and the brightest worked there plus people from think tanks and universities and corporations. The chairs of the boards of big global companies were always involved.

Val, I wanted you to know they're real because you'll encounter UFOs during viewings. I don't want you to freak out. We can't risk losing good viewers. I don't want you to hit something you can't handle. It won't be seeing a flying disc that'll be a jolt, it's what happens next. If you do view one come to me. Tell me everything you remember. That's the official part. On a personal level, I wanted you to know what it can do to a relationship. What it did to mine."

"What's the bottom line, Brian? What do we know?"

"Not as much as we wish. We don't know their history, we don't know how they think, and we don't know what they want. They're deceptive. We use AI to analyze their patterns and come up empty. We're failing in two ways: we need to know their intentions, and we don't, and we have to hide our own intentions when we probe them and we can't. We put everything on the internet, and all they have to do is download it all and map the patterns. We can't keep our enemies out of classified systems but we think we can keep out a race that might be thousands of years older than we are? We can't let people know this, Val. Think tanks have done studies, what might happen to the fragile bonds of society, and it isn't pretty. They would break. The aliens have been careful not to do that, and we better not do it to ourselves.

"But that's incidental. I don't want what happened to my marriage to happen to you and Nick."

"So you're divorced."

"Yes." He finished the nuts and tossed the bag onto the table. "The day the movers took our stuff was a bad day. When the last lamp was loaded, I walked through the empty rooms of the house where we had spent so many happy days. It was like a corpse, with none of the light and warmth that gave it life.

After I locked up the house for the last time, I stood on the lawn until the sky grew dark. It was October and a chilly wind was blowing off the lake. I crossed the road and walked to the edge of the water. There were dry leaves underfoot and clinging leaves on the maples, their colors more vivid under the cloudy sky.

I waited for something to happen. Nothing did. The sky kept its secrets close. The sky is a lens that looks both ways, you know. They can see everything we do. We look out and all we see is how small and young and ignorant we are.

I thought I was smarter than I was. The dots I thought I had connected were scattered into the sky like jacks flung from the hand of an angry child. Maybe I broke some universal rule, like stay in your lane. Maybe the spirits heard how happy I thought we were and taught me a lesson. Maybe I simply ignored the warning signs at home because I didn't want to know. I mean, I was a spy, Val. What was I to do? Not lie? Tell her what I did?

In retrospect, maybe. Maybe this, maybe that. Or just maybe, nothing."

Interlude

"I am convinced that most people can learn to move from their ordinary mind to one not obstructed by conventional barriers of space and time. Who would not want to try that?"

- Russel Targ, *The Reality of ESP*. Co-founder of the CIA-sponsored Stanford Research Institute's investigation into remote viewing. His work was published in *Nature, The Proceedings of the Institute of Electrical and Electronics Engineers* and in *Proceedings of the American Association for the Advancement of Science.*

Chapter 13
Short and Sweet

Nick here.

When I worked at the agency, I used my analytical brain, I used my intuition. During viewings I have to suspend both and just stay calm and steady. It was good practice for life in general which I needed, I admit, after my breakdown and have never stopped needing. Anxiety is constant. Sometimes I can manage it and sometimes I feel overwhelmed. The traumatic aftershocks continue to plague me. I can feel sudden dread when the right triggers bring back memories of torture or what they did at the agency after I told the truth, which was a kind of torture too. My former colleagues are not amateurs, after all, and know how to "take care of" people. Maybe that's our real job description: manage and manipulate. Make our enemies, real or imagined, inside or out, know they'll feel the sting of the lash if they step out of line.

Staying steady, staying detached, is not easy. I was glad to have people around with whom I could talk about our issues. Everyone at Dasein—Joe, Hal, Brian, Val of course, and even Syl, became part of the posse. I trusted them all, perhaps naively. My gratitude for their hiring me diminished my suspicions. I shrugged a lot, dismissed a lot, and worked alongside them as if everything was on the up and up. I chose not to notice what I should have brought to consciousness.

I was shooting the breeze one wintry day with Sylvia, who was sitting in the alcove called her office, her desk obscured by piles of folders. She used computers for all her work but printed out everything. In the past she would have opened one and implied I'd better let her work, but she was getting friendlier. She engaged in convivial banter and when someone does that, they become more attractive as a person, they become almost a friend.

She asked what I was learning, now that I had done a bunch of viewings, some of which had decent results. How was it affecting me? And Val, too, how were we as a couple, both engaged behind the curtain as we were? Was our work impacting our relationship at all?

"Surprisingly," I said, "the viewings help me learn how to live. You watch your mind begin to form patterns, and it forms them more quickly when you're anxious or afraid, which I often am these days. You see how those emotions distort your perception. You have to step back and observe your reaction and include it in the data. You have to watch yourself watching yourself. You have to see the back of your head with your own eyes. You have to let yourself patiently wait as the darkness begins to glimmer, then reveals a landscape, a structure, a person doing something. Sometimes feelings flood into your brain and you have to hold on for the ride. I don't know yet how feelings adhere to a time or a place or an object, Syl, but they do. We learn that past and future are markers for states of consciousness. Not only in dreams, but in the vast landscape of memory-space, everyone is an artist. Time is an illusion, Einstein said, and even if he was only consoling someone, it didn't just slip out. He had to have thought of it. Time seems like a roundabout with entrances and exits and we try to enter or leave as we circle, depending on our intended destination. We organize events in a sequence but it's based on links and loops. It's arrogant to call ourselves shamans, but that's how we feel. Val and I get lost in our discussions, what we're doing, what it means. I think we're handling the impacts okay."

"That's what you and Val talk about over drinks at the end of a day?"

I smiled. "Sometimes. Sometimes we just have great sex."

"You wish."

We laughed and for once I did not give voice to the inappropriate images that bubbled up in my brain. I knew Syl had had partners but I didn't know which she preferred. I learned long ago, people don't choose what they like, they like what they like.

Sylvia preferred mathematical abstractions as gateways to the truth. She loved numbers, she said. She was quite literal and found our metaphors amusing.

"Math is not a metaphor," she said. "It describes the real universe."

"The universe is nothing but math?"

"I didn't say that. No one knows. I said it *describes* the universe better than anything else."

She said she was the only one at Dasein who knew that. "There's nowhere to hide on a spreadsheet, Nick. I see everything. If I tell you what I see, I'm being helpful. If I tell someone else, I'm a whistleblower."

"Are you?" I asked. "Who do you report to, Syl?"

"Nick, please. I saw what they did to you. I'm not crazy."

She had seen *The Insider* and asked me if it was true to my experience. I told her it pretty much was. Everything but a bullet in a mailbox.

She was warming to me I thought after months of working

together, once she realized how hard I worked, how I had their backs, how much better I was getting at accessing information and above all billing clients. Because I added value to the enterprise, she treated me like a human being. At any rate, that was my interpretation.

She worried more than the rest of us. "One day there will a reckoning with cash flow," she said. "When you look at the hours you spend viewing compared to what we can charge, it doesn't pay the bills. And one of you is always doing charity. If someone is in pain and hasn't got much money, you do the viewing for free. You're good human beings, but can a business work that way? There's a bottom line, you know. Police departments, attorney generals contact us about kidnappings or lost children or trafficking, and you never charge for that. No one will ever know how many lives you save. You work with people at the FBI but it's always individuals or department heads and they do it on the QT, never official business. Your relationships are helpful in getting work, but you can't say who they are. You could blow up their careers. It's a shame that you can't talk more openly about your successes. You'd be fodder for the tabloids and silly memes like staring at goats."

Syl smiled. "Wasn't it you, Nick, who told the story of the surgeon who couldn't tell anyone why he was so good?"

I nodded. He had gone to my old friend Penny for help when he got depressed. He said he was a brain surgeon and used to teach at the Feinberg. She asked why he left and he said he didn't dare tell the residents why he succeeded so often. He said he would sit at the heads of patients scheduled for surgery and wait until a soft white light appeared around their heads. Then he knew the surgery would be successful. If he told that to the residents, he'd be selling insurance.

"So yeah, we're in a bind. We count on word of mouth, but clients sign agreements not to talk. Thank God they do anyway. But once upon a time, before the agencies buried the programs, they even did public demos."

"I heard that too. Tours in other countries with one of the best viewers. He did viewings on television. He did them live with double-blind protocols so there was no way they could be faked. No one could impugn the methodology.

"When he was on tour in Japan, some professor said he would quit if he couldn't find the trick. The viewer did a double-blind target live on television and the audience judged it 95% accurate. The professor came in three days in a row and all he saw was the viewer sleeping on a tatami in the green room. He couldn't see any tricks. Of course he never resigned."

"My favorite story was two live viewings he did in England," I said. "One was the brand-new MI6 Building, a supersecret building, that created such a row that they were not allowed to use the material on television."

Syl sighed. "Yes, but that was then. Policies changed and they stopped touting success. They denied what they had promoted. That doesn't help us, does it? I do worry about the future. It would make a huge difference if a prominent company went public and said, yes, we've been using remote viewing and it's made us a quarter of a billion dollars."

"I know who you mean," I said. "It certainly would. And they certainly won't. Still, the word gets out. We're not the only ones in the game. Other countries use viewers for intelligence. That legendary viewer–another Joe, a different Joe–talked to his counterparts in Russia when he went there for three weeks. He did a remote viewing with their best and they targeted one another and did a drawing that was a mirror image which blew everyone's minds. They got along because neither bought into politics. The Russian said they met on a different level, he actually called it spirituality; he said he wished he knew another word that meant the same thing but he didn't. I mean the world of an Expanded Self, he called it on TV, and adepts in Tibet, India, Japan, related that to their own traditions. There were discussions online about that. I found them at the Internet Archive."

"Getting back to the other topic," Syl said, "remote viewing does change you, doesn't it? Hal said it's like going down a rabbit hole. What did he mean?"

"He meant working more and more between two worlds that operate differently, using different logic. Yes, it changes you," I said. "Alterations in our brains show up on MRIs. They're similar to scans of monks who meditate for years. But scientists still insist it's a fraud. They don't know that the scientific method is only one way to get at the truth. They don't understand their limitations. The want psi to dance like a trained dog. It doesn't work that way. Psychic episodes aren't predictable, you can't make them happen. They happen to happen. But you can make it more likely that they will happen by knowing that they do. Your conscious mind can invite your unconscious to help you out. Turning cards in a lab is the last place to find psi, but even there, it does occur. AIR, that DC consulting firm, did a pretty extensive study for the CIA and their bottom line was, yes, the hits are more than chance would produce. But even then, people twisted their conclusions and made it sound like nothing was found. I talked to the head of AIR and he said that real hits happened. Their study confirmed it. And like you, he was a math guy. He had degrees in math from the University of Chicago."

Sylvia said, "It's changed me too, hearing all these stories. I needed evidence. You guys made the case, and the times it doesn't work throws into relief the times it does. Your honesty about failures gives credence to your success.

"Damn!" she laughed. "I sound like one of you."

"God forbid," I said. "We need your analytical mind. Don't drink the kool-aid."

She laughed and opened a folder and lifted a paper. "I better get back to analysis," she said. She raised the page. All I could see was a printout of rows of numbers.

"Remember, Nick, numbers never lie. You want the truth? Here it is. Just do the math. Even if it says we might have only a couple of months before we need more capital.

"Thank God for eccentric millionaires," she said with a wink. "Where would we be without them?"

I told Val about our conversation. She picked up on what I said about her psychic gifts. She didn't think they were gifts but a part of normal functioning. Some just did it better. She didn't like the word 'psychic.' "But what else should we call it?" she said.

"Think of Elizabeth Myer," I said. "When a dowser found her daughter's stolen harp, it blew her mind. She said it changed everything. She risked her position at Berkeley to tell the truth. Either she's a liar or the world is not what she thought, she said."

"She was courageous, yes," Val said.

She paused and then said:

"Something happened this morning that I can't explain. I was waiting to tell you."

"You shouldn't let me always talk first," I said.

"It's how I grew up. It's a hard habit to break.... Anyway, I told you that Simone's mother was in a nursing home and pretty sick."

"Yes, you said that last week."

"So I wanted to support her, and for the last several days, before I went to work, I went there the first thing to see how she was doing. I didn't notice any change in her mother. She was often asleep.

Simone was grateful that I stayed in touch, checking in, which is all we have sometimes, right? Showing up?"

"Yes."

"So this morning I followed the same pattern. I went to see them and went to work and after I met a potential client for coffee, I was driving back to the office. You know the route. I was in the lefthand lane approaching the light, with the turn signal blinking, but as I slowed, I felt this strong urge to return to the nursing home. I had never done that before, never went back a second time. I thought, I better get back there. I had to wait for traffic to let me cross four lanes to the right and turn at the comer, opposite the way I intended to go. So it stood out, not my usual pattern. I went back to the nursing home and as I pulled into a visitor space, I saw Simone coming down the walk, tears streaming down her cheeks.

'How did they find you so fast?' she said. 'Mother just died and I ran to the nurse and said, you've got to find Valerie.'"

That was her story. Short and sweet.

"So how do you explain it?" Val said.

"I don't," I said. "I explain less and less, the more we do this. I know less and less. I marvel more and more."

"Yes," she said, coming into my arms for the kind of long-holding hug that dissolved into gratitude that we had met, that we had fallen in love, that we were on this incredible adventure together. That the pacemaker still worked. That we were so alive.

"Yes," she said. "So do I."

Interlude

"An uncontrolled agent is like an unguided missile. We have no hook, no handle, to manipulate his behavior. The uncontrolled agent can go running off in whatever direction he pleases, talk to whomever he likes, do or not do what we request – as it suits his fancy. It's better not to deal with such a person at all, regardless of how well placed he may be. Only work with people who are under discipline."

- David Ignatius, *Agents of Innocence*

Chapter 14
An Unguided Missile

In the deep cold Midwest winter, there is nowhere to go but inside. Inside ourselves, I mean, not inside the arid steam-heated rooms that reduce humidity to desert level. When I had a stay on Maui for a bit too long, the horizons closed like a vice by the time I left, thanks to island fever. Tropical weather does not drive introspection. A seed has to fall to the ground, they say, before it can sprout and bear fruit. That didn't happen in the tropics, but it did in Chicago in the long cold winter. At least we tell ourselves that to make it easier to endure.

But you do wonder sometimes why you're living here. Your forehead freezes unless your hat is so far down it covers your eyes which makes walking into a lamp post more likely. Your cheeks feel as if they might crack if you warm them up too fast. Ten minutes of ungloved hands is an invitation to frostbite. You stand at the window watching it snow, which is beautiful, yes, but after a few months, it feels confining.

So we watched more television shows, sometimes streaming two or three episodes in a single night, balancing the urgency to finish a series with wanting to save some for another night. We stopped watching "news" because violence and close-ups of weeping women were triggers I wanted to avoid. The news is not good for anyone with PTSD. If I hear one more time, "the following images may be disturbing" before they run the video, I will throw the TV out of the window.

Val and I searched through literature to learn more about what was going on when we did a viewing. That meant learning more about psi in general. There was a treasure trove of material from the Society for Psychical Research at the turn of the century in Britain and plenty more here. SRI had good and bad examples, charlatans and shamans. We erred on the skeptical side; we weeded out accounts that didn't have good documentation. Like UFO reports, calling them "anecdotal" did not invalidate claims; anecdotes, in any other context, are what we call "history." It helps to know the person telling the story, their character, their real bio. The most compelling accounts from the most credible people were like gold nuggets panned from a stream. We wash the other pebbles back into the water.

For psi and UFOs alike.

I trust Val's accounts. She trusts mine. When a fighter pilot told me that "we chase UFOs and we can't catch them," I knew he meant it. I may be making remote viewing sound like science fiction too, but believe me, we are not making these stories up. Extraordinary knowing is not extraordinary. Nor is the fact of visitation by a superior species. We have gone to all the neighbor planets, after all. When I was growing up, we feared that we would sink in the dust if we landed on the moon. We thought there were Martians and canals. We're mapping thousands of exoplanets, the low-hanging fruit of gas giants and hot rocks. I wonder if Martians file UFO reports about robots roaming the landscape and a copter in the sky?

The more viewings we did, the better we got—our percentages of hits increased, although they never reached a hundred per cent, or even near it—yet we understood less about what was actually happening. We wanted to know how consciousness worked, how the universe worked. Yeah, right. Every generation believes its own models of reality, then the models change. Models always leave out a lot of data.

Our language seems to illuminate the world but dims our view at the same time. At twilight the movement of shadows makes them seem like living souls. Hal's faeries prowl the perimeters of our lives. The world plays shell games with us and we never find the pea.

A paradigm is a prison and we inmates are the guards.

That was true in our little Dasein world as well. There were lots of conversations, but they didn't all include me. I knew I was missing key pieces. As a result, my cognitive dissonance increased. I grew frustrated by my lack of insight into the origin or real purpose of Dasein, beyond making money. Joe said only "a few of us began this new company," and that was all. My spidey-sense suggested there was more to it than that. Innuendoes, whispered conversations, debriefings in the scif that Val and I could not attend, suggested a hidden agenda. Over those long winter nights, the data points went drip drip drip and wore away my trust.

Call me a cynic. I began to wonder if my meeting with Joe at the Barbican was really accidental. Later I went to the owner and asked if Joe came in a lot. He said he did, he came in every afternoon and sipped a drink as if he was waiting for someone.

I wanted to know what was going on. I learned there were files in locked metal cabinets and on computers. I had accepted what Syl said about our hand-to-mouth existence. The end of the month, she said, was nail-biting time. We never knew if we'd make the rent and payroll, but money always seemed to come in before it was too late, sometimes just before. I knew there was one major investor who had bankrolled the enterprise but I didn't know his name. "You don't need to know," I was told. I thought he might be like Bigalow who funded ill-conceived work on UFOs and fruitless searches for life after death. Was our angel the same kind of guy? Or was the money, some of it at least, funneled from agencies and hidden in black budgets? I knew that things did not add up. I began to suspect that Syl's anxiety about cash flow was not the entire truth. My years of learning not to trust appearances went deep. My new way of living, accepting things at face value and telling the truth, was eclipsed by former habits. I began to think I couldn't trust anyone at Dasein except Val.

I didn't know what I didn't know. But I trusted my sixth sense.

I decided to cut a few corners to find out what was going on. It was justified, I believed, because Val and I were part of the narrative, part of the plot, and while the narrative was compelling, we didn't know where it was going or how it would end.

The high degree of mutual trust in our small group made listening to confidential conversations easy. We said we respected each other's privacy and thought that was adequate security, but it wasn't enough to deter a motivated snoop. We never scanned for listening devices or looked for back doors. Tribal loyalty diminishes due diligence, lowers the sense of threat. Security inside our group was assumed and therefore given short shrift. We counted on obscurity to keep outsiders out and never considered an insider threat. In that we were a lot like the agencies, preferring to ignore red flags. I counted on that practice to learn what was happening.

I planted bugs in the scif. Unless they scanned the room, they would never be detected. I sent the audio feeds to servers in the cloud. I read some of Joe's files. He kept them in a manilla folder before putting them into a computer and shredding the notes. Computer files were hard to crack. I had friends who could do it but chose not to call on them. That would only add more risk. Joe's folder for files waiting to be transcribed was a good start.

There is no rush like breaking in and finding something cool. Every hacker, every spy, every good journalist, knows that rush. I was like a kid breaking into a candy store, gobbling chocolates and filling his pockets, hoping his mouth wasn't smeared with the evidence. The material I discovered blew my mind.

I didn't tell Valerie at first what I was doing. I knew what she'd say (don't). I showed her the spoils after I had some juicy bits I knew she couldn't resist. Sure enough, she was chagrined, but she listened to every word. She said "you should not be doing that, Nick" but didn't tell me to stop in a way that said she meant it. "I don't need to know that," she often said when I reported something interesting, but she often added, "well? what else did they say?" Then her pretty head would tilt while she listened with attention, often going tsk tsk tsk. Having her cake and eating it too.

"OK, damn it," she said, "now we have to pretend we don't know."

"Welcome to my world," I said with a smile.

I tried to be subtle when I talked to Joe, hinting at things I wanted to know in more detail but trying not to suggest I knew all about them. Joe would tense and ask how I knew some detail or other. Who have you been talking to? What have you been doing, Nick?

I created trails to plausible sources at the agency, never using names. I was back at inventing narratives as I had done with Penny. A spy is a spy is a spy. Joe knew I knew something, but didn't know what or how. I tried to keep my questioning opaque. More was at stake than sources and methods (i.e. him); I could lose my job if he found out what I had done. My reputation, already on probation, would never recover.

Hal's explicit behaviors made him seem like an innocent. When you're open about being a shaman in an ancient Celtic tradition and believe you get information from faeries and other invisible people, instead of thinking you might be self-deceived like channelers who think they're getting the straight poop from angels only they can hear on high, your revelations are fun to read but not convincing. Hal wrote down what his discarnate mentors said during sessions of automatic writing in a barely legible hand and he shared them with us openly. Bor-ing! One can only read so much about higher realms before the accounts are repetitious and devoid of meaning. Nothing was verifiable. Nothing added to our self-understanding or suggested that the "wisdom" of discarnate beings was anything but a fantasy.

All that blather covered his real interest. Hal's' real interest was UFOs. Hal had interviewed numerous witnesses to UFO events on military bases when they came to take his courses in traffic analysis. He had his own folder, thick with reliable first-person accounts. I heard him discussing those with his many trusted sources.

Joe used encryption to make calls in the scif, but I didn't need to crack his code, only hear his words before they were encoded. It was like an el train on the high track before it dove like a roller coaster into the subway system. You don't need to go underground to catch the clatter and rattle of the cars before the dive. Joe was talking, I discovered, to people inside the agency about our work and about us, about our viewing, yes, but as often about UFOs. Our remote viewing, our stated reason for existing, was a real enterprise but also a means to another end. It was dual use. It was like the search for manganese modules by the Glomer Explorer. The ulterior search was the Soviet sub but manganese was good to find. The public claim was that remote viewing had been shut down inside several agencies, that Dasein was a private group that went out on its own, so the agencies and Dasein both had plausible deniability. We did remote viewing exactly as I reported, but we also used it clandestinely to learn more about UFOs. That warren of rabbit holes turned out to be deeper, more extensive and more concerning than I thought.

Brian was the ultimate insider. His official role was never revealed. He was always "an associate" or an "adjunct resource" but I learned that his transfer to working on UFOs after the fuck-up with the Booz Allen contractor had been in the works, waiting for a pretense. They used that infraction to account for his transfer. The story made sense as an explanation. He told it to Val so plausibly, she took him at his word. In the warren of offices to which he was sent, reached through doors that went through doors, he moved from one "above top secret" compartment to another. He had clearances for them all. As best I could infer, he did CI, disinformation, even deception against the aliens, and he sponsored useful idiots who filled You Tube, Tik Tok, and instagram with videos that were watched thousands of times, all related to UFOs and all complete bullshit. He discussed advanced projects that were reported as UFOs and kept the stories in circulation. We say we don't fly experimental craft over populated areas, but that was a lie. Where else would we test them? Only at Tonapah, White Sands, Eglin, far from facilities that birthed them? That was too much trouble. You could track a lot of our test flights by the dots on the map that callers said were UFOs. Most UFO web sites gather reports uncritically and total numbers of "sightings" that have little to do with reality. To move with some sanity through that morass, you had to know what you were doing. The UFO fanatics as a rule did not. But Joe and Hal and Brian did. Good civilian researchers like Swords and Aldrich and Powell and Greenwood and their troops did good respectable work and put it into a huge book of history. They used primary sources, most from the government itself. We managed that level of unusual competence by ignoring them. Silence was as effective as debunking and used fewer resources. Clark's encyclopedias were top-drawer stuff, but who reads encyclopedias? Meanwhile claptrap filled the mental space of our sadly diminished society. From conversations captured by my bugs, I learned that Brian had worked in R and D, space war, and with a secret inside group that monitored the whole program. Ersatz groups like MJ-12 were created to keep the bloodhounds off the scent. They had to do that, don't you see: if people knew thst UFOs are real, if they knew that remote viewing worked as well as it did, they might act on what they knew.

The scope of the UFO enterprise suggested its importance. It was not a game, this UFO business. It was way above top secret and the stakes were startlingly high and had been for decades. A Canadian minister who was right when he said that UFOs were a major concern of our government also claimed there had been a meeting. Us and them. He didn't mean Ike meeting tall whites at Edwards. He meant a sit-down approved at the highest levels. I asked Edgar Mitchell about it and he went to a friend on the Joint Chiefs. All his friend would say was, yes, and don't ask anything more.

Why had we debunked UFOs for decades? We had to get there first. "There" meant a number of things. We had to undermine the efforts of enemies to reverse engineer the baffling craft. We had to colonize the moon, and monitor Lagrange points, and colonize Mars, and find asteroids to mine at reasonable cost, which was still out of sight. We had to intensify the military use of space so the bad guys didn't have an advantage (a bad guy, if you haven't figured it out, is anyone who is not us, and "us" is a moving target).

The layers of obfuscation, distorted stories, false documents fed into the mainstream, the resources needed to do all that, suggested a strategy on the level of the Manhattan Project, with consequences just as bad if it wasn't done well.

Still, all I heard were hints. Who were these intruders? They had apparently evolved on different planets or colonies or collaboratories scattered throughout space. There are different visitors with different agendas, not all of them benevolent. There was no written history, no official record. The minutes of meetings were written in invisible ink. Cover stories were stacked on shelves to use as needed–like blaming the Roswell crash on a weather balloon and flying debris to a press conference overnight.

Brian referred to "the Hugo event" and a record of it was in Joe's file. He also said things that were classified above top secret and if I divulged that information, I'd be eligible for a long stay in a supermax. I have no recordings, no extant documents. I would love to tell you everything, but I have to say what I know without telling you what I know. I will tell you the least untruthful things I can. I will dodge and weave and scatter seeds of doubt. I will protect sources and methods, yes, but mostly I'll protect myself.

Crashes gave us alloys, dead beings and broken robots that only confused us more. Their brains were bigger with more lobes and folds and billions more connections. We didn't understand how they fired or how the electrical signals were experienced as cognition and consciousness. We didn't know how they perceived the world. Analyzing their brains was like taking apart a camera without seeing the images it produced or dissecting dolphins to determine how they built an image of their world. We were like the proverbial blind men handling an elephant. We simply wanted to know what was going on in our galactic neighborhood, but the more we learned, the bigger the neighborhood became and the less we knew about who they were, where they came from, how their societies worked, and what they intended.

When Brian debriefed me and Valerie about UFOs, he told us only enough for his purpose, not ours. He wasn't talking out of school as we had thought. He was doing what he was told to do, keep control of the narrative, keep control of us. He was very adept at mixing truths with half-truths and lots of outright lies. His omissions were significant. They wanted to use our viewing for at least two things, besides the intelligence gleaned from our work which was sent to all the usual suspects. Brian told Val we were likely to encounter UFOs during viewings and that when we did, we were to tell them everything. That might fill in some blanks and add to the big picture. In that respect, we were two more sensors in a vast array. But on top of that, they wanted to know what viewing did to us. Our health and well-being was no more important to them than the health of the guinea pigs our agencies had drugged or brainwashed or tortured or sent to Montreal to have their minds wiped. Their major concern was getting our sworn acquiescence and having plausible deniability if we went off the rails.

We were expendable.

I found in Joe's folder one complete story, the Hugo event. I didn't dare mention it because he would know how I knew. So I asked about the story Brian told Val and Joe laughed. "The one about the UFO entering the lake?"

"Yes," I said. "That one."

"Nick, that was based on a story he read. It didn't happen to him."

"Oh, really? What magazine was that?"

Joe googled and after a minute of thumbing buttons told me the name of some minor literary magazine that hardly anybody read. Something called The *Puckerbrush Review*. "And this is interesting," he said. "The story was fiction but based on a real event. But it wasn't a married couple, it was two brothers fishing on a lake. One filed a report and the other had no memory of it at all."

"And the reason for his divorce?"

Joe laughed. "Brian was never married, Nick. He was smarter than that. He was married to his work."

I played my recordings for Valerie and showed her the Hugo file. We were baffled, and she was of course angry at Brian for lying so blatantly. She was angry at herself as well for not seeing through his lies. We couldn't ask Joe or Brian direct questions. We could only sneak up on the narrative and hope we got enough to connect some dots. We couldn't push too hard.

You have to understand that when two-letter compartments stack on top of one another like cargo containers, you know you don't know and will never likely know the truth. Some containers are intentionally empty and some are loaded with contraband. Take reverse engineering. You may be tasked to recreate a recovered part (from a UFO or a Chinese jet) but then it goes to someone else, and then someone else, once it has been fitted to another part that comes from someone else, and on and on. Only the directors see it whole and sometimes not even. Your compartment is sealed tight.

But people do share stories, and the gossip I had heard at the agency fit what I was learning. I was way out of my comfort zone. When that happens to someone like me, I try to control my anxiety by talking to someone I can trust. If they're not available–Val didn't know any more than what I told her, so she couldn't help–I write it down. That's what I am doing in this book. I am trying to manage the impact of what I learned, what I know, by writing this book. I am telling you the least untruthful things I can. I swear to God I am. I am motivated by the same imperatives that made me a whistle blower: the people of this country, the people on this planet, have a right to know what's going on. Our self-appointed "guardians" do not have the right to shut us out. Thinking that we deserve the truth is what got Snowden and Manning into deep shit, but my commitment like theirs is to the truth, however much I surround it with a bodyguard of lies. As it says at Langley, "the truth shall set you free." But I think they mean it another way.

All I ever wanted to do in my life was see clearly and say clearly what I saw. I wanted to understand as much as I could, clearances and classification be damned. I milked every cow I found in the barn. My opportunity to learn was racing by. I did not want to end my life like Koheleth saying, meaningless, meaningless, everything is meaningless. I wanted to communicate some of what I knew as a legacy, a tired word but a good one when you're aging. Despite all the questionable things I had done, I wanted to contribute something, however insignificant, so my life meant something. A short span of time, a brief opportunity, is all we have. I fear I'm almost out of time. I hear the ticking of the clock. I hear the ticking of my heart with its finite number of allotted beats. I hear the mortality express dopplering down the track.

When you're in white water and see rocks up ahead, if you look at the rocks, you hit the rocks, but if you look at where the water goes, you go where the water goes. I want to help you see where the water goes. The rest is up to you.

Here is my account of "the Tonapah event."A visitor had apparently landed at Tonapah and was welcomed to a scif. And here is the full story of the Hugo event, named after a part-time barista of all things, a wood carver, not Hugo Gernsback or the prize of the same name. Val and I had watched a series streamed on Netflix about an odd little man named Hugo who claimed to have met with aliens. The story was fanciful and hard to believe at face value. But I think it held some truths among its wild claims. That his account was in one of Joe's files in its entirety suggests it wasn't irrelevant. There was something to it; the truth or some of it was in there somehow, in some form. The account as Hugo told it sounds like a fable, but a fable like a myth is meaningful, maybe not like history, but meaningful in its own way.

Hugo and the visitors supposedly met in some kind of flying apparatus where they discussed the weirdest things. It sounded absurd in a sci-fi way, but it wouldn't have been the first time a fictional account hid real details in plain sight. Jelli told Val that one part of her believed what she thought she remembered, one part of her thought she imagined at least some of it, and one part of her feared the whole episode was a hallucination. We have the same multiple choice options. I concluded that Tonapah was real and the Hugo-event actually happened although not exactly as he said. It's best to let you read it in his own words and decide for yourselves.

But first, Tonapah. Stranger than fiction, yes, but it's likely it happened pretty much as Joe said.

I finally lost patience and demanded that Joe own up. I gave up being subtle. I felt like Redford in the film telling Deep Throat to stop his chickenshit games. I want to know what you know, Redford said, and so did I. Joe was massively pissed off.

"How the hell do you know about all this in the first place?" he said. "Who have you been talking to?"

"Joe, calm down," I said. "You know I can't tell you who I spoke to. I have a life outside these rooms. I still have friends at the agency. After Val and I hit the same UFO target, we were spooked. I called someone I knew. He told me enough to make me come to you.

"So that's how I have a clue. I don't know the details. And if you do ..." I turned the tables on my friend. "If you do, you're more involved than you said and your role at Dasein is not what you said. You never left the agency, did you? Dasein's a cover for something else, isn't it? In addition to being a remote viewing enterprise?"

That strategy pretty much worked. He muttered a bit but settled down and led me into the scif. He locked the door behind us. Did he look around suspiciously and wonder if all I had done was call a former colleague? Was he thinking there were bugs in the scif? Later I learned he did scan the scif for bugs, but after I removed them. He did look around, but he didn't do anything more. He pulled out a chair for me and took one for himself, and when I had my back turned, he pushed me into a rabbit hole and once again, I was falling, falling, falling, outside of time and space in a quest to understand the mysteries of the universe, the myriads of beings that Hugo said evolved, endless creatures most wonderful.

At a certain point, our conversation dealt with the ultimate meaning of ... well, everything. What other kind of meaning is there, after all? I made a note to call Bill Webb and tell him I wanted to talk. Now that he left the ministry in a formal capacity, what did he think? Now that he didn't need to repeat the party line, what did he believe? Was there more meaning in existence than the meaning we make with our meaning-making brains? Was meaning intrinsic to existence? Was the fact of information a signal and a clue?

But first, the Tonapah story and then the purloined Hugo file.

Interlude

"What is truth?"

- Pontius Pilate, *John 18:38*

Chapter 15
You Can't Handle the Truth

"In any case, you aren't cleared to hear it, so you'll never know if you can handle it or not." That's what Joe told me in the scif.

"Do you know the whole story?" I responded. "Do you have all the pieces? If you don't, who does?"

"No," he said. "I don't." He settled down. "Brian might come closer to seeing the bigger picture. I suggest you not approach him the way you did me, like a bull in a china shop. Anyway, he's onto you. Christ, Nick, I thought you'd grown up, after all you went through."

"Fuck you very much, Joe."

"Look, I'm taking a risk just by having this conversation. It's premature. It shouldn't have happened this way. We planned to fill you in at a later date. We had a timetable for a good reason. This project needed to ripen. Had you waited, we might have been able to arrange clearances. Now you fucked it all up. I can't request higher clearances for you unless I tell them why, and now I'd have to report what you did."

"How should it have happened, Joe? What did you intend to do?"

He shrugged. "Let's not go there. It's moot. Let's get down to brass tacks."

"OK," I said. "Let's."

I didn't think I had done something awful. I was trying to understand the players and I didn't have a program. How could I do my job if they lied to me and Val? How could I trust them?

"Let's start with the recovery of material," I said, "from vehicles that crashed. Val and I both saw wreckage scattered all around. Do we have that material, or not? Do we know what it is?"

"It depends what you mean by 'know what it is,'" Joe said. "Has some been retrieved? Yes. Do we analyze it as best we can? Yes. Is our analysis good enough to reproduce the alloys? No. And why is that? Because we can see the atoms, we can see how they're arranged, but not why they do what they do in combination with the uniforms they wear. It doesn't make sense to us yet."

"Do we have bodies? Val saw a body on the ground. Was she right? Are those stories true?"

Joe shook his head as if I was too dense to get it. "If we did, you wouldn't be cleared to know, Nick. So maybe yes, maybe no. If we did, and if we sent them to Ohio for dissection, we wouldn't understand what we saw. It's like looking at a machine invented hundreds of years ahead of our own technology. It's like an ancient Celt finding a radio."

"What about contact? That's a simple yes or no."

Joe named a bunch of two-letter compartments where I might find hints of some answers. "You have to put the pieces together, Nick. No compartment has it all."

"And I'm not cleared for any of those," I said. "You know that."

"I do know that. So what do you want, Nick? Want me to tell you what I think? I can say what I think Brian thinks, but what good is that? His access is way higher than mine but it's still hearsay. Some of us are disciplined and observe proper protocols. Do you know the names of the files you want?"

He was toying with me. I knew how we filed reports. Cross-filing with false labels was common, often used to frustrate FOIA requests. If you can't name what you're looking for, it won't be found, even if the file is right there under a different name. You'll get a standard reply that the file could not be located. Which is technically correct. Knowing the names that link the names is not in files we can get. It's in a file, but not in a file I could find.

The absurdity of it all made me laugh.

"What's funny?" Joe said.

"This whole damn thing is funny. It's crazytown, Joe, this wilderness of mirrors. It can drive a person nuts."

"It can," he nodded. "We know people who went off the rails."

"Angleton, for one."

"Yes. Hillenkoetter, Helms. Vallee, of course, lost his compass long ago, once he was recruited. Double agents have to be crazy in just the right ways."

"I did a viewing, Joe, of the site that Val had seen. I didn't know what it was when I sketched the scene. I drew lines randomly. When they connected, I saw what looked like debris, pieces of a crashed vehicle. I thought it might be Russian or Chinese. Maybe a plane like the one that Carter said was found by a remote viewer. As Valerie had, I sketched what looked like a being. When I came out of the altered state, I rose back to awareness as if I was ascending into more and more light, and I was shaking. I told my controller what I saw. I know what I saw, Joe, so don't bullshit me. You're telling me that story has not made the rounds? That's like telling a fighter pilot not to mention a UFO encounter. It's all over the squadron in a matter of minutes. We know what we recovered, some of it at least."

"You know a few stories, and some might be true. Others are yellow scarves the gnome tied on all the other trees. You're not planning to blow the whistle again, are you, Nick? Reveal the contents of this discussion? We would just debunk the story, you know, and shred your reputation. That is, if you didn't go to jail. Which you most likely would." He paused and had a look on his face I had never seen before. "You have no idea what you're dealing with, Nick. This is way above your pay grade."

I looked at him with anger, helpless and afraid. I admit it: I was afraid. A part of me did not want to know the truth, now or ever. "Thanks for the advice, Joe."

"You and Val discuss what you see, what you do, don't you?"

"Of course we do. We tell each other everything. That's why agents are encouraged to marry inside the fence. Relationships with normal human beings are damned near impossible."

Joe sighed. "Nick, you have some details right and some wrong. Do you want to know the Tonapah story? As much as I can say? A sketchy account with lots of blank spaces?"

"Yes," I said. "I certainly do."

This is the story Joe told:

"I wasn't there. That's the first thing you need to know. Yes, I am still with the agency, but I wasn't read into that debriefing. When we started Dasein, we were told enough to do our work and nothing more. Brian had Ken Bolin help me do the paperwork. He was sheep dipped for an assignment at Tonapah. No one knew he came from the agency. Why he told me about that event, God only knows. I think the event itself knocked his judgement for a loop. I thought he was a good soldier until he did that. He was practically kidnapped by OSI when they realized he was at the scene. Those guys handle black operations at the highest levels, the X-files stuff, the weird stuff, and the worst stuff like trafficking, pedophile rings, and even, I understand, snuff films. Bolin did some of that and was sickened by what he found. For an honest-to-god snuff film they had a regular Hollywood set with all the latest equipment and a little girl. You know why? They want realism, and when they get to the point where they kill the guy, they use a rape of the little girl as a pretext. They want his fear when he realizes they're going to kill him to be real. The victim thought he was in a run-of-the-mill pedophile film. He didn't know until the end they planned to kill him. They let him do what he wanted with the girl, then the 'good guys' barged in and rescued the girl and shot him dead. Then it was a wrap."

"You're telling me the truth?"

"I'm telling you what I heard. They hand those films one to another so the minute you take it, you're a criminal, so customers don't go rogue. It would mean they go to jail."

"And what happened to the little girl?"

Joe shrugged. "We can guess. A lifelong struggle to regain sanity. Dissociated states. Confusion about what's real. You know, the human condition," he tried to smile.

"Why would any alien, knowing who we are and what we do, want to even talk to us?"

"That's one more data point I haven't got. Anyway, that's what OSI deals with. Bolin said he never got over clicking through images of children abused in every imaginable way to desensitize him for the work. A number of his colleagues couldn't take the constant assault on their sensibilities. Bolin endured. He had been at Tonapah on a mission related to a space plane and was standing back in the shadows at the door, 7DF, unnoticed by the rest who were staring at the gate. He should not have been there. They thought they cleared the area. Someone fucked up so he was there when the alien came in.

"The gate opened and in came a silent slowly-moving teardrop-shaped machine and the gate closed behind it. A door opened and then ... out came a large creature. That's what he called it, a creature. With a big head and large shiny eyes without pupils or any expression. He watched them lead our 'guest' to a scif and that was that, as far as he was concerned. He never learned the gist of the discussion and neither did I. Make something up if you want. No one can contradict it. It's better for disinforming, too, to spread as many stories as we can.

"So yes, Nick, an alien was at the base, alive and kicking. The dead ones would go to Wright Pat to be examined and stored, if any were ever recovered, that is. That one was very much alive.

"Look, I've known Bolin for years. We worked on an exfiltration that took a long time and a lot of planning under the watchful eyes of the Russians. We barely got out of Dodge with our lives. We got the guy and his family out and they live happily in Omaha. If you say that I told you any of this, I'll deny it. As far as you know, it's just a story. You weren't there. You'll never talk to Bolin, who was transferred after interrogation to the north pole. Last I heard he was counting penguins."

Joe looked at me with narrowed eyes. "I really want to know who you talked to, Nick."

"Forget it, Joe. You know I can't tell you that."

He knew not to push. "Whoever it was, this stops here and now. Do you understand how fucked you will be if you breathe a word?"

I let that pass. "Sure, Joe, but we do need to talk about Dasein. You fed me a false story, Joe. You lied to us. We can't work under these conditions without an explanation."

"I can't tell you that, Nick, unless I am cleared to do so. You have no 'need to know' the back story, why it was done this way. You know how it works. The likelihood they'll give me permission to tell you anything at all is slim to zero, given how you left the agency."

"Then why did you recruit me?."

I watched him closely to see if he was lying–again.

"We wanted you as a viewer. Valerie was a bonus. We were happy to have her. We consulted the shrink you saw after your breakdown and he told us what to expect. He talked about the consequences of trauma–so we could manage you, Nick. Manipulate you, one might say."

"I thought those conversations were confidential."

Joe smiled. "Yeah, right. We thought you might be pretty good as a viewer and we thought you might be good with clients. But that was secondary, Nick."

"What was primary, Joe?"

"Nick, we've been doing viewings for some time, but the impact on viewers varies. Good viewers are sometimes borderline marginal and viewings add to their distress. Given your condition, we knew it might not take much to–how can I put it–intensify your symptoms. We wanted to monitor your reactions. We want to better understand the impacts of remote viewing. When Valerie got into it, it was perfect. You two interacted all the time and you were both good viewers. Valerie was a star so we added to her load. The intelligence did have value, both here at work and at the agencies where–of course. duh–we shared everything."

"You're saying that Dasein was a petri dish and we were the specimen."

"I wouldn't put it so crassly, but, yes, that's a major reason you were recruited. You filled the bill on multiple points."

I wasn't surprised, not really. It all fit what the agency I knew so well had me do before. But I had to sit still and breathe deeply until my anger abated.

"Is that the whole story, Joe?"

It wasn't, but that was all he was telling me, that day. Or ever.

"That's all I can say. We knew what we were doing. You were watched carefully. If we grew alarmed, we had protocols in place to handle whatever happened. Val was a good test case in her own right since other than abuse in a prior relationship, she was pretty clean."

"Tell me more about Tonapah."

Joe shrugged."Not much more to tell about that. They cleared the deck while the alien waited out there in the desert. Then he was cleared to land. If the story leaks, we'll make you sound like an idiot. Put you into the same category as Lear or Greer. Or Jacobs or Mack. They have their own cultic followers. One's on the side of bright light and the other's on the dark side and mildly deranged."

"Bolin really told you the truth, you think?"

"He did. I think. Luckily he came to me. I reported him right away and the OSI guys came down on him hard. He disappeared in the middle of the night. I wasn't kidding. I heard he was way the hell up in Alaska. The closest we get to a gulag," Joe laughed. "Maybe at Eileson, near Moose Creek."

"I hope he brought his mittens."

"Nick, I'm telling you what I can. I know what you did ten years ago when I was caught up in Amsterdam. You think I'd forget that? But you can't know everything. You know that."

"Who are they, Joe? Where are they from?"

"I think they're a species so far ahead of us we can't even grasp

it. I believe–that's hearsay, too, like everything else you're getting–
that the Tonapah meeting was a kind of first date. Maybe there have
been more. I heard that we learned that they enhanced their
capabilities genetically to adapt to an environment we can't even
understand. We don't know what challenged them to change their
abilities."

Joe put his hand on my arm with a semblance of comradeship."I
should report this talk. You know that. But I have my own agendas.
I want Dasein to work out and fulfill its intention. I don't want the
higher-ups to think our decision to bring you on board was a
mistake. You weren't the first and you won't be the last. We know
what we're doing. So it didn't work out as planned. Hell, few things
do. But I have to trust you to keep your mouth shut. Can I?"

I was back in the rabbit trap that agencies set so well. I felt that
sinking feeling that comes when I realize how deep it all goes, how
little I know, how beyond my control it all is. No wonder we have
religions, ameliorating our helplessness, our fears. The shock of
new knowledge can be way beyond the telling. When I learned
things at the agency that forced a revision of what I thought was
real, it pulled out the cornerstone of everything I believed and I felt
like I was living under water for weeks. Trying to tell someone what
it's like to experience that is impossible. Normal people just don't
understand. They believe in their beliefs.

So where could I turn for solace?

Where else? There may not be a God, as Woody Allen said, but
we know there are women. Thank God I had Valerie. Valerie keeps
me as sane as I can be kept.

Joe did not tell me the whole story. Bolin had in fact told one
other person about what he saw. I heard that from someone else
who knew a guy who knew a guy. By the time the story reached me,

it may have left its original form far behind.

But the story I heard kind of matched what Joe said. And the fact is, you know as much as I do, now. You still have no idea what's really going on. You probably never will. Valerie and I did pick up a lot of bits and pieces here and there and we put them together as best we could but I don't think you want to know what we think. I mean that. We have lots of sleepless nights or sometimes one of us will notice the other staring off into space, but not really, staring into the future in light of what we wished we didn't know.

We can't do a damned thing about it, so we say the serenity prayer a lot. With history as our guide, we know that if humans can do something, however horrid or heinous, the likelihood is that they will. Writing history is a way to tame the past by making it seem meaningful, like looking at Medusa in a mirror, making reality bearable. The earth is a sponge that has absorbed more blood than we can imagine. We think that's true for at least one alien race as well. Based on what I learned, I know it is, as much as I know anything.

The scenarios we extrapolate from viewing UFOs—and their larger platforms far away—are hard to put together. There are too many variables. We don't know how they experience time, so we can't know their long-term intentions. I think they take their own sweet time to bring things to fruition. The closest I can come is Maori time. A Maori taught me when I worked inside a Five Eyes compartment how differently they think. They think something important can take a thousand years to accomplish. They walk slowly, but they don't walk backward. I'm a creature of the white western world and I can't think like that, much less like our visitors. So even if I wanted to divulge more than I am in this narrative, it would be speculative and your brain, trained in our provincial habits of thought, would never grok it. It wouldn't help you see the big picture. Anyway, you don't really want to know. Get on with your happy little lives, like they said with a wink in *Men in Black*. 'Tis the season to be jolly. Especially now, at Christmas time, wrapped in our furs and fables, we don't want to know what lies ahead, do we? Ring, ring those bells and sing those joyous songs. The future already exists, the future has already happened, and speaking for myself, I have to say I prefer the past. The past is a done deal, packaged and wrapped, so it really can't threaten us. It may cause nightmares, but that's why we have sedatives. There's something about a finished era, however wracked with pain, that is comforting in its way. World War II and the Holocaust are subjects now for patriotic movies, not the horror that they were. Talk about Medusa seen in a mirror! And maybe another future will emerge from the blood and dust and rubble of the past. It can, you know. Entropy sometimes decreases. I can't do the math but that's what they tell me. And at least two of those species have our backs or say they do, and that's good enough for now.

And as I keep insisting … now is all we have.

Interlude

"There are many worlds and many systems of Universes existing all at the same time, all of them perishable."

- Anaximander, in Simplicius,
Commentary on Aristotle's Physics, 1121, 5–9

Chapter 16
Hugo Blau: His Story

O K, that's one of the stories, the Tonapah incident, short and sweet with a lot of blank spaces, but that's how they often are. The world does not come to us complete and unredacted. There are lots of black marks obliterating important parts. That, I'm afraid, is the human condition. We are listening to a symphony in a hall with a lot of dead spaces. I am writing a book that is true to the way life comes to me, fired into my face at point blank range. There are a lot of missing pages. As Hal said, it's like going to a movie after it started and leaving before it's over.

Here in its entirety is the tale told by Hartmut (Hugo) Blau:

My name is Hugo Blau.

I am writing down my experience. It wasn't a dream. I dream a lot. I know when I am dreaming. I know when I'm awake. Like Santa Claus, in reverse.

This account is true, as best I can remember. I am writing it because Colonel Reid asked me to. Colonel Reid is a bird colonel in the Space Command, he says. I have no reason to doubt him. His uniform which may be borrowed says that's his rank. I didn't request his bonafides and took him at his word. Although I am a civilian, I acknowledged his authority during the event. I respected him for what he had done (he was heavily decorated for heroics during one of our many wars but never spoke of that himself) and I did as I was asked.

Dreams are inside our heads. When we wake up they pop like bubbles. Most are hard to remember. What happened in the Bin was not like that.

I use the name "Hugo" because it means mind or spirit and that's where this takes place, in my mind. That doesn't mean it did not happen in the "external world," only that everything that happens there is filtered into our minds. We create mind maps of events and believe they are the events themselves.

Some of the things that happened were symbolic, that is, they were literally true but also conveyed meaning beyond their factuality. They had more meaning than things that just happen to happen. I believe the meaning was designed to make sense to a human mind. The aliens used human symbols derived from hundreds of years of observation to replicate what they overheard eavesdropping on our planet. Nevertheless, at one point, all of the symbols seemed to rise into the air like the deck of cards at the end of Alice's story. A phantasmagoria morphed into a seemingly literal history. This may sound like a fable, but it is literal history too.

Once a bat crawling down from the floor above my basement apartment was caught in the ceiling fan in the bathroom. I thought the high-pitched sounds were from metal pieces that had come loose instead of a shrieking bat being shredded. That's how the symbols sounded when they rose into the air. I covered my ears until the sounds stopped. The silence afterward, the clarity it engendered, was stunning. The contrast—chaos first, then serenity—was intentional, I believe.

The silence expanded like a warm glow, a generous invitation, a welcome to the universe. I had never before been invited into a group. That's how I know it wasn't a dream. In my dreams, the screaming never stops. In the Bin, it stopped and an invitation was extended. The Visitors said, in effect, Hugo, come on in.

I accepted. I said yes.

My real name is Hartmut but I prefer Hugo. I live in a basement apartment I have lived in for years. It was easier and cheaper to stay than go.

On a bright day, the light in the basement is like twilight. So I installed bands of bright fluorescents that crackle above me when I carve, hissing like bug zappers, me the ever mindful moth, an erratic percussive rhythm above the soft chunk of my blade whittling wood.

I carve for a living, and I carve because life seems to work better when I carve. I would have carved even if no one bought the creatures I release from their wooden sarcophagi. Some are based on games, some on the world of Marvel and other graphic novels, some on toys. Vampires, witches, goblins. Demons from anime. Trolls and dwarfs like the kind that scared my grandmother Sophia in the old country.

The aliens pulled me into a looking-glass world. I like to think my carvings do that for children. And for adult collectors, too, of which there are many, especially now, who gaze, I like to think, on their subtle faces until the magic happens. My little wooden figures are like spells incarnate, needing only a human to hold them up and look at them to generate their power.

When I carve, my mind, my imagination, is like a snow globe, trembling with the tension of creativity, a little blizzard falling on elves or mini-dragons. I coax what I see from the wood, but at some point, the wood speaks for itself and tells me how to find the right form. Then I become its partner, its servant.

My head is bent up around because of scoliosis. My family could not afford surgery or even a brace. I didn't know any better and took life as it was. My symptoms developed early, at twelve or thirteen, compared to the norm. I was very self-conscious, naturally. My shoulders and hips were uneven. Straight-ahead people as I call them never know if I'm coming or going. I have adapted. I have compensated for my affliction with compassion toward others. It was that or the reverse. I listened to others tell their tales and if you do that, if you really listen, you wind up with compassion.

My childhood had not been normal, as you may have guessed. My parents tried remedies advertised on the internet, hoping for a cure, with predictable results. I remained bent. Until they found a special school I could attend, I amused myself at home. I first learned about wood carving on the Hobby Channel. I begged for wood and a knife and began whittling. When the first vague shapes emerged from blocks of wood and little nubs of wooden eyes looked back at my own, I was hooked. I consumed the myths and legends of my heritage, the stories of the northern forests. Ancient images made their way down my twisted spine to my fingers and through the chunking knife into wood.

Others liked my little people. They bought them and I made do. I showed them, I think, the gods and demons inhabiting their souls. Comic and game shops sell my painted creatures. Then I pay for more wood and make more. Rent is low. I hear buses and cars outside and when I climb up and look out the half-window I see through the bars the feet of the plodding masses passing by. I have lived in that twilight world like a troll.

Still, I need people. Engaging with others makes me feel more human. When I first moved here, I went to the coffee shop every morning just to be around human beings, and after a couple of years I was asked to fill in as a barista when Jessie got sick. With my head at an odd angle, I looked comical to some and alarming to others. Even the worst disabilities, though, disappear when someone engages with a cripple like me and my appearance becomes translucent to the Hugo Blau inside and my personhood comes out to play.

I learned to take a step back from conversations and listen not only to others' words but to their underlying feelings. In addition, getting complex orders right was not easy. Listening to a foursome describe their specialized drinks, one pump of this and a half caf that, taught me to focus intently. Because I was barely above the counter, my head twisted away from their downward gaze, I picked up feelings in a way that felt like iron filings in a magnetic field. I came to rely on that talent. I developed an almost psychic ability to know what others need and respond in a calming way.

Sometimes it *was* psychic, when I paid close attention and entered into the flow of our fields merging into a flux where the origins of thoughts and feelings were unclear. I loved flowing into that state. Over time I made myself open to it, I got out of the way and then it happened more and more.

Knowing how to do that prepared me for the Bin.

Is that why the aliens picked me? I'll never know. The colonel and his cadre were flummoxed too, trying to understand why. Everyone guesses, no one knows. I ignore the distorted versions of my story that circulate online. Some claim, for example, that the knock on the door was at midnight. No, it was in the afternoon. Another error in their now-mythical narratives is, I knew the colonel was coming. Some say it was psychic, others a text to my phone. I did not know he was coming. The third is the conversations they invented, the words they put in my mouth, to make the story more interesting. Their descriptions of the aliens are comical. They are like Ripley's monster on the Nostromo. No physical description captures their diaphanous morphing forms.

The simple truth is, I met the aliens in what we called the Bin and I confronted the threat of the Other with openness, acceptance, serenity, compassion, understanding, and excitement. I beheld a different race. I was curious and interested. I didn't fight or take flight. I stood my ground. I beheld their oddness as I beheld the oddness of all the people around me for my entire life.

The knock came on one warm day in June. June 16, to be exact. Fluorescents hummed above my head as always, and I was twisted around to watch the knife in my right hand whittle the wood into a long-nosed elf with a green mushroom cap on his head. My hand had a life of its own and I was a spectator at my own play, a tourist in my own territory. I watched the part of my brain that is creative do its work as if it listened to a muse.

Knock. Knock.

"Who's there?" I said, startled. I did not expect a visitor.

Knock. Knock knock.

"Who is it?" I said more loudly.

"Hartmut Brau?

"Blau. Not Brau. Yes. Who is it?"

"Colonel Nate Reid of the Space Command."

I waited.

"What do you want?"

"I want you to open the door," he said, "so we can talk."

I slid off the stool and scuttled sideways like a crab to the bolted door. I unlocked and opened it and looked up around at a tall officer. His immense bulk filled his blue uniform. I thought of a large bullet with eyes and nose painted on for a face. Through his legs and the sharp creases of his blue trousers I saw the steps behind, the concrete wall in the summer light. I could smell his after shave.

"Talk about what?"

The colonel stooped and pressed his face against an invisible pane just inches from my nose.

"I would rather explain inside. May I come in?"

I could have said no. But instead I backed in and he followed, closing the door with a soft click.

He looked around at my studio, the unmade bed, the dishes in the sink. He correctly identified a chair under some clothes. "May I sit down?"

I hobbled over and removed some shirts and threw them into the corner.

"Thank you," he said, settling as best he could into the low seat.

I looked him up and down and decided to listen. I think you get the information you need in the first minute or two. I sized him up and judged him to be a military officer, straight as a rail.

The colonel asked about my work, my background, my life. I discussed my childhood, how I learned to imagine all sorts of creatures in the absence of friends. I talked about learning to use my emotional reactions as sounding boards when I engaged with others. I told him how I listened with my ear to the ground as it were while others walked about. Because I was so distorted, I posed no viable threat. I was a harmless quirk of nature.

Then I asked why he came.

"Do you believe in intelligent life elsewhere in the universe?"

"Of course," I said. "I also think we have been visited. We have been sending smoke signals for hundreds of years. If anyone cared to look, if anyone else is curious, they had a look. Wouldn't we? "

The colonel smiled, his grave face reminding me of an egg breaking when he did. "Yes," he said. "Most of the stories about visits are silliness, disinformation, the confusion of useful idiots, a cottage industry thriving on lies. Most is that."

"And the rest?"

"The remainder consists of a cultural intrusion by a complex civilization into our conscious awareness. We've known they were here for a long time but didn't know why. Couldn't do a damn thing about it. Now they want us to run some tests on their behalf. They want a formal sit-down with a human being and devised a means of choosing who it is."

I turned off the fluorescents and we sat in the twilight of the warm summer afternoon. This well-pressed fellow was as out of place in my cave as a gourmet meal. Made me feel a bit peckish. Still, I sensed his commitment to the job he had to do and drew myself closer.

"So why are you telling me all this?"

"Because they used the data they extracted from our global systems to whittle down their list to two. Their AIs made the choice. They asked to meet a human face to face."

"Is that cool or what!" I felt like a little kid. I know I sounded silly, but it *was* cool, damn it.

"It is," he acknowledged. "They chose two people based on their deep probing into the nature of the human psyche. They want to pick one. One is Luisa Martinez from Union City. The other is you."

There was more than a roaring in my ears. There was a maelstrom, as his words turned into disbelief. The twilight in the basement dimmed, the walls shattered into pieces. But I was still on my stool, somehow, head bent up toward an officer sitting improbably in my chair. I was Hartmut the harmless, the neighborhood cripple, the improbable part-time barista. I understood what he said, but I sat in a cone of silence. The world tilted. The Colonel observed.

I enabled. I allowed.

Yes, I said. Oh yes, Colonel Reid. Yes yes yes!

Nothing I have told you makes sense. I concede that. But then, that's the point. The way we think, nothing makes sense.

Besides, they play with us. They understood us, from their point of view (you can never escape your point of view) as well as an alien could. Then they began this end game of contact and communication. But you'll find no evidence of this. Everything has been erased. NORAD shrugs and says, say what? NASA says, we'd love to help but we're so busy, maybe another time. DOD says, gosh, we have our hands full finding new weapons. The colonel prefers it that way. His superiors prefer it that way. The President, I believe, prefers it that way, and the Homeland Defense top brass and anyone else who counts, they all prefer it that way. For the moment, they do not want the world to know that this event happened.

Nothing I can do about that. I told my story and it was wildly distorted by news outlets. So it goes.

I am telling you the least untruthful things I can. This account may sound fanciful but it contains the larger truth.

In retrospect, my memory plays tricks. Was the Colonel in uniform when he called or did he wear navy slacks, a light blue shirt, and a windbreaker, collar up? I prefer that he be in uniform, and so he is. He also wore opaque sunglasses, which I neglected to mention. I saw my twisted self reflected as a miniature. I later carved the way I was mirrored by the glass darkly.

He arranged for me to begin the tests. We arrived at the airport in a black SUV. Instead of following the public road, we entered a restricted area and then a hangar and then went down a ramp into a tunnel and came out in another hanger where we entered a waiting plane. The windows were blacked out, it was dark by then, anyway, early evening, and we flew into a dark sky. We turned this way and that and climbed above the clouds, then headed what I guessed was north. We flew for at least two hours. The colonel was silent despite my questions. Then we landed at a secret base.

If you look at satellite photos you will not see the base. The base is not on any map. From above it is hidden by camouflage and forests. Pines and aspens, I believe. I am sure our enemies' sensors detect signatures of heat, communications, all those things. Or maybe we are better at masking it than I know. Reporters looked later, and you can look if you like, but you'll never find it. The reporters never did. And if you drive all around the north woods on existing roads, hoping you'll find a fence, you will find yourself twisting and turning this way and that and coming to dead ends. Roads go only into denser and denser groves of trees. You'll never see a trace of human endeavor. You will always return to where you began. It is like a Mobius strip.

Look as closely as you can. You'll never see where I went.

They settled us into plain comfortable rooms and explained the plan. Luisa Martinez and I would be given tests, first written, then medical. That was it.

Luisa had little to say in English. I had little to say in Spanish. We groped toward a viable connection, nevertheless. I loved the way she smiled and how she folded her hands in her lap in the creased folds of her flowered dress.

"How did they select us?" I asked again and again until it was clear that no one had an answer. These aliens were sophisticated beings from a remote star system. They weren't capricious. The simple truth was, the military didn't know. When I figured it out, and I did, even had I said it clearly, the soldier types would not understand. They couldn't think that way. We can't escape our myopic vision.

As I said, I had mastered empathy and compassion. Luisa had

mastered servanthood. For much of the world, those talents are not features. Our lives were not based, as most seem to be, on avarice and greed. We knew better, me and sweet Luisa, and the aliens knew better too. Those qualities burn in their world like a bonfire at night. I believe they want us to understand that they ought to burn in ours as well.

The agencies responsible for observing near-earth space, monitoring everything, knew there were artificial observables behaving with purpose but they didn't know what they were. Nothing makes a four star madder than knowing they haven't got a clue. How can you get to five stars if you haven't got a clue? (OK, scratch that, it has happened many times).

My hunch is that the aliens understand us in a way that we can't imagine because they know that information comprises the essential structure of the universe, but a particular kind of information. They know that relationships determine identities. Everything is connected, and the patterns that we see constitute what we call "cultures." We have no idea what their culture is about; we can only cobble together bits and pieces and hints and hopes from the little that we know. For heaven's sake, we barely know ourselves.

The data they used was our data, linked in ways we couldn't understand, related to points of reference that were alien (duh!). I am trying to say that the process was not something any of us understood. It was a black box.

After answering their questions, Luisa and I endured tedious medical tests. We obeyed orders like good little lab-rats. Poke poke poke. Oops, sorry. Poke poke poke. They ran us through scans and that was the quiet part because we could rest in the tube, except for the MRIs which banged on our heads like heavy metal music.

Luisa grew on me, and I think she was fond of me, too. She worked in a cafeteria in Union City High School, serving macaroni and cheese and chocolate pudding to hoards of raucous students. I concluded that she did it the same way she went through the tests, with a smile and genuine kindness. She served, I think, because she loved to serve, finding fulfillment in dishing out scoops of food to kids. I searched in vain during our truncated conversations for guile or deceit. I never found any. She was simply kind, and that was that.

We were like Hansel and Gretel, hoping we weren't headed for the oven of a wicked witch.

After the tests, I returned to my carving and waited. A month passed, and one day Colonel Reid called and said it was time for the next step. We returned to the base in our shadow flight.

The aliens showed us a recording. This is how we draw you, they said, and we want you to learn how to draw us. If nothing else, it will erase your false impressions.

We stood before the wall of knowledge, the Colonel called it, watching screens update. On four of sixteen monitors appeared the quadrants of a face. It was more or less human, with reasonably attractive features, lively and expressive eyes. The mouth said human words. That's how they saw us. They used, I think, a very good AI. Then we took the controls and drew pictures of standard alien forms, with big heads and big eyes. We were told the aliens laughed.

They said they had been waiting for the right time. They never said why that time was now. They sketched an image of their origin planet, the planet that spawned the !kiii−^6, they called it, several spiral arms across the galaxy, orbiting a yellow dwarf like ours. It looked to our untrained eyes like another planet, that was all. Details were obscure, historical facts in short supply. My questions focused on economics, politics, social and cultural life. They ignored my questions. This is not a tutorial, they explained; it is an announcement and a process. Policy and wonkiness can all come later. I am sure you know, they said, they don't matter much, despite how many people make a living spewing out big words.

We need a name for this encounter, they said, because you like names. Let's call it Nexus.

"Nexus Six?"

"Certainly," they said. "As you like."

So?" I said. "Now what?"

"That's it," Nate shrugged. "They have enough data, they said, to make a choice. And they did."

The Colonel smiled. "Hartmut, the aliens would like to meet you. Luisa will be a backup."

"Bueno," she said, her hands folded in her lap.

I couldn't breathe. The perspective of the human race widened like a dilated pupil. I was the aperture. I was invited to take one small step on behalf of the planet but I had better find another way to say it, not echo Armstrong. Try this: I was invited to climb a stairway to the stars.

The PR team agreed that *Nexus* was the perfect word. "I am Nexus," they wanted me to say. They already had thousands of T-shirts ready to distribute. Nexus was emblazoned in red on a black background. No one on earth knew what it meant, but when PR teams get going, they have their own momentum, whether it makes sense or not. I agreed to say Nexus during public appearances, but, of course, I never did.

I was moved to another part of the base. With my physical infirmities, blasting off into space in a primitive earthly rocket would have been impossible. The aliens had a better idea.

We called it the Bin. It looked like a storage container. The means of uplift was not disclosed. It wasn't propulsion as we knew it. It was a magical means of countering whatever was in the way.

When you remove the resistance, they said, there is only motion in the direction you choose. They did not understand why we went with coal and oil and gas when electromagnetic fields were so much cheaper and more efficient. Is your nuclear research only for killing? I explained about money, how much it mattered to most people, and they said, oh.

I sat comfortably in a padded seat facing a window. I relaxed as best I could.

This is what I remember:

The entire Bin rose soundlessly into the sky. Through the window the landscape fell away. I was suspended in the air at a very high altitude, held there by inexplicable energies. There was no feeling of movement. Not a creature was stirring, not even me. I sat in my chair as if perched on my stool in the studio, waiting for what was next.

There was a slight shivering behind me and then a sound as the wall folded into itself. It was like origami. I knew somehow that aliens were near. I detected their presence by a sixth sense. The Bin became bigger. Everything expended with a sense of white liquid light. I felt their presence like a density in the air. I tasted something coppery and had a hard time swallowing. I felt cold and shivered and I thought I smelled sulfur. The atmosphere felt heavy. Had I not been strapped into the seat, I might have plunged through the window to escape the smell. Behind me, three of them approached. I felt them there, is all I can say. I think there were three, they were three in one and one in three. Their identities were baffling, a gestalt, a collective intelligence, I don't know. Not like the Trinity but equally weird, equally illogical. I never knew who I was talking to or who was speaking. I experienced a wordless greeting. Their words brightened inside my mind. They wisely came around the walls in a mist which hid their essential forms from my sight. Were they humanoid? Barely. Something else? Maybe. I didn't know. I focused on what looked like heads and arms and what I thought were torsos, making them seem humanish. They were a mishmash of multiple personalities presenting themselves as one.

"Do you remember what happened in the driftless area?" a voice said. It was a voice in my head, not my own thoughts.

I flashed back years before. I sat in a van at the top of a hill in the driftless area, land untouched by glaciers, huge humpbacked hills. The van was packed with others like me on an outing from our special school. I was looking toward a river in the distance. I felt all alone. It became very quiet. An image formed in my mind, the face of a creature I never carved, a face unlike and like my own, human more or less. That being and I entered into a kind of communion. My companions in the van disappeared from my awareness. There was only a privileged view, an entity from somewhere, out of nowhere. I was rapt. The only word I felt was "love."

"I thought it was a hallucination," I said.

"It was one of our random scans of your planet. We introduce ourselves that way, leaving impressions in many minds at once. Over time, the way we look, the fact of our presence, becomes commonplace. 'Hello! Here we are! We are here.' You are like ants learning that dogs exist. You don't know what to do with that, naturally, but in any case, now you know something new. A critical mass of data tilts your understanding. Most humans now know that we exist. You know you're not alone. You may not consciously know that you know, but believe me, you do know.

"Some revolutions are noiseless. New paradigms enter hearts and minds without fanfare."

"The readiness is everything," I said. "Is that it? Our species is ripening? We are becoming aware that there are lots of apples on the tree?"

"Do you remember what happened next?"

"Yes. I returned home aware that I had become a little bit more than human. Knowing you existed made us feel like kin. If my psyche is like a house, speaking metaphorically, there was a large addition added on. Kinship made it feel spacious. Our tribe was bigger than we thought. We had to, in effect, drop our buffs and choose a new name. I don't think we found it yet."

"Yes. And that was just us, one little species penetrating your psyche. Think what it means for millions to interrelate that way and share impressions of one another in their single mind. Imagine a galactic cluster with millions of different living entities joining arms in a cosmic dance like a hora around a black hole.

"One day, Hugo, you will see the universe."

A vision flashed and vanished. The sight was dazzling. More, I cried, I want more. It can wait, I felt they said. We have other things to do.

The chair turned slowly. Three creatures with their arms as it were through one another's arms stood dimly in the half light of the Bin. They were certainly different. I felt they were assigning me a role in a cosmic play. Godot had arrived and was having tea. I didn't know what to do but I remembered the rule of improv: say yes and.

I could feel their difference but did not recoil in horror, as many do from the Other. They morphed back and forth like a hologram, their forms flexing and translucent. They were, frankly, beautiful. The display, their presence, was beautiful. What were their pronouns? They didn't say.

I endured. I stayed. I discovered what it meant to "keep it together."

Then I felt shotgun blasts of meaning, communication, all at once. Boom. Boom Boom. Each blast made me recoil, then twist back to my pretzel shape. I was lost in the process of trying to grasp their ... meaning? What did they want me to know?

They wanted me to let the Colonel and everyone else know the truth.

Then that communication ceased. I remained in a state of readiness. I was all tingling and dimpling. The pastel colors of the sky shone through the walls of the Bin, bathing me with an iridescent light.

Questions, I thought. *Ask questions.*

"What is it like to be a child in your world?"

I saw what looked like anemones flowering with pastel colors. Growing from spores, dispersed in space?

"Do you have families? When you travel, do you miss others?"

Family or something like it manifested as an image, a shared point of reference, a tribe, a clan. Myriads of creatures glowed like reflections on soap bubbles being blown through space, an infinitely recursive form or foam that made me want to cry, it was so beautiful. Then I did cry, quietly. Beauty can do that to a human.

When I was able to speak again, I said, "When did you grasp the immensity of the universe? For us it was very recent. Not long ago, we thought our little galaxy was the whole shebang."

"Long before. Long before."

"Do you feel wonder?"

"Wonder is the doorway to mystery. Every mystery that is resolved uncovers more mystery. Mystery is recursive. More and more galaxies tumble into the dark and disappear. You can go forward forever, and like a Mobius strip, you will return to where you started. Your momentum generates the illusion of time. Mass makes gravity."

"What is most fundamental," I asked? "What undergirds everything?"

Something like a smile slid along the viscous skins of the bubbles, a rainbow shining like water in oil, skimming through the foam. Foam, I thought. Fee fi fo foam. Quantum foam. Cosmic flux. I heard the crackling and popping of billions of bubbles in a universal foam.

I was changed in a twinkling. I stayed available to a genuinely alien presence. I passed their final test.

The Bin filled with kinship and joy.

Then it emptied. They disappeared. The walls folded back and became opaque once more. Suddenly, sadly, I was alone, going home. The window became bright and I arrived on the soft grass inside the fence of the base in the north woods. The Bin opened and I was helped from the chair and through the door. I smelled a pine forest, the damp earth. I was back in Wisconsin, way up north.

Rain blew into my face. I crept, cold and wet, into a crowd of waiting expectations. They hurried me inside. Debriefings began at once. I was debriefed for weeks. They had trouble understanding what I tried to say. The process devised by military minds was imperfect.

When they finished they told me the plan. It was pretty simple. I was to say nothing. Because nothing had happened.

"It's better that way," said the Colonel. "Then we can study their strategies using the data you provided. We can evaluate the threat, if there is one, and how to counter it."

"Am I only a sensor, then?"

"In a nutshell," said the Colonel, "yes."

That's as far as he could reach. Strategies to counter threats.

I was taken to a hangar and flown home.

Who leaked it first? No one knows or, more accurately, no one is telling. The media found Luisa and her smile played well on the screen, her big brown eyes without guile. Then they found me and I tried to explain what I believed had happened. One late night talk show was enough. The goofy host made silly jokes about my new friends. No one understood. Everyone made me into an icon that represented their own projections.

I told my story without variation. I just said it, again and again. Then I wanted to be alone. I wanted to stay in my cave and carve what I had seen, now that I knew that there are worlds without end, endless forms most beautiful pouring forth forever. I was not built to be a celebrity.

The Colonel denied everything. The event was spun as the fantasy of a lonely mole. Fantasy, alas, plays at the multiplex better than documentaries. They made movies of the event, distorted narratives or anime with actors paid millions to say words mouthed by toons. Reporters scoured the north woods and found nothing. Instead of concluding that we know how to hide secrets and secret bases really well, they concluded the base did not exist. I took what came my way: all of that publicity boosted my prices and sales. My reputation, which wasn't tethered to my real life, became a meme morphing from mind to mind. I blew up on Tik Tok and made a fortune.

I, Hartmut, Hugo, an influencer. What a world. You would not believe the offers I have had from men and women alike with scoliosis fetishes.

I am now and will be forever in the minds of many a half-mad recluse inventing stories every bit as fantastic as his carved hobgoblins which multiplied in price and are featured in galleries and juried shows. Boxed sets sell for plenty. Last year I was awarded a Dupray First Prize. Private commissions pay even more. I refuse to move to an aerie, however. I like my twilight world where I am free to carve. My memories are turned into images of so many different aliens, variations of the forms that morphed before me. They apparently told me a lot in those bursts of communication and somehow my brain plays it back.

If fiction is the only way to tell the truth, then fiction it is. I can live with their false stories because I have always lived with their stories. I am serene. Life is painted now with bright colors.

I connected in the Bin with ambassadors of another civilization. Our exchanges sound inane, but hidden in our words is a groping for a larger understanding. When they left, the explicit part of my role was over. The next part began when my carved idols were disseminated widely and became part of the psyche of all humankind. Had Jung been alive, he would have had to add a new archetype to his list.

Sometimes at night when I am done working, I outwalk the city lights and scan the skies for stars. I see and imagine planets, the inhabitants of which they whispered. My dreams are alive with creatures with silvery wings hovering over oceans aglow with iridescent scales, with the heads of dragons, fire-breathing, and with gargoyles and angels, their glass skins the colors of amethysts, sapphires and rubies. I don't know if I am remembering or dreaming. But I know, and you know too, that the angle of our consensus has shifted. I know and you know too that the future is past and the days to come are already here, that the bridge we built or became in the Bin is crossed in all directions, myriads of beings of a thousand shapes and hues streaming in the light of setting suns.

Interlude

"Those who adapted best after trauma operated within 'positive illusions,' not delusions but stories that gave meaning to or put the best spin on things, thus mediating reality and our vision of it in a compromise between both."

- Shelley Taylor, Professor of Psychology, UCLA

Chapter 17
Got a Minute, Bill?

"Hello!" said Bill Webb as he opened the door and stepped back. "It's been a long time, Val. Come on in."

"Boots off? They're pretty sloppy from the slush."

"If you don't mind. Do you need socks or slippers?"

"No, I'm good," I said, pressing the back of the right heel with a wet black toe, then standing on the bootless foot to pull off the other with an *oof*. I stood both wet boots neatly in the hallway before I closed the door and pulled up the thick socks that had squashed down.

"Want some coffee?"

"Thanks, no, I'm good." I looked around at his newly constructed habitat. Since leaving the ministry officially, he had redone his decor to reflect his evolving identity, using pictures, posters, and mementos to remember who he was.

"Looks nice,"I said. "How's the adjustment been?"

"Effortless," he said with a smile. "No looking back. I had to get some ducks in a row, and as I did, I was filled with such a sense of liberation. So much gratitude for having the guts to move on." He laughed. "God called me in and just as clearly God called me out.

Long live God."

"That sounds healthy," I said.

"Come sit down." He offered a choice of chairs or a sofa and I picked the straight-backed chair. I wanted to be alert for the conversation, even though I wasn't sure what I was going to say.

When we were settled, he lapsed into a familiar mode from years of counseling. His body language said, whenever you're ready. He invited, I accepted, just like Hugo Blau.

"Thanks for seeing me, Bill. I'm sorry to put you back in the role, but I needed to talk to someone who would understand."

He opened his hand in a gesture of, whatever you got, bring it on, and so I did.

"I want to understand what's happening when I do remote viewing. When any of us do it. And what it might be doing to us. I know you meditate–"

He shrugged, as if he was a beginner. Of course, everyone is.

"So you must know what it's like to find yourself in a different state. Suddenly your sense of yourself is different. It feels like your awareness extends out in new ways. That's what I want to understand. What is happening, Bill, when it feels like our consciousness becomes part of something bigger? Can you help me sort that out?"

Bill uncrossed his legs and leaned forward, cradling his near-empty coffee mug in his hands. His eyes were bright and I felt his lively intelligence, liberated from the organizational constraints of a vocation that became so limiting. The freedom to grow is intoxicating; I know how good it feels to be open to the future.

"Damned if I know, Valerie. Honestly. I don't know."

Somehow that relaxed me and I laughed. "That's some help."

He sat back and laughed with me, then. "I hear what you're saying. The first thing is, be grateful you can do this and have the support of Nick and other viewers to keep you on track. But as to what's happening? I don't think anyone knows how to describe that. They say those who know don't speak and those who speak don't know and they're not being cute. You can know and know you know, but you don't have the the words because it doesn't translate from one domain to the other. All religions have explanations, and they're all in the domain of speaking, not knowing. They all use metaphors because that's all we have."

I was disappointed. "I guess I should be glad you're not a buddha who explains everything. If you were, I'd have to kill you, right?"

"If you meet the buddha on the road and all that, yes. You would. Val, all I can do is tell you to pay attention to what you learn and be grateful for the experience. Are you thinking of joining a religion? To have someone define your experience for you?"

I thought for a moment. "No. I appreciate the spiritual metaphors and the tools and techniques they've tested over time, but no. You were the only one we could listen to, Bill. So no, not really. Why do you ask?"

"Well, you can cherry-pick tools from any tradition, so long as you filter out the craziness. There was one prayer I said a lot, Val, that maybe speaks to your question. Almighty God, unto whom all hearts are open, all desires known, and from whom no secrets are hid...." He paused to let it sink in. "See, that's describing the same expanded consciousness, or non-local-consciousness, that you're talking about finding when you do a viewing but it jumps right away to God instead of staying with your experience, your sense that our hearts are open, secrets known, and remote viewing is one way we know that. You described it pretty well on the phone, what you and Nick are doing, what kinds of amazing things happen. So pay attention to your experience. Talk it over with Nick and other colleagues. Reflect on your experience."

"Trust the process, is that what you're saying?"

"Yep. If I knew more than that, I'd tell you, Val."

He was right. There was nothing more to say—about that.

When he saw that I was finished, he took a last sip of cold coffee and put the mug on a table. Then he sat back and folded his hands on his little paunch, which I think had grown since he left the fold, and suppressed a tiny hiccough. "Sorry," he said. "GERD." He smiled. "Okay. So that's that?"

"That was helpful. It validates my experience and you don't try to explain things you can't. It helps me know, too, that I am not nuts."

"Oh, you're not nuts," he said. "You're blossoming, Valerie. You and Nick were lucky to cross paths at the right time, too. Coupleness helps. A couple can often do things that neither one alone can do."

"We were. Lucky, I mean. We do. Things I wouldn't have ever done alone. I mean."

His expression changed as he made an intuitive pivot to what he was discerning, things I hadn't said.

"So ... how are you guys doing these days? Everything copasetic?"

There was no hiding anything from Bill. He had x-ray vision like Jelli's new pals.

"Yes, yes we are, but like everyone, we have our challenges. Honeymoons end. Six months of chemical highs are followed by reality."

"So what's it like now?"

"It's mostly good. When I watch him, when he's doing something and not noticing me, I love who I see. So there's that. After the pacemaker thing, though, we're both more anxious. Sometimes I'm afraid he'll keel over. I hooked into someone twenty years older, I knew what I was doing, but I think of that too. We have both lost friends and family. It has an impact, Bill."

"Of course it does. The older we get, the more we lose."

"I can see the future coming, Bill. It's not here yet but it's like a semi coming toward me on the interstate. In my lane, I mean."

He looked intently at my face as if searching for something. "You're still young, Val. You've got miles to go."

I sort of laughed. "If you say so." I waited and felt the emotion of everything I hadn't said. It swelled inside me until it had to come out. "His PTSD events are disconcerting, Bill. He gets upset more easily. He's hypervigilent. He isn't sleeping well. I think it's contagious. The viewing is making me squirrelly too, depending on what I hit. I'm doing more and more and I'm not sure that's wise."

"What do you mean?"

"Well—he's not as much in control as he was. As a spy, he prided himself on keeping everything clear. It's not as neat now, he forgets things more, and then he gets angry with himself. And at work, besides the impacts of so much viewing, we think the ones who recruited us didn't give us the whole story."

"Is that a surprise, given that they're spies?"

"I guess not. But we wanted to be part of it. We wanted to be on a team. We trusted them. They said they set up the business on their own but now we think they never left the agency."

Bill waited. Then he said. "So? What can you do about it?"

"Well," I looked around and found nothing to look at. "We can choose to stay or not. Or keep digging. We want to know. What was their motivation? And—OK, this may sound crazy—what does it have to do with UFOs? I always save that for last, but it's part of the conversation. We're thinking now, it might be the most important part."

"UFOs ... how? What do you mean?"

A chill slid into my gullet like super-cold ice. I was suddenly afraid, almost panicky, that Bill had been recruited too and was part of the cabal. That's how crazy you can get, suspecting everyone, especially the last ones you'd suspect. Nick had told me how often they used clergy, therapists, journalists, even travel guide staff who could go everywhere and ask all kinds of questions.

Appropriate paranoia is a curse. The agencies don't talk about what it does to people to do the work. They brush off suicides as one-offs, like they say assassinations are always done by lone wolves. They treat trauma in-house to make sure agents are under control. If they can't, Nick said, they watch us very closely. *Very* closely.

I chose to believe that Bill Webb was who he said he was.

"People talk about UFOs as it's nothing but the craft. It's not about the craft. It's about the existence of aliens. That's the bottom line. UFOs are real, they've been here for a long time, and they're security threats for good reason. A lot of people know that, Bill. They—the aliens—are much more powerful than we are. And now we think there might have been contact. A conversation. We think we have a right to know. Not being able to discuss what I know makes it worse."

"Makes what worse, Val?"

Go ahead. Tell the truth.

"I have symptoms of trauma too. I'm much more anxious. I dwell on things I can't get out of my mind."

He took it in.

"I've looked at UFO stuff online. People turn it into a religion. It's comforting because they think they know. That's true of all conspiracy theories.

"They want to believe that someone is in control."

"I know. No one is in control. Nick calls it a chaotic system. Anything can pop from any bubble any time."

"That's how a clerical vocation begins. You don't see it coming. We didn't get drunk one night and decide to become clergy. There was always an experience that moved us. Most of us, anyway. There certainly was for me."

I waited. He didn't want to sound crazy, either. Finally I asked, "What was your experience?"

"It wasn't one thing. It was a process. It came to a climax ... how do I say it? ... I never talked about it, Val, even in the ministry ... " He reminded me of Jelli searching for words to describe her experience. I leaned forward on the chair and looked intently into his face. "For me it was falling down, falling down in a hallway, although it can happen anywhere. It wasn't *like* falling down, I literally fell down before the manifestation, the sudden presence of transcendent power. It was overwhelming. I hid my face. I couldn't bring myself to look directly into the dazzling light. It was real, Val. That's what happened. Here and now, it's just another story. Then and there, it was real."

"That really happened to you?"

He took a long time before he said, "Yes. It did."

"Did you tell that to people when you preached?"

"Of course not. They would have thought I was a lunatic." He smiled. "They were Episcopalians, Val, not Holy Rollers."

"I think I know what that's like. I can hardly talk to normals now. I don't know who to trust. I feel helpless, and angry, and anxious. Nick made me watch a video on YouTube called "Playing Through the Pain" about what intelligence work can do to you. It was based on real life stories. The guy who gave the speech said you could hear people crying in the room."

Bill looked concerned. "Valerie, what is it doing to you? Seriously?"

I didn't want to cry, but his compassion nudged me over the edge. Tears streamed down my face and gasping sobs gave voice to everything I didn't want to say. Bill leaned and held my hand until I stopped. When I could speak again, I said, "It's making me crazy, Bill. I can't not know what I know, I can't unwind time. I can't understand my own experience and I can't deny it. It's traumatic, all right. People try to suggest what might help me deal with it. It's always the same things. Get into nature. Listen to music. Hang out with nice people. Go to beautiful places. See friends. But we both do all that and we still wake up in the middle of the night with nightmares, Bill."

For once he had nothing to say. But his job was to say something, so he did.

"You're doing everything you can, Val. Work with Nick on this. Don't try to do it alone."

"Yes. We do. But it's bigger than we are, Bill. We talk ourselves into exhaustion. It's not academic, Bill. It's personal, and it's getting to us both." I forced a wry smile. "Waiting tables and pouring drinks seems so innocent. The Valerie I was seems innocent and long ago."

How much good does talking about it do? Who knows? I did not want to feel any more of the pain I had buried. I needed to stop talking. I gathered myself together and rose.

"Are we done?" Bill said.

"We're done," I said. I walked to the door and slid back into my boots. "Thank you, Mister Webb," I said. "Send me a bill."

"Of course," he laughed. "Use venmo."

Nothing was resolved, but I did feel better. I don't know that I felt hopeful, but I did feel that human beings can endure anything.

Bill gave me a hug.

"All will be well," he said. "I mean it, Val. All will be well, and all manner of thing will be well."

I wanted to agree, but I knew better.

"Yes," I said. "Isn't it pretty to think so?"

Interlude

"There are more things in heaven and earth, Horatio, Than are dreamt of in your philosophy."

- Shakespeare, *Hamlet*, Act 1

"Quantum theory will be 'common sense' for the next generation. Things do not have a unique history but every possible history, each with its own probability. A particle can be anywhere because it can have any path or history."

- Stephen Hawking, "Science in the Next Millennium" presented at The Second Millennium Evening at The White House - March 6, 1998

Chapter 18
Time, and Time Again

Nick often picked up on feelings or changes in me a few days before I did. Sometimes he asked, 'what's that's about?'–the feeling he was getting when I was still oblivious. He did that after I met Bill and I told him all about it.

I told him how the work was affecting me. My need for a high level of trust at Dasein was completely blown. Nick listened patiently, nodded empathetically and said the right things. He was in open-and-listening mode and I got how much he cared. I got how much I mattered to him, one more time.

Still, talking to Bill Webb and Nick was not enough. I needed someone with a clinical background because, to tell you the truth, I was more anxious by the day, but I guess I wasn't ready yet to make an appointment. I wasn't talking to normals much, lest my conversation edge into taboo subjects, and now the world of work on which I relied for stability was filled with suspicion.

Once I learned that Dasein was a cover and they hid things from us, I felt as I did when Pilgrim was gaslighting me. Joe and Syl and Hal and Brian still worked for the agency and were using us. I started to question everything. Then I had a viewing session that knocked me off track.

Remote viewing in its most vanilla forms takes you to unusual places. Most times we touch the target, scan it, describe it, and come home but once in a while, we immerse ourselves so deeply in the site we have to be hauled back home. It feels like the walls of spacetime quiver like rubber. We can actually feel the control pulling us back into breathable air.

I hit a site that took me to a very dark place, the darkest I had ever known, and I had a hard time coming back. While still there, I began to scream. I screamed myself back into the arms of my control and others he called for help and I opened my eyes on all of them around me, looking concerned, looking afraid. I stayed in the chair until I felt I was back, back at Dasein, but above all, back inside myself. But the world around me was skewed. In the viewing room I was lost in a hall of mirrors, the images disconnected and lacking lucidity, in contrast with the place I had viewed that seemed to be real, coherent, and terrifying.

That night it was Nick's turn to hold me as I trembled in his arms, as I do him when his flashbacks grab him by the throat. We were quite a pair, helping each other stumble down the rocky paths we had chosen.

Those paths required hypervigilence attuned to the slightest shift in perception or feeling. Call it a consequence of trauma if you like, we found it helpful to pay attention. But that took a lot of energy. Sometimes I yearned for my early days in Des Moines where I never questioned anything, where an owl hooting in the woods as I walked to the Raccoon River was only an owl, not an omen of darker things.

I do not intend to take you to those dark places but please don't forget that they exist. We all swim in the same murky water. If we find the waves breaking over our heads and the current too strong to fight, we might be in danger of drowning. I want you to make it back to the beach. You don't need details of what I saw to know you construct of necessity a more benevolent world than the one that exists. That's just what's so. Don't live in denial, please. The stakes are too high.

During another viewing. I relaxed into the soft, dimly lighted space and felt the target right away like a fish taking the bait. The line jerked and I held on with both hands. I followed impressions to the site. I sketched quickly and the paper filled with an image of a bombed-out room. Nothing you don't see on TV every night except the pain I felt in that room was intense. My breathing quickened. My leg involuntarily jerked. Then I began to see what was causing the pain ...

That's enough. I'm dealing with my experience by telling you what it was like, but telling you the details might trigger you and it would certainly trigger me. Use your imagination. Or don't. I'm trying to say, the good things we do and the evil things we do both matter. Our choices matter. It's really that simple. Karma is real. Jelli said that if the aliens intervened, we wouldn't learn from experience what we need to do. But we are such slow learners. I can't forget that Elie Wiesel, when asked what we learned from the Holocaust, said, "we learned we can get away with it."

Back in the office, I cried like a lost child.

I knew I needed help. You must understand, good things were happening, many more than the evil I had touched so deeply. Many more people were happy with their lives, including us a lot of the time. But those quieter times were marred by remembering that kind of pain. Living on the edge sounds exciting until it cuts you like a knife. Our work, I was starting to think, was death from a thousand paper cuts. I wanted to rebalance so I didn't lose myself entirely.

Then this event happened. This is how I remember it. Parse it as you like.

❖ ❖ ❖

I had finished a viewing, an innocuous one for a client looking for information, and decided to walk home from the office. I thought the cold wind would wake me up. I was walking north toward the corner when I realized I had lost myself in thought and I looked up at the traffic light to see if it was safe to cross the street, but there was no traffic on the street. The normal mid-day flow had been there, I was sure, a moment before, and now it was gone. The street was silent, empty, and I crossed, confused by what was happening. Then I saw a cyclone fence around the entire next block, inside which was a parking lot. I walked along the fence to find a better vantage point. But before I had gotten very far, I saw a guy walking with his phone in front of his face and I was afraid he would trip and fall. I called to him to watch out and he looked up. He thanked me when he was near enough for me to hear. "I was googling for pictures of the old Sidney Hih, the building that was here. Did you know the Sidney Hih?" I shook my head, bewildered. "It was a great place," he said, "it was like a maze because they smushed three buildings into one and the stairways and hallways didn't always align. You could seriously get lost. I actually did, once. I could hear music faintly and tried to find the source but couldn't find the way.

"Great bands came through before they were known. I saw Green Day there."

Milwaukee. This is Milwaukee.

He said, thanks for the warning and walked away.

If that wasn't weird enough, I went down to ... where I had parked the Prius? Really? When? But sure enough, there it was on the street. In a daze I returned to Chicago and got back to the Dasein office. Syl was at her desk and and said, "I thought you left for the day."

"I forgot something," I said, and went into another room and gave it enough time to make it seem I was retrieving something. I sat and thought and drove myself crazy trying to understand. I said goodbye as I left and drove home. Nick was already there and looked up when I came in.

"You look like you've seen a ghost," he said. "What's going on?"

I told him. I said I had better see a shrink. He went out to check the Prius. The gas had been at half full and now was close to a fourth of a tank. The mileage was consistent with that: I had put on two hundred miles.

I got the name from Simone of her shrink and made an appointment for the next day.

I won't bore you, or myself, with the inconclusive results of my sessions with Dr. Fred Guzman because he was as baffled as I was. There was no explanation for what happened other than a hallucination and they don't rack up two hundred miles. "Of course," he added, "it might have been a run-of-the-mill fugue state. That might explain it. The problem is, nobody knows how events exist in time or out of time or get mixed up in memory. Our interior worlds are unique to each one of us. On top of that, it sounds like you had what someone called 'an experience anomaly.' That doesn't tell us much, but it gives us a label to use."

I talked to Nick about it. He was more concerned with how my work was assailing my sense of self. Maybe your trip existed only in your mind. Maybe it was out of time. Maybe you went somewhere that existed in another dimension. All we know is you had a trip. Valerie, I don't have a clue.

I'll condense a lot of what we said and see if it makes sense. If it doesn't, message me and I'll try again. I think I'm sort of OK now, I think the trauma of the viewing and that odd journey have faded. My brain is making it all seem like a bad dream.

Guzman told me to wake up every morning, get dressed and get into my day. Use routines to organize your time. Believe in something, whatever it is. Belief is what matters, not the object of belief. Believe in tomorrow, believe in a future. Believe in the love you've found with Nick. Believe that the world is mysterious and you'll never understand it all.

Valerie, he concluded, hang on. And please, don't kill yourself. This too will pass.

The more I thought about time, the more perplexed I became. Nick did his best to share his random thoughts. Thinking about time is difficult for physicists and harder still for normals. If time is embedded in consciousness and memories cause the sense of passing time and reformulate each time we retrieve them and go in confusing directions like the hallways in the Sydney Hih ... how do we know when something happened? And does it matter? Minutes are something we invented to tick off time. Clocks are inventions. Other cultures construct time and space in radically different ways.

Nick tried to paraphrase physics books written for kids. Books like "Meet Mister Atom" with a quark on the cover hiding behind a tree so you couldn't see it directly or a page that said "this page intentionally left blank" which was really a picture of a neutrino shown at "actual size." Hiddenness. Every time we look, we change what we see. If we don't see it, it hasn't happened. Maybe this or maybe that. Or just maybe, nothing.

Arrrrrrgggggghhhhh!

Nick said, OK, sit down and have a drink. Let's review what they think they know.

Space and time establish intervals between events. Time passes at different rates relative to the speed of an observer and their frame of reference. Mass slows time down like a record player losing power, turning a tenor voice to a bass. Time maps uniquely to every point in space. All events are permanently located on those points, so nothing happens simultaneously. The word simultaneity has no meaning any more. There is no flow from past to present to future. All is always now. Making matters worse, time passed more slowly in the early universe than it does now. Time undergoes quantum fluctuations. Quantum equations don't require time. Past and future are not present in a basic grammar of the world. Time is a stubbornly persistent illusion.

Putting it poetically, we can't step into the same river twice.

Does that help?

Uh-uh, I said. Not one bit.

"I totally understand," he said. "It doesn't help me much either. It's all metaphors, anyway. 'Curved space-time' is a metaphor. So is 'complementarity.' We don't know what elementary particles are made of. Point particles - occupying no space - don't and can't exist. In a nutshell, Val, we don't know what we're talking about, but somehow we can use the words to move mountains. No one understands quantum physics. Everyone agrees with that. But faith in its precepts is rewarded. Most of the stuff we make these days, works, and we use quantum theory for more and more. And when we know what those guys know, as Edgar Mitchell put it, our models will be replaced and we'll do things that look like magic to us now."

"And this relates to remote viewing how?" I said. "How does that help me adjust?"

"Science needs a new mental model. So do we. Understanding time means understanding how our brains work, because we give time meaning.

"So memory—and UFOs—and remote viewing—are all kinds of time travel. This is my point: Your trip was a dislocation in time, a detour in consciousness. That doesn't mean it wasn't real. It was real in a different way. 'Experience anomaly' is not a bad label.

"I haven't told you everything I saw, myself, during a bunch of viewings. I wanted to protect you. It was like seeing strange luminous creatures in the ocean at great depths. It was fun at first; now it's disorienting. Do we want to keep doing this?"

"You've had a lot of unusual trips?"

"Yes," Nick said. He said he filled notebooks with what he remembered afterward, all the places he had wandered but hadn't sorted out yet. He had them stacked in our bedroom closet. I was shocked when he said, "Maybe I'll do another book."

"A third book? Really?"

"A fourth. Didn't I tell you? I must have forgotten. I'm thinking of a third to make it a trilogy. It would let me address things people never talk about."

"A third book? And maybe a fourth? Where will you find the time?"

He shrugged. "I have a lot of notes. A trilogy is three books. What do they call a fourth?"

I googled. "A series of four books is a tetralogy."

"The question is, am I running out of time? I don't know if I'll live long enough to get it all done—"

"Don't say that," I said, suddenly frightened, feeling what life would be like if I were alone. "And stop picking at that, will you?"

I meant where the pacemaker had been inserted. Nick kept fiddling with it, palping it like a pet. He did that with other healing spots and scars.

He lowered his hand from his chest. "It's a nervous habit," he said. "Making sure it's still OK."

"Believe me, you'll know if it isn't."

"Or not," he said.

I didn't think it was funny.

"If you do try a fourth book, based on extra material, I might have things to add from other trips."

"That would be great. *Life in the Twilight Zone* by Nick Cerk and Valerie Patchett."

"I think that title is taken."

"We can work on a title. Maybe just *The Mobius Legacy*. It would read like science fiction, except it's all real."

"Everything we talk about is like science fiction these days, and yes, it's all real, too. But can we please stop talking about this now? My head hurts."

He raised his hand to the implant and I pushed his arm down. "Stop it!" I said.

I sighed about as deeply as I ever had in my life. "I need to focus on something that has nothing to do with this. I need a vacation from our lives. Play that Gymnopedie by Satie that we like, the one that concludes *My Dinner with Andre*."

"He would understand."

"Who? Satie?"

"No. Andre Gregory. He went to some pretty strange places. His entire life was an experience anomaly."

"I need to be in the ordinary world. I need to chop celery and peppers in the kitchen. I need to boil water for pasta. I need to make sauce. Just find the Satie, please."

He watched me go into the kitchen and turn on the bright fluorescent light. I heard the first notes and drifted into the calm the music induced. He watched me open drawers and fetch utensils and get vegetables from the bin. He came to help chop and slice. The rhythm and the sound of the knife on wood was a soothing soporific. I thought of Hugo Blau, the chunk of his carving knife on wood. His whittling blade, my chopping knife: the sweetest things that labor knows.

We carried on in customary spacetime, preparing for dinner, trying not to think of what we knew.

Interlude
Life in the Pit

"Whoever battles monsters should take
care not to become a monster too,
For if you stare long enough into the Abyss,
the Abyss stares also into you."

- Friedrich Nietzsche, *Beyond Good and Evil*

Chapter 19
A Sit-down with Former Friends

They called it an all-hands meeting, but that was a misnomer. Some staff weren't there, and besides, we had never had one of those before. They were trying to make it sound normal.

Brian wasn't there. Why? Nick asked. Well, Joe said, he's not really on staff, not officially. And Syl doesn't need to be there. The issues we need to discuss do not concern Syl.

So Joe and Hal and Nick and I sat in the main conference room and waited for the axe to fall.

Hal looked genuinely sad. He liked us, I think, and we liked him. His crazy ideas were fun, and when he let us know some of what he had collected over the years from credible people about UFOs, it filled in some blanks. Their interest in our military sites, our missiles, our nuclear weapons, was obvious from the start. Hal told us how they hovered over bases all over the country and played with the launch codes just to show us that they could.

Hal said the sit-down reminded him of his days in the pit. He said he spent several years in the pit and had some great stories to tell. Joe kept us on track, though, not letting Hal digress. Straight in his chair, sober-looking and grayer than ever, Joe filled the chair with his ever-widening body. We couldn't help but notice how much weight he had gained, but we weren't there to discuss obesity. We were there to talk about us.

Joe had deduced that we had access to some of his files. He concluded correctly that the ones on his laptop were safe. His crypto pals at the agency had seen to that. If enemies couldn't penetrate the code that protected our nuclear weapons, we sure couldn't do it.

He inferred correctly we had listened to his chatter. He inferred correctly that we knew more than we let on. He inferred correctly that we had violated protocols. He concluded correctly that our future with Dasein was in the past.

"So what were you after?" he said, beginning the meeting without formalities. "Why did you do it, Nick?"

"For obvious reasons," Nick said. "You lied to us from the start. You didn't just happen to be at that tapas bar, you had been there for days, waiting for me to show up. Then you led me to Dasein with an offer you knew I couldn't refuse. You knew how badly I wanted back in the game and that I was done with the agencies. You must have thought I still had value, or you wouldn't have done it but you clearly had more on the agenda. So for the record, be explicit: what did you have in mind?"

Joe nodded.

"Yes, we knew what you had done at the agency. Until you cracked or whatever you call it, your work was good. When Valerie came along for the ride, it was even better. We hadn't thought about Valerie but she self-selected into the group and was damned good at viewing. You both produced, you were good earners, as they say. I told you what we had in mind. I have nothing to add to that, Nick."

Val broke in. "It had a cost, Joe. I did more and more and you did less and less. We were guinea pigs, weren't we? You noticed that Nick and I both had symptoms of trauma, you had to, but never suggested getting help. You were as bad as those bastards at

Langley that wiped people's minds and dosed them with drugs until they jumped out of windows. You lied, you deceived, and you didn't care what the work did to us. We heard that people who went to that out-of-body place sometimes killed themselves. There were no safeguards on our trips."

"Yes, I'll concede that. And yes, that was a major agenda. We wanted to know the long term effects of remote viewing. Other recruits weren't–"

"Expendable?"

"Expendable, yes. Call it like it is. And we did get good results along the way, and we did learn a lot about the ways it affected you. You told us everything in those late-night sessions, and by the way, as long as we're talking, you didn't know Syl was not just an accountant. She was watching you closely. It never occurred to you, I bet, to look for her files, did it? That's where all the notes were kept."

"No, it didn't," Nick said. "What assholes you are, really."

"Nick, come on. You know the nature of the game. You played it for years."

Val interjected, "OK, so you're worse than I suspected. I was naive. But let's not get off track. You did want to see what viewing might do to us. But more than that, Dasein was dual use. The enterprise was a cover for UFO research. Wasn't it?"

"Triple use, really," Joe said. "The results of good viewing were important, the effects of viewing over time on viewers were important, and adding to our knowledge of UFOs was important and this was one way to get it. When we detected them during viewings, the aliens responded. Their psychic sensitivity allowed them to know we were there and interfere with our probes. Their responses and strategies added to what we knew of them. That was critical and one of the few ways we could get it. When we targeted them, they felt our presence. You can't do good CI unless you fit all the pieces into a puzzle. Our research into UFOs has lots of pieces, more than we can integrate. Now we know a bit more than we did. Your reports afterward contributed to that. So thank you for sharing."

"Which means," Nick said, "you still don't know what they're doing here, what they intend. Isn't that right?"

Joe shrugged. "I can understand why you would say that. Maybe yes, maybe no. We have more intelligence on them than ever before. We do the best we can with what we have. And we've been at it for seventy-five years, almost."

"Things were getting dicey out in public, weren't they?" Nick said. "When the head of NASA says it made the hair stand up on the back of his neck to get a classified briefing, it made my hair stand up too. The carrier group reports were credible as hell. That's why the government finally said aloud that UFOs were real, but then you shut the door on sharing data just as you have for decades. You think it's your right to know, instead of trusting us with what's happening on our planet. You think you own the truth, don't you? All our bases belong to you."

"You're worse than scientologists," Val said.

"Depends on your definition of 'worse,'" Joe said. "Everything we do is a means to an end. We claim no moral high ground, but neither can you. Everyone is complicit."

"That's how you have to think of it, to justify what you do. Get to the point, Joe. What do you want from us now?"

"Just an acknowledgement in writing that you understand that you violated your NDAs and your tacit acknowledgement that you don't want to spend years in solitary confinement so you'll leave quietly, take a fair severance from Dasein, and keep your mouths shut. That's all we ask. If you say one word about what you did here or what you know, we'll bring the hammer down. I'm not kidding."

We wanted more on the record. We knew we couldn't divulge what we had learned unless we wrote fiction, but we wanted the narrative to be as complete as possible. Three books wouldn't even be the tip of the iceberg. I thought I might need seven.

We wrote this account for you. We wanted to unlatch the door of your cage, the consensual reality in which you pace back and forth. When a concentration camp was liberated and the gates were open, some of the captives staggered out, walked in circles for a while, and went back in. They didn't know where else to go. Don't let that be a metaphor for what you do after reading this.

"What did the Tonapah event lead to? That's not too much to ask, is it?"

"Of course it is," he said. "You know better than that. You know they're here, you know we've engaged with them, and the whole enterprise is multi-layered. You would gulp if you knew how many layers. You have no idea how many of the documents and stories you believe are part of that process. We prioritize what's important. Our job is to protect the country, protect the agencies, and above all, protect ourselves. Ideally we can manage all of that successfully."

"Right," Nick said with a snort. "Like you have in the past?"

"Don't be cynical, Nick. We can always do better. We know that."

Nick exploded. "How many times have I heard that after a major fuck-up. After something leaks, we say, 'Yes, we can do better. And we will.' And then, nothing."

Joe shifted in his chair which had grown too small during the conversation for his comfort. "Well, that's just your opinion, man. There are other points of view."

"Hal?" Valerie said. "Haven't you anything to say?"

Hal shrugged and smiled in a way. I think he genuinely felt badly that this is where we had arrived. "I regret this happened. We had a better scenario, but it didn't come to pass. I'm fond of both of you. I wish you hadn't pushed. In time you would have learned as much or more and not gotten shown to the door."

"That's so kind of you," Nick said. "And when are we leaving?"

Joe looked at his spiffy new Apple watch. "Five minutes, maybe. If that."

"So we're done here?" Nick said.

"Finished," Joe said.

So we were thanked for our service, warned again of what would happen if we said a word, handed documents to sign, and given paper sacks with our few personal belongings in them. The locks had already been changed so they didn't care if we handed in our keys or not. None of us shook hands. The mutual bad feeling was so thick, you could cut it with a knife. They held the door as we left and we made our way down the stairs to the outer door and the freezing Midwest winter.

Interlude

"The dream of a man's heart, however much we may distrust and resent it, is that life may complete itself in significant pattern. Some incomprehensible way. Before death. Not irrationally but incomprehensibly fulfilled."

- Saul Bellow, *Herzog*

Chapter 20
Twiddler's Syndrome

We're never ready, are we? No one knows when they're out of time.

Twiddler's Syndrome. That's all it was. Something as trivial as that. I knew Nick palped or teased the sites of prior damage from surgeries like Mohs or frozen actinic keratosis. I tried to break that habit, but had no idea where it could lead. He did it a lot at the site of his pacemaker implant, but I didn't know it had a name: Twiddler's Syndrome. Makes it sound kind of cute.

It was a beautiful winter day with icicles on our windows glittering like crystal in the sun and fresh white snow quieting the city. It had snowed all night and the snow was a foot deep. I knew driving would be difficult but the beauty made it worth it. Nick and I often said we loved four seasons and the upper midwest certainly delivers those.

I rolled over away from Nick and looked out the window through the ice. Maybe we'd stay inside all day. Maybe we'd phone it in. Maybe we'd recapture the spirit of the snow day we had after we first met. I rolled back over and looked to see if Nick was awake. He usually snored a little, but I didn't hear anything. I expected my turning in bed to wake him up.

It did not. So I shook his shoulder.

"Nick?" I said. "Nick, you do not want to miss this beautiful day."

Nothing.

I shook him again, harder, and I kept shaking, which wasn't very intelligent, right? but I didn't know what else to do. I just kept shaking. Shaking him and shaking him.

"Nick!" I said loudly into his ear. "Nick!"

It began to become apparent, what had happened in the night. I don't even want to say it. Nick had always said I could have the last words in *Mobius: Out of Time* but this is not how he meant it. He planned for me to write a conclusion and at last the trilogy would be done. Then we would go out and celebrate. Negroni time, followed by making love.

The trilogy was done, but not in the way we expected.

I put my hand on his cheek the way he had always loved and it was cold. I lowered my voice. There was no need to shout. There was no need to ... anything. To do or say anything.

I burst into tears. I sobbed and sobbed, it felt like forever.

"Oh Nick!" I said in a whisper. "Nick, please don't. Please don't! I can't live without you. Rick, please, please don't."

I blurted out his real name, that only I knew, I think.

Then I was crying again, I was crying again and again like a record that skipped and played the same notes over and over. I came up for a gasp of air and then went down again. I cried until I was exhausted. I knew I had to get out of bed and make a call, but I stayed beside my beloved until noon. By then Nick had already turned into something else. His face was like a mask. There was no breath of life.

There was no Nick. No Rick. No ...

tick tick ti

Interlude

"He who learns must suffer. And even in our sleep pain that cannot forget falls drop by drop upon the heart. And in our own despair against our will comes wisdom to us, the awful grace of God."

- Aeschylus, *Agamemnon*

Postscript:
The Last Word

Nick has the last word after all—the last words of the first book, actually. He wished those words were not accurate, but he knew better. This is what's so, he said. This is the way it is. Then he quoted Dick, that reality doesn't go away just because we refuse to believe in it.

The silence of the grave is not an answer but a question to which we must find our own answers. That's what Nick said.

"Most of our history goes down the memory hole and what's left is arranged in a narrative that suits whoever writes it. Everything we thought, everything we believed, is consumed in the fires of Orc, and the ashes of our histories uplift into the smoky air where they darken the skies and blow in all directions and at last drift in an easy wind like black snow onto the landscape we inhabit in a trance, lemmings happily headed for the cliff."

Almost verbatim, but not quite. As Nick said, the editor has the last word.

Appendix
Species, Lost in Apple-eating Time

B elieve it or not, it was Hartmut/Hugo who found this short story in a stack of dusty old sci-fi magazines in a used book store that was going out of business. Many stores were moving to the internet, and we could browse online, but it wasn't the same. It didn't come close to the smell of old paperbacks in stacks, sorting through them all, and suddenly finding a treasure.

"Species, Lost in Apple-eating Time" is an odd story. It's about a big Self and a little self in dialogue, as if a Self includes the smaller self we think we are, and the tale suggests that the universe itself is a Self, in a way, and spawns civilizations one after another, and when they hook up, they discover a new identity that includes and transcends their former ones. That happens again and again until the universe fulfills its destiny and all civilizations are fused. The universe takes its sweet time getting there, but it has, after all, all the time in the world.

The end of the story may confuse you so let me spell it out. When the Self or self-consciousness that finally fills that entire space of the universe believes it is done, it notices a tiny pinprick in the fabric of the skein—its name for the unified everything—and stoops down, as it were, to look through it. That's when it discovers that what it thought was the end was the beginning, that the little hole is a speck of foam in oceans and oceans of foam, each its own container for not exactly a universe, but a separate universe-like thing, and the Self/self that thought it had mastered everything is traumatized, to say the least. What it thought was the whole universe is one tiny dot among trillions. That shocking realization made the Self regress to a self like in a game of chutes and ladders. It slid back to its primitive state, the way we are now, here on earth, thinking so much of ourselves but barely out of the tide pool. The Self once again consoles the little self which has to begin growing all over again, knowing who it isn't more deeply than who it is.

Hugo thought it captured the vision he had been trying to articulate: the glory and the majesty, the wonder and the vastness, the endless parade of sentient forms that are apertures, looking out and looking in (which was the same thing), despite the impossibility of grasping who we are from the inside and the equal impossibility of stepping outside ourselves sufficiently to turn around and see ourselves as a whole. He also thought it was a very odd story, like his own, and he liked that. Finding other bent minds is comforting for those who live a twisted life on the edge. Take my word for it.

My beloved Nick served the gods he knew with honor. He dared to speak the truth. I was the only one who knew his real name and I promised not to tell, but sometimes things do just slip out. It should not have been a surprise.

This story is offered in honor of my darling and his quest. All whistle blowers are like Quixote, tilting at windmills. They impact the collective ethos for only a moment, like that guy in Quixote that resumed beating his servant once the knight moved on. Nick knew the game was rigged but he knew it was the only game in town and he loved to play. You can't say he didn't have fun. He had a wonderful time. I know he was grateful to everyone who helped him become who he was, everyone he touched, everyone who touched him, everyone who loved him, everyone he loved.

I miss you, darling. I miss you so much.

Species, Lost in Apple-eating Time

The moon was the first step down from our front porch.

We were so proud to navigate that top step, letting ourselves down carefully, knees scraping on the rough wood until we could stand up and see the world from a new perspective: the tops of the trees a little higher, the edge of the step against our legs like the ledge of a cliff.

It seems like a dream, that time when the planet mattered, when we were as gods. We were young then, just buds, full of the pride of life, our outward migration a cloud of bats pouring out of a cave at twilight. We called ourselves humanity or humankind, and we had the audacity to make up names for other species. Whales. Lions. Elephants. <laughter> We believed in our distinctions, dividing everything up so it could be owned. We followed the contours of language into space as if what we described "out there" was independent of ourselves. Our words wrinkled and slashed into the spaces between the worlds and we came tumbling after.

Now we know better.

Let me explain. Forgive my primitive images, please, and please forgive my archaic language. I am not talking down to you. I am using metaphors preferred by children learning their first words because that's what humankind needs. The Froth overflows your tiny cup of cognition like bubbles on the lips of a nursing child. Of course we are not limited by Ourself(Itself) to such a small container. And yet we are. We are the smallest bubble on the corner of that baby's mouth. So drink, my precious child, my beloved child, drink all of your milk and you will grow big and wise and strong.

Out here, in the expanding space of (y)our outward migration, we encountered trillions of windows that open onto the universe. Even on our home planet, our small precious world, there were millions of perspectives. Yet we had the arrogance to think that the window through which we leaned, craning our necks like immigrants in a tenement to see past the laundry that hung between the buildings, was the only aperture that mattered.

We called everyone else an "alien," as the ancient Greeks called everybody barbarians. Even after Contact, when the Little Truth became obvious, when decades of periodic encounters with intelligent beings had finally drip-drip-dripped into a steady trickle and percolated through our defenses and denial died at last, even then we called them "aliens" instead of Wrzzzzarghx or Lem-Lem-Three-bang)! or HellenWuline. And that was just the Tight Group from the few stars in our neighborhood. The Skein was the stuff of legend then. We gave it hundreds of names and celebrated them all in story and song. In our innocence, we spoke of "wormholes" as if beings of massive size could squeeze through them and blip blip into hyperspace. <chuckle> We felt ourselves Big then, bigger than anything else, which happens as a rule just before the bubble pops. When the down-a-thousand offspring of the HellenWuline twice-twisted showed us how teleportation really happens, humanity died dead. Yet memory (as we called that wrinkling in the diaphanous fabric of the Skein) flows that we celebrated in the streets of thousands of cities on hundreds of planets, so excited were we all to be free of our local star-allegiance at last. The geodesic was so interlaced with cross talk that everyone became. The Skein emerged in our consciousness like the grin of the Cheshire cat.

Now, when I say "we," I mean the beings who had coalesced into and around our common purpose then, however dimly we glimpsed our reflected image. "We" were what we had made of ourselves, a Being(we) that made Accidental Humanity look like a small primitive tribe. So humanity – for all intents and purposes – was long gone and we were more. But we still hadn't grasped the true nature of the Skein.

Teleportation turned us into toddlers coming down those front steps, ready to hop skip and a-jump around the all the way around the long way around the block.

But not alone. No, not alone. Once we had exchanged data with the down-a-thousand twice-twisted spliced pairs, with the *66^^^ (the six/six) and the Yombo-wh-!~~ from far beyond the clouds in our local groups of galaxies, we were no longer remotely human. (Do I repeat myself? Very well, I repeat myself). Humankind had vanished into the Strands of the Hundred-and-Twelve. Only the museum (a crease in the Skein like a memory) preserved molecular clusters of how it felt to think like primitive humanity, placing ourselves at the center of the universe, as happy as rabbits scampering in the grass and as dumb as a box of rocks. So we use the museum to enter again into those primitive languages. When we do, we immediately feel the constraint of our childlike thinking binding us like wet rawhide, shrinking in the sun. The cultures of Accidental Humankind had once been comfortably snug. Then they grew tight and then they became suffocating. Time to breathe. Time to be free. You would think we would have bolted for the opening door and leaped from the edge of the cliff, but humankind is a funny duck. Even on the edge of surrendering, we experienced the expansion of possibility as something to be resisted. Humankind resisted it's own destiny, even as it arrived. As if to become more was in fact to become less.

It is no wonder then that traits like that were discarded and the attitudes of the Nebular Drift, as they were called, those thousands of trans-galactic cultures that had grown into a single Matrix, were integrated instead into the way we made ourselves make ourselves. The Hundred-and-Twelve was a single thread, humankind a recessive gene in the deep pool of the Matrix.

Once we had engaged for millennia in multiple replication and had manufactured the attributes we preferred, we were no longer at the mercy of molecules that had piled up willy-nilly to create an interesting but pot-bound species. And along the way, you had better believe, now write this down! Yes, I mean it! This is important. Along the way, we made plenty of mistakes. Now we can see they're what they(we) called funny then. They can still be observed in a simulation of a replication of a holographic set in the Skein that anyOne can access. Unhappy humanitads unable to laugh, horse-laughing humanitoids unable to think, chip-whipped hummans unable to dance. We did not know that laughing and thinking and dancing made humans human, then. The trick was getting the mix just right. And that, we discovered through trial-and-error <yes! spell it for me! Good!> meant a mix that was right for the Skein, not just a species or planet or galaxy. A mix that made the trans-Matrix a rich broth of diverse possibilities. We became adept at pan-galactic speciation only when we learned to think macro, manage multiple millions of stars and planetary systems swarming with sentience. We finally identified consciousness, intensionality, and extenuation as hallmarks of a mature being(people)-or:species and the necessary attributes of any viable hive.

Consciousness is a field of possibility, self-luminous, unabstracted, boundless. It is a way the wrinkles in a diaphanous fabric (as it were) invite self-definition. Our subjectivity is our field of identity, shaped by the Skein.

To review, then, my little ones: <I know how tired you are. Believe me(me)[me]{me}, I remember!> We gave species names. Thousands of cycles later we discerned a pattern of trans-galactic distribution and nested disintermediation and called it a void Warp. At last we called ourselves(=Self) the Skein and were ready to take that first tentative step off our front porch.

We had expanded plenty by then, into ourSelves, hollowing hundreds of inhabited galaxies, filling them with Nothing. We began to understand that there was neither out nor in, there was only the Skein becoming aware of itSelf. All of the names were arbitrary vocables, but even that simple fact was beyond the capacity of a human brain truly to grasp. I know, because I fed the primitives into the simulated human mind and the Skein belched. So even as the Skein continued to manifest itself at all levels, a remnant of humanity like an eddy, a backwater, on a single planet continued like the tip of a whorl of a swirling fractal to think one thing. The Skein, of course, knew many things, but knew too they were really One. The Skein had a theory of everything.

How could we-it, how could the Skein, manifest at every level? An excellent question! Because how we define the system depends, dear ones, on the level at which we choose to observe it. Everything is nested, connected. Yes. Messy and messless. Very good! The cosmos is layered in countless steps from its tippytiptop to subatomic particles, which now we know, aren't particles at all.

Well, my dearly beloveds, let us continue: The Skein was more than context, the Skein was/is the content of whatever we had no longer happened to become. Now we became. Our languages fractured once and for all when we tried to name ourSelf in the Skein. Looking back at the nested levels of linguistic evolution, we can see how we were spoken by our primitive language, all unconscious that we were carried along for the long ride outward, oblivious to how language was made. Then we learned how to make progeny that made language that made progeny that made language and so on and so on, down-a-thousand-thousand. Accidental Humanity had to vanish, so do not grieve for what is only never lost <twinkle>. We learned how to extend ourselves until we were singular, flexing inside ourselves(ourSelf), our awareness nearly identical to the molecular enterprise we had chosen to become. When we look back or across the translucent folds of the Skein or–as some say–when we look into the Emptiness and see what we created out of Nothing–no wonder the new skin/Skein growing all the while under the old was experienced as something new, when in fact it was always the Skein, a field of subjectivity within which we had always been woven, always dimensioned. Yet even then, our arrogance persisted, because the Skein was aware of itself as a journey moving outward at increasing speeds, rather than a spiral closing in on itself.

The more matter was ingested and became the frame of the evolving Skein, the less able the Skein became of saying anything at all. The Skein fell into Mute, when the edges of the known universe were discerned not in some simulation but as the finite-but-unbounded possibility of Skein itself. There was, after all, nothing more to say; language no longer served a useful purpose. The numbers of differentiated apertures through which the Skein experienced itself had advanced to something like 2 to the 32nd power, but every single one <laughter> was Skein and aware of itself as Skein. Except the ones that weren't, but they were Skein too. <Remember yourselves! Remember that planet!> The configuration of energy and information that had animated itself so many millions of eons ago had reached the near-term goal of expansion. As we understood or defined it, of course.

We knew by then that we had chosen only one way to expand, filling spacetime co-extensible with our awareness, we knew there had been millions of other possibilities, each a perfectly good way of being the Skein. But then we arrived at the edge of the front porch for the first time and slipped going down and landed, whapht! on our ass on the second step. We hadn't seen it coming but (obviously) in retrospect, it was inevitable.

What the Skein boldly called the Known Universe was in fact merely a bubble of Froth that Second Contact dimensioned some/what so immense that we had to regress, we were so confounded by the Bigger Truth of it all, so aghast at the muchness of it, the wildness of it, the sizes and sizes! We were like a child(Children) called suddenly (prematurely? No, I did not say that) to advance to a level of comprehension and self-responsibility unimaginable to our little brain. So we stuck our thumb in our mouth and began babbling. Yes, the Skein started speaking again, just before it disappeared.

We know now that the Skein had no choice, and of course, what I call "speaking" resembles primitive utterable tongues as an exploding galaxy resembles the darkness of a limestone cave in one of your green hills. The Skein needed to differentiate itself in order to extend itself through the aperture that disclosed new possibilities that the Skein had been unable to imagine in its finite-but-unboundedness. Now, of course, we just call it "reality." Then, it blew the mind–literally–of the Skein. Mind disappeared, and the Skein experienced itself as a field of consciousness, unabstracted, self-luminous, boundless. More important, the Skein saw that it too was merely an emergent reality, a Self as illusory as that which humanity had called ourSelf/itSelf.

It had to happen. We know, we know it did. But forgive us please a wispy remnant of wistful feeling. The way the Skein dreamed was childlike. The Skein planned Little, while thinking it was thinking Big. Now we understand <smile> Pause. <smile> We met ourselves in the Froth like a child with paper and pencil doing sums while the Froth was more like oh, lets say a Supercomputer(s), a dimensionless web of quantum computers that networked forever, indistinguishable from its means. The Froth was like an old Apple under a tree on a morning of giving/receiving gifts. Or perhaps an entire planet under a heaventree of stars wrapped in the fabric of spacetime. Oh, more. More. The Skein reached its limit because it experienced the Next Step as limitlessness, while the Skein had built itself to manage only finite-but-unboundedness. However many possibilities we had included in our/its schema, the fact that they could be numbered however numberless the numbers was simply a careless mistake.

Back to the drawing board, boys and girls. Trial-and-error means we make mistakes. The Skein over-reached itself through the aperture into the Froth and became the Asymmetric Foam that now is flowing with growing confidence in its capacity to enhance the possibilities that glow with nascent mentation on the outer inner edges of the Froth. We are the emptiness of the Froth. Our destiny has been to become Nothing. We understand at last (we say with downcast eyes and chastened demeanor, knowing we understand nothing, nothing at all, knowing that we are like children standing on our front porch, looking down at our skinned knees and the first step). The Froth looks to humankind in its planetary crib like a hydra-headed fractal, the Skein like a bubble in the Froth. We believe the Froth Knows Whereof it Speaks, while the Skein, bless its heart, has outgrown its worn yellow one-piece sleeper. It is time for the Skein to buy itself a new suit.

And die to being the Skein forever. Yet within the Froth what was the Skein meets and embraces what had been ... even Our/its language breaks, the billion Skein-like non-Skeins smiling at the sheer impossibility of saying anything at all. We are the Froth and the Froth is evolving toward the Second Mute. We must try. Why? Because humankind tries. Humankind tiny but laughs and thinks and dances the Froth. Small and so adorable, humbled now, humankind on its wee planet. Tip of a swirl. A swirl in a whorl of a spiral. A dot in a galactic cluster, faint. Very faint.

Try. Try again. Fee fi fo foam.

<sigh> <smile>

The Froth dimples and gimbles, mimsy as the Skein, laughing and dancing, ola! Loa! High! High! Leaps over the fire of life to become twice blasted twice undone.